### "I thought you were busy,"

she protested as Joe yanked her back into the stable, down on top of him, sprawling on top of the soft bed of hay.

"I could never be *that* busy," he teased, crushing her breasts against him. "I'm sure I have time for a break . . . in the hay."

"Is that anything like a *roll* in the hay?" Alix asked, still pretending to fight him off.

"For a city girl you sure are quick to catch on to the country ways." He planted light, tender kisses along the column of her throat.

"I've always been a fast learner," she murmured, her pulse throbbing wildly.

"Then let's forget about playing doctor. We'll play school instead."

"I get to be the pupil?"

"No way," he answered, his body tensing with desire. "I have the distinct impression you came out here to teach me a thing or two. So go ahead, sweetheart, teach me . . . "

Dear Reader:

Romance offers us all so much. It makes us "walk on sunshine." It gives us hope. It takes us out of our own lives, encouraging us to reach out to others. Janet Dailey is fond of saying that romance is a state of mind, that it could happen anywhere. Yet nowhere does romance seem to be as good as when it happens *here*.

Starting in February 1986, Silhouette Special Edition is featuring the AMERICAN TRIBUTE—a tribute to America, where romance has never been so wonderful. For six consecutive months, one out of every six Special Editions will be an episode in the AMERICAN TRIBUTE, a portrait of the lives of six women, all from Oklahoma. Look for the first book, *Love's Haunting Refrain* by Ada Steward, as well as stories by other favorites—Jeanne Stephens, Gena Dalton, Elaine Camp and Renee Roszel. You'll know the AMERICAN TRIBUTE by its patriotic stripe under the Silhouette Special Edition border.

AMERICAN TRIBUTE—six women, six stories, starting in February.

AMERICAN TRIBUTE—one of the reasons Silhouette Special Edition is just that—Special.

The Editors at Silhouette Books

# MARANDA CATLIN
# Prisoner of Love

*Silhouette Special Edition*

Published by Silhouette Books New York

**America's Publisher of Contemporary Romance**

To everyone we've ever known in our entire lives—
but especially to
Silhouette's "How to Write a Romance" Workshop
and to Mary Clare Kersten,
who brought us together . . . and gave us a chance.

SILHOUETTE BOOKS
300 East 42nd St., New York, N.Y. 10017

Copyright © 1986 by Barbara Craven and Martha Hix

ISBN: 0-373-09303-9

First Silhouette Books printing April 1986

America's Publisher of Contemporary Romance

Printed in the U.S.A.

## MARANDA CATLIN

is actually two Texas women—close friends, both firm believers in life's romantic spirit—who sometimes write as a team. Which one is the "better half" of Maranda Catlin? They take turns, each making the claim on alternate days.

NEW MEXICO

OKLAHOMA

ARK.

Fort Worth ● ●Dallas

TEXAS

LA.

Johnsonville ●

Bandera ●
San Antonio ●

Houston ●

MEXICO

GULF OF
MEXICO

TEXAS

Underlined places are fictitious.

## Chapter One

Now, after more than a year in prison, time was finally on his side.... Samuel Joseph Sinclair's search for his brother had brought him to the stately Texas ranch house that stood high on a sun-parched, cedar-dotted hill nine miles east of Bandera. The Ferrells might not know any more about Charlie's whereabouts than he did, but this was the logical place to look.

Closing the door of his pickup truck, Joe lifted his face toward the cloudless summer sky and took a deep breath of the clean hill-country air. Its fresh warmth seemed to hold some kind of magical healing powers. Comfort for a weary soul. He would have liked nothing better than to camp out on this very spot, but he needed to find what was left of his family, to make peace with himself, to start life anew.

Taking a last, thoughtful drag from his cigarette, Joe glanced first at the house and then toward the familiar

path on his right. He felt a strong urge to head down to
the water, to kick off his boots and wade in the swift
current where Pipe Creek flowed into Red Bluff Creek.
Hesitating for only a few seconds, he ground out the
cigarette with his heel and started toward the house. He
would ask his questions first, he decided, and maybe go
to the creek later. With the recent spell of dry weather,
it might not be running anyway—but just knowing he
had a choice in the matter was enough. More than anything else, he looked forward to making his own decisions again.

Joe rapped loudly against the carved oak door. And
he was startled—pleasantly startled—when it flew open
immediately. The woman standing in the doorway, fists
planted firmly on her curvaceous hips, was a knock-
out. Tall, but not too tall. Beautiful and ultrafeminine,
but at the same time, not too perfect. She projected a
radiance that promised spirit and style and sophistication.

If he had had to describe her in only a few words, he
would have called her a man's woman. The kind of female a man dreams of... like he'd dreamed of. And if
this woman was a Ferrell, she didn't look like any of the
ones he'd known. Her appearance was too fresh, too
natural.

He couldn't take his eyes from her oval face and her
wide-set green eyes flecked with gold. Beautiful, yet
haunted eyes. Eyes that were a mirror to her soul, that
spoke the language of bitterness and wounded resignation. It was a language Joe Sinclair knew well.

She was saying something, expecting a reply.

"Well? Are you Joe?"

How'd she know his name? No one knew he was
headed this way. Besides that, no one on the outside

knew he had started going by his middle name. He had never really liked the name Sam anyway, and being referred to occasionally as Sam Junior or Sammy was bad enough at six, and downright unbearable at thirty-six!

He had to find out what she knew. "Uhhh . . . yeah, I'm Joe."

"This is hardly the way to start our relationship!" Her high-cheekboned face lifted indignantly, her manicured nails tapping against the expensive-looking gold watch on her wrist. "You're very late. I expected you four hours ago!"

*Our relationship? Four hours ago? Who the devil are you, lady? Whoever you are, you're gorgeous.*

"Uhhh, sorry, ma'am." A ray of sunlight bounced off the huge emerald on her right-hand ring finger, but there was even more fire in her brilliant green eyes.

"Let's get this straight right now, Joe. I won't tolerate irresponsibility!" Her full breasts rose and fell, straining against her cream-colored silk blouse as she gave a sigh of exasperation. "I'm a punctual person, and I expect the same of you."

Joe had no idea what she was talking about, or what she was doing here. But what difference did it make? What he was really concentrating on was the beautiful color of her shoulder-length hair. Combing his fingers through those soft chestnut-brown waves was a habit he wouldn't mind acquiring. And what would you call a dazzling complexion like hers? Peaches and cream? Yeah, that was it.

He wanted to tell her exactly what he was thinking, but figured she would slam the door on him. Or maybe pull a Smith & Wesson and run him off the place.

"Ma'am, I think—"

"I understood you'd be arriving by ten-thirty, Joe. Thanks to you, I've missed an important luncheon."

Joe noted her indignant sniff, but to him it only added to her charm. He had always been a soft touch for a high-spirited woman, but this one was in a class all by herself. Why wasn't he speaking up? Telling her he wasn't the Joe she expected?

Samuel Joseph Sinclair knew exactly why he wasn't making an effort to come clean. Because if he did, he'd find out what he wanted to know and then be on his way. He hadn't been with a woman for more than a year, and this was no ordinary woman. The last thing he wanted was to leave. In fact, the only thing he wanted right now was a chance to develop this "relationship" she'd talked about.

"Listen," she continued, "I don't know what's the matter with you, but will you please stop staring at me? You're making me very uncomfortable! After all—" she straightened to her full height, which he guessed to be about six inches short of his six-two, and moistened her coral-tinted lips "—you're the one who ought to be doing the talking and explaining."

*Explain what? That I finally understand the old cliché, "My God, you're beautiful when you're angry?" That I've just spent a year in hell, and that all of a sudden I couldn't care less about finding my brother... about anything except getting to know you?* "Uhhh, I don't know quite what to say."

"Well, it's too late to alter the situation now. What's done is done." She stepped back and motioned toward the area Joe knew to be the formal living room. "Please come in. Apparently, there are several of your duties we need to discuss."

When he didn't immediately follow her into the entryway, the click of her heeled sandals stopped and she pivoted toward him. A look of worried concern creased her brows, and her thick-lashed eyes widened in alarm as she spoke.

"Are you okay?" With quick steps she hurried to him, one hand gently touching his forearm, the other tightening on his elbow. "Are you ill? Have you had an accident or something? Oh dear, let me help you to the sofa and—"

"Hold on. I'm not sick," he reassured her as she guided him toward the living area. "I'm fine." *Finer than I've been in a long time, Green Eyes.*

The tenseness in her face eased, and she breathed a sigh of relief. "Thank goodness!" Her hands dropped abruptly, and she suddenly looked very self-conscious about her actions. "W-well, if you're sure you're all right, then we'll discuss your duties."

Duties! Things were definitely looking up, Joe mused. He wondered if she would feel as good in his arms as she looked and smelled, if her voice would sound as good whispering his name—or moaning against his neck—as it did when she was overly concerned about his welfare.

"I'm sorry you missed your luncheon, Ms.... uhhh." He paused expectantly.

"You say 'uhhh' entirely too much, Joe. I hope you won't make a habit of that in front of the children."

The mention of children brought his thoughts crashing back to earth. Kids meant a husband. She wasn't wearing a wedding band, but that didn't mean a thing nowadays. No man in his right mind would let this one get away; he was sure of that.

Yeah, if she had children, there would definitely be a husband lurking around somewhere in the background. Now was the time to do some explaining, and fast. "Ma'am, the—"

"Please don't call me 'ma'am'! For heaven's sake, I'm not seventy-five years old. And I'm not really Mrs. Smith anymore, so you may as well call me Alix. There's no reason for us to be so formal with each other."

Not really Mrs. Smith anymore? He hoped that meant what he thought it did. "Alix? Is that short for Alexis?"

"No, my name's Alexandra." Her line of sight traveled up and down his physique, but then a cold mask seemed to fall over her features. Her voice took on an equal coolness. "I'm in desperate need of your services, but I must be honest with you. As a woman alone with two children, I'm a bit apprehensive of having a single man living on the premises." She hesitated. "And at the risk of sounding chauvinistic, I have a problem visualizing a . . . a man like you working in such a capacity."

So that was it. She was hiring this other Joe. But in what capacity? Obviously, she was way ahead of him. And right now, he thought, he would give anything to do some catching up, especially since she'd made her marital status clear.

During all those months behind bars, he'd thought of little else besides the changes he would make in his life as soon as he was free again. Among other things, he had preached to himself about setting some priorities of his own. And by damn, she was going to be Priority Number One!

Maybe Alix had bought the house from the Ferrells. She might even be a friend of theirs, someone who could give him a lead to his brother. For that matter, why did he have to have a reason or an excuse? He'd simply play along till the real Joe showed up. He had nothing to lose at this point, and maybe everything to gain.

He realized she had started talking again, and he hadn't heard a word she said. "I'm sorry, Alix, you lost me. Would you repeat that?"

"I said, I will appreciate your not staring at me. It's rude, and it's certainly not a good example for my children!"

Instinctively, Joe glanced around the room. Were the kids hiding behind the sofa? "Oh, sorry."

Her voice rose in pitch. "Have you been drinking?"

"Absolutely not, ma'am. I mean, Alix." If he had ever seen a scowl as appealing as hers, he couldn't recall it now. "Would you mind spelling out my duties?"

"Are . . . you . . . serious?"

What did this wonderful creature want? He could think of a lot of duties he'd like to perform for her, like fanning her dark, wavy hair over a pillow. Kissing those full, inviting lips and then tasting the sweetness of her mouth. Making slow, beautiful love to her.

That perfume of hers was turning him into a maniac, making him think like a love-struck teenage boy! And this "playing dumb" business wasn't making things any easier, he thought ruefully, but he had to keep her talking long enough to find out exactly what kind of work he was supposed to be doing for her. Joe lifted his shoulders and palms in a questioning gesture.

"Don't you remember anything?" She tilted her head as she spoke, and her hands were back on her hips again.

She sure knew how to get your attention. Never had any woman intrigued him so totally. "Well, I'm a little sketchy on a few points, Alix. Would you—"

"What am I getting myself into?" she grumbled in a barely audible voice, rolling her green-and-gold eyes skyward and then back to Joe's gaze. "I expect you to keep this house relatively clean, do a reasonable amount of cooking, give me a lot of help with the children and teach them a few things about riding and ranch life. That's all."

The look on her face spoke volumes. Clearly, the woman had no idea how much work was involved in the duties she had listed.

"Now do you remember?" she asked.

"I'm getting the idea."

"After all, if it weren't for your ranching background, I would've insisted upon a female in the first place. Goodness knows, if you were a woman, this conversation wouldn't be necessary!"

He couldn't suppress the grin that played across his lean face. "Ms. Smith, I do believe you're a sexist."

"You can believe whatever you like." She was obviously trying to hide the look of amusement that lit up her eyes for a brief moment, but Joe hadn't missed it. She lifted her chin again, as if the action itself would give her words more conviction. "As long as you remember who's the boss here."

Without a doubt, she would be a helluva lot more fun to be with than the bosses Joe Sinclair had been around lately. "I can handle that."

"Good." Her features softened, her eyes momentarily dropping their guard and reflecting a decided look of relief. "If you'll follow me out back, I'll show you to your quarters."

This, Joe Sinclair thought, must be something like dying and going to heaven. "Lead the way, boss."

He had had twelve months and four stinking days to reflect on his past and think about his future. He had resolved to live each day as though it were the last, to make each minute count. And at this particular minute, with this particular woman, he felt a strong stirring of desire...and bewilderment.

She put on a pretty convincing show of bravery, he mused silently, but it wasn't bravery he had seen behind those beautiful eyes. Just before she'd lifted her nose in the air, for no more than a split second, he had caught a glimpse of the vulnerability she tried so hard to conceal. Alix needed his help more than she knew, he suspected—and he'd help her. At least until the real Joe arrived.

Never in all her thirty-one years of living had Alexandra Smith encountered such a strange man. Admittedly, they had been sheltered years, but not totally sheltered.

She had hired Joe Tobin sight unseen. But only because Luci Noonan, her most reliable and trustworthy friend, had recommended him highly and then insisted on arranging the whole thing. Luci assured Alix that she would be hiring him again herself if they hadn't sold their summer place. She'd sung his praises loud and long, swearing he was indispensable last year and "an absolute marvel" with her children. Even Mr. and Mrs. Ferrell knew of Joe Tobin's reputation, and they had been thrilled to hear he would be helping Alix watch over the Bar F in their absence.

Nevertheless, Alix thought as she watched him inspect his accommodations, he had acted dazed! The way he had stared at her so openly made her wonder if there was something wrong with her appearance. And now that he had finally stopped eyeing her, she had to find out. Reaching up, she casually dabbed at her mouth and then moved her hand to the back of her neck. No. No cereal or smeared lipstick on her face. And no tag hanging out of her blouse.

She was still rather embarrassed over the way she had rushed to him. She hadn't meant to act so familiar; she was simply worried about his well-being, just as she would have been for anyone, and Alix hoped he hadn't taken her gesture the wrong way.

And though she wasn't totally convinced he hadn't been ill, at least he appeared to have made a quick recovery. At the moment he was touring the small house, opening closets and cabinets and doors. Unaware of her scrutiny, he seemed to be taking mental notes on what was where, as well as on what items might need to be added to the stock.

The man was an enigma; he certainly didn't fit the picture she'd drawn in her mind of her summer helper. She had conjured up a mental vision of someone older, someone more like the trailride cooks she'd seen depicted in artwork of the old West. She would have guessed Joe to be a rancher, or at the very least, a rancher's foreman. But never a hired hand. Despite his earlier trancelike behavior, the man had presence.

She had almost forgotten how to laugh, and his playful smile and quick sense of humor intrigued her. Her life had been so serious for such a long time now, it seemed. How wonderful it would be if she could learn to laugh and have fun again.

Leaning against the doorjamb, Alix wondered why this seemingly capable, undeniably virile cowboy would accept a position as a housekeeper. As much as she hated to admit it, the man simply exuded sensuality— from the fluid, graceful way he moved to the bottom- less depths of his cobalt-blue eyes. His hair was trimmed a bit shorter than was the current fashion, but it was thick and almost black, with no traces of gray whatso- ever.

Alix studied his tall, muscular frame, looking away quickly each time his eyes locked into hers. And yet, as if driven by some unknown force, she was compelled each time to steal another glance as soon as she felt it safe to do so. His shoulders were wide, tapering to nar- row hips and powerful thighs. He was wearing close- fitting jeans that appeared to be brand-new instead of well-worn and faded as she would have expected.

She liked the firm, masculine set of his mouth. But what was it, she wondered, that made him so attrac- tive? His face wasn't movie-star handsome. Rather, it was lean and rugged, with a faint, vertical scar cutting through his left eyebrow close to its outer edge.

Alix was sure of only one thing about this man. He wasn't anything at all like the men she'd known in the past. She had grown up with most of them, watching them as they continually tried to prove their masculin- ity by a lot of show and talk. But they had never grown out of it. Joe gave the impression of having an innate sense of self-confidence, one that mere words couldn't alter one way or the other.

How she admired and envied that quality in him. If only she could be that sure of herself. Yes, Joe was one of those rare men whose bearing was, if possible, even more enticing than his physical presence.

His physical presence. If there was anything amiss on that score, it would have to be his lack of a suntan. But it certainly didn't detract from his sensual magnetism. Alix remembered how her breath had caught in her throat when he stood close to her. She remembered the clean, warm essence of him. For a fleeting moment, she wondered what it would be like to make love with him. An unfulfilled warmth brewing in her lower abdomen—long dormant until now—and the involuntary tightening of her nipples were reminders of her own sexuality. Painful, hurt-filled reminders.

A familiar ache shot through her body, and she blinked against the burning moisture in her eyes. Hadn't she learned her lesson? A man like Joe would never be interested in her. Not Alexandra Powell Smith, the woman who hadn't even been able to keep her own husband interested!

How odd, she thought, that she should refer to herself as a woman, when she had never really *become* a woman, when she had never fully understood the sensations her body was experiencing right now.

Suddenly determined to compose her thoughts, Alix straightened. She would forget his raw appeal. Or if that didn't work, she would at least ignore it. He was here to work for her. Employer and employee, nothing more, nothing less.

"This is a nice little place, Alix." Joe walked into the living area of the servants' quarters, rolling up the sleeves of his soft plaid, western-cut shirt and exposing the wealth of dark hair on his forearms. A bright smile lit his face. "I'll be just fine out here."

"I'm glad you approve." She looked away, finding it difficult to ignore his firm jaw, his intriguing smile.

"Tell me, Alix. How long have you owned this ranch?"

Once again, she felt compelled to look at him. "Well, it's not really mine. The Bar F belongs to one of my father's old alumni friends; he and his wife are on vacation, so they're letting me stay here for the summer." It wasn't necessary to tell him that the free use of the ranch had been a godsend. "Actually, I live in Dallas."

"Bandera's a long way from Dallas. What brings you here?"

"I needed to get away from it all, so to speak, and I thought it would be a wonderful experience for the children. But mostly, I'm here to work. I'm . . . a landscape artist."

"Then this place will be perfect for you."

He sounded genuinely interested! How refreshing it was, after all the pat-on-the-head comments she'd had to tolerate in the past.

"From what I've seen," Joe continued, "it's a beautiful piece of property." He joined her in front of the wide east window, pulling the drape aside. Time was suspended for a brief moment as they stood side by side, gazing toward the hill, laden with cedar and oak, closest to the house.

Alix had spent the past few days blending and reblending paints, studying her every stroke, trying to capture the countryside's multitude of rich green hues. When she finally spoke, it was in a reverent whisper.

"Yes, it's breathtaking. I only hope my work will do it justice."

Why had she let those words slip out of her mouth? She had more than a few doubts about her talent, about her decision to start painting again, and especially about trying to make a living as an artist. But until this very moment, she had never even hinted about them to anyone but herself. Hopefully, she thought, the comment had sounded innocent enough.

Suddenly realizing how close he was to her, she took a step backward. But just as she had found it easy to confide in him, so had his nearness seemed so right, so natural. If he had taken her statement as modesty, she wondered if he thought it was false or genuine. Not that it mattered, but—

Joe turned around to face her. "Have you had much experience running a ranch, Alix?"

"Well, no. I was counting on you for that."

"I see." His look was a bit skeptical. "As I drove in, I noticed the pastures need grazing. Are there any horses? Any livestock?"

"No, there's no livestock. From what I understand, this isn't a working ranch. The owners do have a couple of horses, but they're being boarded at another ranch near here. You'll need to pick them up sometime in the next few days."

"I see," he replied quickly. "That shouldn't be a problem."

Was she imagining it, or was his skepticism turning to condescension? Alix tried to shake her nagging worries. She couldn't waste this chance for a new beginning. In order to have that chance, she needed Joe to take care of the house and the children. Whether or not the man liked her didn't matter. She couldn't let his personal opinion of her interfere with what she needed to do. He was her employee, period. And if she had to keep reminding herself of that fact, then that was exactly what she would do.

"Have you been here long, Alix?"

"A week." One week down and ten to go. It was the middle of June, and she had the use of the ranch for the entire summer. But foremost in her mind was the fact that if she were going to prove to the world and to herself that she was a serious artist, she had to reach her goal of half a dozen paintings by July fifteenth, exactly one month from the following day. And the only way she could accomplish that feat was to stay away from Dallas for a while.

"You've been here alone all week?"

"No. My mother's housekeeper was with us until this morning. I rather expected that you'd be here before she left."

"What about the owners of the Bar F? You must know them pretty well, huh?"

"Well, yes and no." She hesitated, feeling she had already told him more about herself and her present situation than he needed to know. "Why do you ask?"

"No reason. Just curious." He shrugged his shoulders. "By the way, where are your children?"

"I'm not sure. Probably down by the creeks."

Joe's eyes widened. "By themselves?"

"Of course!" she answered quickly. "I didn't say they were *in* the creeks."

"Aren't you concerned for their safety?" He studied her for a long moment. "How much do they know about country living?"

Why did everyone in her life, including this total stranger, seem so intent on questioning her judgment? A hot remark in her own defense was squelched by the sound of her son's voice coming from outside the house.

"Mommy, Mommy! Where are you?"

Turning, Alix opened the door with a jerk and called to her five-year-old. "I'm in here, sugar." The little boy scampered through the doorway, and a smile crossed Alix's face as she bent and opened her arms to him.

"Hi, Mommy," Michael exclaimed as he returned her hug with enthusiasm. He lifted his face, his eyes alight. "Guess what? I caught a butterfly but it got away. But that's okay, 'cause Kim said we could catch another one."

"Of course you can!"

"I'm hungry, Mommy. Did that terrible man show up?" The towheaded boy pulled away from her, miming her earlier words.

"Michael!"

She heard Joe's laughter from over her shoulder, followed by his deep voice. "Yes, Michael, I'm finally here. And don't worry, I'm actually pretty nice when you get to know me."

"Good, 'cause Mommy said you'd fix us some lunch when you got here, and I'm hungry!" He managed to stretch out the last word dramatically as he clutched his stomach in the most pitiful of starving-children poses.

Alix forced a smile. "How can you be hungry, Michael? Mommy fixed your lunch." If he tattled about it being a bowl of cornflakes, she would crawl under the rug! "Remember?"

"No," he answered solemnly.

If Alix had inherited one thing from her father, it was his strong sense of pride. And Joe was on the way to finding out her so-called "important luncheon" was nothing more than the futility of getting a hot meal prepared for her children! "Michael, it's not nice to fib."

Ignoring her, the little boy peered up at Joe again. "Are you please going to fix me something to eat, sir?"

With a toss of her head, Alix turned to Joe. "This is my son, Michael Smith." Better known as Benedict Arnold, she thought as she flashed her son a warning smile. "Michael, this is Mr.—"

"Why don't I call you Mike, and you just call me Joe?" he interrupted, then grinned at Alix. "As you said, there's no reason for us to be so formal with each other."

"Nobody ever calls me Mike, 'cept my sister Kim sometimes. But I like that name, Mr. Joe. Will you please fix me something to eat?"

"Sure, Mike. What sounds good to you, son?"

"Something hot!"

Why did her youngest child have this irritating habit of telling all? The old riddle about the three fastest forms of communication had become a family joke: telephone, telegraph and tell Michael. But right now, it was ceasing to be funny.

"You couldn't be too terribly hungry after that nice lunch we had, Michael. But we can have some milk and cookies if you like." Eyeing Joe, she wasn't surprised to see his lips drawn in a tight line. He was probably rehearsing his call to Child Abuse Hotline!

The nerve of the man, looking at her in that fashion, she fumed inwardly. She had had enough criticism in her life; she didn't need it from him! Alix flounced toward the main house, young "Benedict" in tow.

"This way to the kitchen," she called over her shoulder. "I'll just have cookies, thank you."

"You bet, Alix," he drawled.

Alix refused to turn around again, but she didn't miss the hint of amusement in his smooth, slow voice.

Once in the large country-style kitchen, Joe literally took over. Domesticity seemed natural to him, Alix mused as she watched him finding his way around the room and setting the table.

Kimberley, displaying all the enthusiasm and energy of a typical eight-year-old, came bounding in as Joe began filling the glasses with milk. She took to him immediately, and within a matter of minutes, both children were hanging on to his every word.

Alix longed to be so at home in a kitchen. Perhaps she *had* been a bit on the defensive with Joe, but her culinary helplessness was a sore spot with her. And she didn't want him, of all people, to know her inadequacies.

Darn it! She had wanted to fix a hot lunch today, but she didn't have the slightest idea where to start. Finding nothing in the refrigerator except foods that needed to be prepared completely from scratch, she had given up in frustration. If only there had been some of those frozen entrées she could have done in the microwave oven. Or maybe some hot dogs.

Alix could remember a time when, as an eager young bride, she had been enthusiastic about learning to cook. But her efforts were less than successful. And from Wilt, they received either snide laughter or not-so-subtle disapproval, or both.

Since cooking hadn't proved the least bit rewarding or enjoyable, thanks to the circumstances, Alix had finally abandoned it completely. She wished now that she had kept on trying, but money had been no problem at the time, so it hadn't been necessary. And quitting had been far easier than coping with the constant strain on her ego.

As it turned out, that was only the first of numerous goals and dreams she had relinquished over the years. And her ego had suffered nonetheless. But her ego and the past were going to have to be pushed to the back of her mind. She had two children, a stack of bills and a chance at financial and emotional independence—no one said beginning a new life at her age would be easy.

"Mr. Joe," Kimberley said, stuffing a third cookie into her mouth, "may I please have some chocolate syrup in my milk?"

"Me too?" Michael chimed in.

"That stuff will ruin your pearly whites. There's already enough sugar in those cookies to choke a horse!"

Michael scowled questioningly and muttered, "What's a pearly white?"

"Your 'pearly whites' are your teeth," Joe answered, smiling.

"Does that mean we can't have chocolate syrup?" Michael seemed to have grasped the general idea, and both children turned to Alix for support.

"They always have syrup in their milk, Joe. It's on the lower shelf of the pantry. Will you get it for them, please?"

Both young heads swiveled back to Joe.

"No, Alix. I won't." His voice was quiet and full of resolve.

Owl-eyed, Kimberley and Michael looked again at their mother. Alix knew they had never heard such insubordination. But Joe had been hired to help with the children, and she also knew she shouldn't undermine his authority. Kimberley and Michael might not have been sure of the meaning of his statement about pearly whites, but she had known full well it translated to "no."

"Mom?"

Her back was to the wall, and Joe was fully aware of it. "Please don't talk with food in your mouth, Kimberley," Alix grumbled.

"But, Mom! We didn't have anything but cold cereal for lunch, and I'm starrrving!" Her daughter was definitely gaining fast in the race for Benedict Arnold of the Year.

Joe was staring at her, and Alix met his scrutiny with defiance. His brow lifted as he shook his head, then flashed her a wink. "Ease up on your mom, kiddos. Just this once, I'll go along with the chocolate syrup."

"Goody!" the duet shouted.

"If you'll excuse me..." Chagrined, Alix left the kitchen. She paced the den for a few minutes, first rearranging sofa pillows that didn't need rearranging, then tapping her fingertips on the fireplace's flagstone mantel.

Alix could see the three of them through the open doorway. She stopped her tapping and listened as Michael told Joe that he really was pretty nice. Kimberley jumped into the conversation then, telling her rapt listeners that the people who named Bandera spelled it wrong. "They call it Ban-*dare*-a," she said, "so why did they put an 'e' in it?"

They were laughing, obviously having a wonderful time, while Joe ignored the jangle of the telephone. Alix waited for him to pick up the kitchen extension, but when the fourth ring brought no response, she rushed over to the big oak desk and lifted the receiver.

"Hello? May I speak with Mrs. Alexandra Smith, please?"

"Yes, this is Mrs. Smith."

"This is Joe Tobin. I'm sorry I wasn't able to call you earlier today, Mrs. Smith. My mother's had a heart attack, and I'll need to take care of her for a while. As it stands right now, it doesn't look like I'll be able to work for you at all this summer. I know this puts you in a bind, Mrs. Smith. I'm real sorry, but I hope you understand."

What! Her line of sight flew toward the kitchen. "Yes," she murmured. "I understand. And I hope she'll be all right." Then who was the man in her kitchen? The man who was entertaining her children, the very man who was now watching her, studying her face so intently? "Please don't worry about it. I'm sure I'll be able to find someone else. Thank you for calling," she managed to say before she replaced the receiver in its cradle.

Turning her back on Joe—or whoever he was—Alix crossed the room and stood in front of the fireplace. There must be something she could do. She made another about-face, only to see that he was still watching her.

Alix turned away from him again, her hands clutching at the mantel, her mind aware of nothing but his penetrating gaze and the throbbing ache that pulsed in her temples. Who could she call, even if she was able to get back to the phone? She desperately needed a minute to compose herself...to figure out what on earth she could do. Whoever he was, she and her children were alone with him. And miles away from help.

Good heavens! How could she have been so naive? She had invited him into the house, literally invited him in to play this masquerade of his. Terror, mixed with anger and self-recrimination, shot through every nerve in her body. He might be a rapist, an escaped convict, even a murderer!

She couldn't let him see her fear, or take the chance of scaring Kimberley and Michael if they detected it. Alix had no choice but to stand up to him. Somehow, she managed to walk to the kitchen doorway. When she finally spoke, her voice sounded far away from her, as if it were coming from someone else's throat instead of her own.

"Children, it's time for a swim. Your suits and towels are in the cabana. Wait for me outside. I'll just be a few minutes, and then you can get into the water."

Luckily, the children raised no arguments. Alix watched Kimberley and Michael run toward the pool area, and then she closed the door. A trace of fright marked her features as she swung around to face the stranger.

He glared at her accusingly. "I'm glad you sent the kids out, Ms. Smith." He practically spit her name at her. "You'd better start doing some heavy-duty explaining! Exactly what is your *real* name, lady? And what the hell are you doing on the Ferrells' property?"

"Hold on a minute, cowboy!" she shouted at him, her hands on her hips and her temper flaring. "Just who in blue blazes are *you*?"

"I'm a friend of the Ferrells. I'm positive that you, on the other hand, never mentioned their name, so I don't think you know them at all." He leveled a harsh look. "And even if you do, I'm a good enough friend to know they'd never leave an inexperienced woman in charge of the Bar F!"

## Chapter Two

Joe Sinclair stood perfectly still, his feet planted firmly apart as he watched the green sparks flying from her eyes. He had thought he'd seen her angry before, but this was something else.

Her fists were clenched, and with an "ohhh!" of pure exasperation, Alix stomped into the den. She pulled open a desk drawer, rummaging through the contents. Then she slammed it shut with a quick shove and moved on to the next one. Joe tried to keep a straight face as he continued to watch her. Whatever she was searching for, she was doing it with a vengeance.

Joe knew good and well that this beautiful woman's name really was Alexandra Smith. But instinctively, he'd known she could handle anger a lot easier than she could handle fear. He had seen her quick temper in action and decided to play his hunch by putting her on the defensive. And it had worked.

He could deal with her anger; in fact, he found it one of her more intriguing qualities. But he couldn't bear the stark fear he had seen in her eyes when she looked at him from the den. At that instant, he knew exactly who was on the other end of the telephone conversation. And until then he hadn't given a thought to what she might imagine when she found out he was an impostor.

Claiming to be this other Joe had been a stupid thing to do. But as soon as she had found him out, he had no choice but to think fast and try to talk his way out of it. He'd hoped she might not be frightened anymore when she heard him mention the Ferrells by name. And evidently it had been just the right thing to say; her temper had taken over, and she looked mad as a hornet now. Still in the den, clutching a piece of paper she had retrieved from the desk, she was rifling frantically through her handbag.

That angry front she put up was keeping her safe from something. But he needed time to find out what it was, and he might just be able to buy that time.

Alix stormed back to the kitchen, cramming a small leather case into her purse. Glaring at him, she shoved her driver's license into his hand.

Joe studied it for a few seconds. "Thirty-one, huh?" Raising his eyebrow, he gave her a slow smile. "I wouldn't have thought you were a day over twenty-eight."

"Not that!" She frowned and leaned toward him, pointing emphatically to the appropriate line of print on the plastic card. "The name!"

"Hmmm. It really is Smith."

"Yes, it really is Smith! And of course I can't take care of this ranch. That's exactly why I hired you. I mean, Joe. I mean—"

Thoroughly irritated, she forced a sheet of white stationery into his free hand and kept on talking. "Here's a note from Mr. Ferrell. It clearly states that I'm supposed to be here, which is more than I can say for you!"

Joe took his time reading the handwritten document, and her patience ran out. "I believe it's your turn now." She straightened her shoulders. "Well? Who are you? And what are you doing here?"

"I'm Joe Sinclair."

"That's not enough, and you know it! What are you doing here?"

"Hold on, Alix! I'll explain if you'll just give me a chance." Obviously, she didn't know the Ferrells very well or she would have bolted when he introduced himself. Half relieved, half puzzled, he patted the air in a calming gesture. "I didn't set out to lead you astray. I answered to the name Joe because that's my name. And I'm looking for Brad and Vivian Ferrell."

"Well, they're not here."

Throwing their first names into the conversation had apparently helped his case; she was beginning to calm down. "Do you know where I can reach them?"

"No, not really." Her voice was still a bit shaky. "They're on a private yacht somewhere in the Mediterranean. Unless their plans change unexpectedly, they'll be gone for the rest of the summer."

"And they left you in charge?"

"The couple who used to work for them retired, and Mr. Ferrell wanted to put off hiring a new caretaker until they got back from their trip. I heard about their vacation plans through my father, and they were kind enough to offer me the use of the property. I'm simply keeping an eye on things while they're gone.'' Her hands clutched her upper arms as she spun away from him. Joe couldn't help but notice the quick shiver that ran through her body. ''I think you'd better leave now, Mr. Sinclair.''

Brad Ferrell must have had his reasons, whatever they might be, for leaving this woman in charge of his weekend retreat. Over and above his own personal interests, it wouldn't hurt to keep Brad's interests in mind. Joe still felt a certain amount of loyalty toward his former father-in-law, despite the way he had spoiled Tammi rotten. He could stay and look out for the ranch as well as the woman.

''Why don't you hear me out, Ms. Smith?''

For a moment she didn't speak, but then she braced her palms against the countertop. Her thick hair fanned softly against her cheek as she turned her head slightly, and her voice was almost a whisper.

''All right. But . . . but then you'll have to leave.''

He had always considered honesty the best policy, but now wasn't the time to tell her about his past, or even that Brad and Vivian Ferrell were once his in-laws. There was more than a trace of selfishness in his motivations. After all, his intentions were to get to know her better. And this woman obviously needed a lot of protection, not to mention the fact that those youngsters of hers were a real handful. She could use all the help she could get.

True, he needed to get on with his own objectives. But he also needed time to adjust to the outside world again, and this would be the perfect opportunity to do just that. Then he could find Charlie, reestablish his veterinary practice and get on with his life.

"Look, Alix, from what I could gather, you had a man lined up to help you with the Bar F, but the deal fell through. It's obvious you'll be needing someone else." Joe paused and cleared his throat, hoping she would turn around and look at him. "Since I'm at loose ends for a while, why don't I stick around and help?"

"I don't think that's a very good idea." Rubbing her arms, she turned in his direction. "But thank you anyway."

"What if you can't find someone right away? I'm available now and I'll be glad to stay, at least until you can find someone else."

She scrutinized him for a long moment and spoke warily. "Why do you want to do this? I find it hard to believe you have nothing better to do than to be my housekeeper."

He could think of something better, but he certainly couldn't tell her about it. "No, I don't. I'll enjoy the fresh air and the kids." *And you.* "I've been...away for a while."

"Away where?"

"Back East." The state penitentiary wasn't very far away, but it was definitely east of Bandera.

"Don't you have a job or family responsibilities?"

"No. I'm not married and I'm between jobs, so this would work out fine for both of us." It seemed as if something, or someone, had caused her to lose trust in other people; he needed to sound more convincing or she would never go for it. "Actually, I could use a little extra money right now."

"And how do I know you're not an ax murderer or something?"

As soon as her words registered, Joe felt the blood drain from his face. "You don't. But I'm not."

Watching her brave-little-girl expression, he knew he couldn't tell her about his manslaughter conviction and then expect her to believe in his innocence and let him stay. No, he couldn't say anything. Not yet.

"All I'm offering," Joe continued, "is to help while you look for another employee. I can guarantee that I meet all the qualifications you listed. I know a lot about ranching, and I raised my younger brother by myself after our folks passed away."

"How do you know the Ferrells?"

"I used to take care of their horses." It was the truth, with only one small omission—that he had met their daughter Tammi when her champion mare showed signs of going lame. He had flown out to treat the horse; unfortunately, he had also fallen under Tammi's spell, and the rest was history.

"Look," Joe continued quickly, fixing his eyes on hers. "I probably know more about cooking and keeping house than most women do. If you pass up this opportunity, then you're a fool!"

Alix struggled with her mixed emotions, trying to reason with herself. She was still quaking from the scare he had given her. But for some odd, unexplainable reason, she could sense this man's strength of character whenever she looked into his serious blue eyes. He had established an instant rapport with Kimberley and Michael, and even if he were exaggerating about his domestic skills, he could no doubt handle things better than she could.

After completing her first landscape the day before, Alix had realized how much she needed the inspiration of this peaceful country setting. And she was practical enough to know that without immediate help, she couldn't possibly finish another five paintings by the middle of July. Her hopes for a career as an artist—as well as the independence she hoped to gain—would be shattered. She would have to pack up and go back to Dallas. And then what?

No! She wouldn't give up so easily, not when her entire future was at stake. And no matter how she fought it, she didn't really want this man to leave.

"All right, Joe. I'll accept your offer, at least until I'm able to find someone else. But I can only pay you a hundred dollars a week, plus room and board, of course."

"You've got a deal."

Joe reached toward her, both of his large palms closing over her right hand in a warm, lingering handshake. Alix suddenly decided that ignoring this man's presence might not be difficult, as she had thought before. Instead, it just might prove to be impossible.

Alix took a quick glance at her watch, noting the time, and squirmed into a more comfortable position on the patio chair. It didn't seem possible that Joe had only been with them for a couple of hours. Resting one elbow on the round umbrella table, she pushed her oversize sunglasses higher on the bridge of her nose and watched Joe and the children. They were playing in the large rectangular-shaped swimming pool, bobbing up and down and splashing each other.

No matter how well the situation was turning out, she hated to be at the mercy of other people. Swallowing hard, she remembered how different her life used to be.

She had taken comfort and privilege for granted, as if they were her birthright. And in a way, they had been. Although she wasn't the prettiest or the brightest in the family, being the middle daughter of a prominent Dallas oilman had opened doors that wouldn't normally have been opened to the average individual.

From her earliest years, she had had the best private education money could buy. Heaven forbid that any of Upton Powell's girls should attend Highland Park's public schools, no matter how venerated! And her mother had insisted on the grandest of productions for all three of her daughters' coming-out parties. Naturally, Daddy had gone along with all the expenditures; nothing was too good for his girls.

She had had her own ideas about college, wanting to attend the state university in Austin instead of Vassar, as her older sister Roberta had done. And after the maternal tears had dried, they allowed her to study art at the school of her own choice. Even then, the battle might have been useless if not for the fact that it was her father's alma mater. Alix realized now that her only fight for independence had been nothing but a farce.

Adjusting to the rigors of studying had been difficult after her whirlwind year as a debutante, but she had applied herself and blossomed into a promising landscape artist. And when she met Wilton Smith at a Tri-Delt social during her senior year, she had fallen head over heels in love.

After their marriage that summer, Alix found her husband to be cold and unrelenting. He constantly reminded her of her weaknesses and inadequacies. And how many times had he told her how unappealing she was?

Nevertheless, she had tried desperately to be a good wife, to form a bond of love between them. And in the final analysis, by leaving a domineering, loving father and a life of expecting and taking and smiling and thanking, she'd gone to a domineering, cruelly unfeeling husband and an existence of trying and failing and hurting. And rejection. Always rejection.

For more than seven years, she had tried to make it work—until he had told her he was leaving, over a year ago.

But that was all behind her now. Alix closed her eyes and tried to concentrate on her blessings. She was young and healthy. With any luck, she still had a scrap of artistic talent. And more important than that, she had her children.

There was no point in dwelling on the past and her mistakes. She hadn't been able to make the grade as a wife and lover, but that didn't matter anymore. Things were going to be different from now on. She was determined to become self-sufficient! As she watched the ease with which Joe handled the children, she thought of the expression, "Today is the first day of the rest of your life." A little corny, perhaps, but nothing could have said it better.

Alix took a sip of her iced tea and settled back on the patio chair. It hadn't taken Joe long to unpack with only two suitcases. She had thought it a bit strange that he'd been so conveniently ready to move in. But if he made his living working on ranches, she guessed it made sense. And he had said he was between jobs. Well, it didn't really matter; what mattered was the way he treated Kimberley and Michael. They had certainly warmed up to him quickly. She hated to admit it, but she had sort of taken to him, too.

Her mother would think him totally unsuitable and beneath Alix's "station in life," but her friends would have a different reaction altogether. Joe was the kind of male they all dreamed would walk into their predictably regimented lives for a few stolen moments. He was raw and rugged and untamed, a subtle reminder of what most of them had never experienced. He was what they would refer to as "a real man," one who was as different from the men they knew as night is from day.

Yes, women of her circle were perpetually looking for an escape from reality and boredom, a gust of fresh air after the cardboard staleness of husbands who wanted nothing more than to make the right business connections, to pursue the perfect tax shelter and to seduce some cute young thing.

In order to compensate for the lack of attention they received, most of them wanted a fling with a man who didn't know Gucci from Pucci, Brooks Brothers from Brooklyn. They didn't want them forever; they only wanted a temporary diversion, without the need to give up any of the material possessions they'd been taught to hold so dear. They would have their little trysts...and then discard their lovers like last season's wardrobe.

Alix could never be so blasé. She had been on the receiving end of that type of situation; she would never intentionally hurt another human being. But, she thought as she watched Joe flipping Michael into the water, you could never predict what somebody else might do under similar circumstances. She had learned her lesson the hard way about expecting too much, about trusting too easily.

Joe shook the water from his hair, the moist beads glinting in the afternoon sun. Standing in waist-deep water, he tossed a striped beach ball to Kimberley. When she caught it and, with a squeal, passed it to her brother, Joe turned toward Alix. "Why don't you join us? The water's great!"

"No, no thanks."

With ease, he levered out of the pool. Once again flinging the moisture from his hair with a reckless toss of his head, he flashed Kimberley a wink and bent to grab his towel from a nearby chair. "Okay, but you're missing all the fun."

Alix couldn't take her eyes from his sleek, wet body. No, she thought wickedly, I'm definitely not missing *all* the fun. She stared with fascination as the water glistened and beaded and rippled down his frame, his feet leaving a direct trail across the wooden deck as he advanced toward her.

Her heart beat faster as she painted a solid image of him in her mind, an image of virile perfection. Her eyes scanned his muscular arms and wide shoulders. Suddenly, she felt the urge to run her fingers through the thatch of dark hair that adorned the broad expanse of his chest, hair that narrowed to a V and then disappeared provocatively into the waistband of the worn cutoffs that rode low on his lean hips.

As she studied his long, powerful legs, Alix found herself wondering about the women in his life. Surely he had someone. Her gaze shifted upward, and for a short, sweet moment she imagined what it might be like being with him.

"Everything okay?" he asked huskily as she stared at the wet material that stretched tightly across his lower abdomen, outlining his blatant maleness.

Embarrassed, Alix looked away quickly. He would think her foolish. A love-starved divorcée hungry for a man! She would have to treat him as an ordinary servant, hide behind a facade of strict business.

"You're getting red from the sun," she commented, managing to keep her tone light. "Don't you think you and the children should call it a day?"

"Whatever you say, boss lady."

He turned and motioned to the children, and they both jumped out of the water and ran toward the glider swing on the opposite side of the pool. They didn't even argue with him. But beyond that, the man didn't even act surprised that they didn't argue with him! He just stood there, looking down at her and rubbing his body with a towel.

The way he was staring at her was unnerving, and she tried to keep her voice steady as she said, "Why don't you go into town and pick up some supplies? And a couple of nice, thick steaks for dinner." Purposely avoiding looking at his face, she rose from the chair. "Let me get you some household money."

"Ummmm," he replied, his voice sounding almost amused.

Alix hadn't expected him to follow her as she walked toward the house. She wished he would get dressed...or wrap a towel around himself or something. Even though he was behind her, she could still visualize his skimpy cutoffs.

Getting to know Alix, Joe mused, was going to be a real challenge. She seemed determined to keep up her guard. His eyes trailed her, his feet willingly following as she made her way to the kitchen.

He wished she would've changed into a swimsuit. Not that she didn't look great in what she was wearing, but his imagination was working overtime. Her silky blouse was tucked into tailored slacks, emphasizing her perfect shape. No, she definitely wasn't one of those straight-up-and-down model types.

"Let's see...." She tapped her fingernail against her bottom teeth. "How about mashed potatoes and green beans to go with the steak tonight? And you could whip up a cake for dessert.'' Grabbing a pencil and pad from the top drawer, she kept on talking. "While you're there, you may as well shop for the entire week, Joe. We need almost everything."

Peering over her shoulder as she wrote, he wondered why she seemed so nervous. She was writing fast, talking fast, as if she were in a big hurry to get rid of him.

The items on her notepad were unbelievable: carbonated soft drinks, starches, sweets and very few staples. If she thought he was going to buy all that junk food, he thought to himself, she was in for a big surprise.

"I'm not listing everything we need, so just use your own discretion. The children love peanut butter and hot dogs, of course. Anything like that is fine—but absolutely no liver, spinach or grapefruit!"

She dug through the contents of her purse, handing him a small stack of twenty-dollar bills as she issued further orders. "While you're in town, will you please stop at the drugstore? I need a couple of personal items: a bottle of shampoo, any brand as long as it smells nice, and some nail polish remover." She swung around to hand him the list. "I hope you can be back soon. The children go to bed around eight every night, so they're accustomed to an early dinner."

"Yes, ma'am!" Slamming the kitchen door, Joe headed toward his own quarters to change clothes.

He had a good mind to call this whole thing off! Sure, she was great looking. And he suspected she might even be hell on wheels in bed. But she was a slave driver!

He wondered if she had ever considered a career in the military, or maybe something in a maximum security prison! Dammit, he'd taken enough orders in the past twelve months to last him a lifetime! And he sure didn't need the money—

"Personal items," he muttered under his breath, tossing a clean shirt across his bed and yanking at the zipper of his wet cutoffs. If she wanted to rule the household with an iron hand, then she could damn well do the work herself. But if she wanted *him* to do the cooking and cleaning, there were going to be some drastic changes made around here!

The sun had crested, but it still beat down in merciless waves of late-afternoon heat. The umbrella was no longer shading her completely, and Alix shifted her deck chair. Kimberley and Michael had begged to stay outside, and she marveled at their stamina as they played a game of tag under the sprawling oaks near the pool area.

Just then she noted Joe's arrival, his pickup truck leaving billowy clouds of chalky road dust in its wake. He couldn't have been gone much more than an hour, but she had looked forward to his return. And when he brought the groceries in through the front door instead of the back, she was oddly disappointed that he had ignored them...her!

She hadn't meant to sound so bossy with him before, but he had had her so rattled standing there in the kitchen, almost naked, so close she could actually feel the warmth from his body. It was all she could do to keep her hand from shaking, and Alix wondered now if he'd been able to read the list.

"Come on, children," she called. "Let's go inside."

She could hear him in the kitchen as she neared the house. Ignoring that route, she entered through the wide French doors that led into the den.

Kimberley took off in a rush with a breathless, "Last one dressed is a rotten egg!"

"May I go to the kitchen and see Mr. Joe?" Michael asked with a tug on Alix's hand.

Smiling with motherly affection, she looked down into the child's big round eyes. "No, sugar, Mr. Joe is busy fixing your dinner. We're having your favorite—steak!"

"That's not my favorite," Michael complained as they topped the stairs. "I like hot dogs more better."

"Okay," she said, gently ruffling his hair. "Then we'll have hot dogs tomorrow."

Joe's distinctive voice called from the bottom of the stairway. "About thirty minutes till supper—"

"Marvelous!" Alix answered, then turned back to Michael. "Want me to help you change?"

The boy looked positively indignant. "No! Only babies need help. I'm a big boy now."

"Just won't let me take care of you, huh?" When he shook his head, she turned him around by the shoulders and swatted him playfully. "Okay then, big boy. Scoot!"

Alix hurried through her shower, quickly blow-drying her hair. Slipping into an embroidered Mexican dress of white on white, she chose a teal-blue sash and stepped into matching espadrilles. Making herself presentable for dinner was not necessarily in Joe's honor, Alix thought as she applied a little more coral gloss to her lips. But since she had some extra time, she might as well take advantage of it.

Smoothing her dress, then adjusting the clasp on her gold watch, she descended the wide staircase and crossed to the doorway of the formal dining room. Both of the children were already seated, patiently waiting for her.

The room glowed from the crystal chandelier, which cast iridescent lights and muted shadows on the platinum-rimmed china and cut-crystal water goblets. A bouquet of fresh summer flowers blossomed from a sterling silver vase in the center of the linen-topped table.

She stood outside the dining room, captivated by its charm and elegance. Indeed, she thought, the man knew how to set a table. All the proper knives, forks and spoons were there, and all were in their correct positions. It really was lovely, but far too formal for a weeknight dinner in the country.

"Is today somebody's birthday, Mommy?" Michael was grinning from ear to ear.

"No, Michael!" Kimberley rolled her eyeballs. "It's just a dinner party, like the ones Mom used to have."

If it was a dinner party, it was certainly the closest Alix had come to one in months. Since the divorce, she had been treated like some sort of an outcast by most of the married women she once socialized with. It was rather ironic that she, of all people, had been stereotyped as the dreaded "divorced woman on the make."

The swinging door to the kitchen opened, and Joe backed in, carrying a large baroque tray of covered silver servers. "Seems the Ferrells go in for a lot of fancy trappings."

"Yes, it looks that way." Alix tried to hide her smile. Even though he was handling things beautifully, he simply didn't look the type. "But I suggest we eat casually in the future."

"Mom, may I ask Joe to dine with us?" Kimberley asked politely, and Alix noticed not only the special emphasis on the word "dine," but also the fact that her daughter had dropped the Mister from in front of Joe's name.

What would it hurt? After all, he had virtually saved her life by taking this job until she could find someone else. And her curiosity and interest in him were undeniable. "Certainly. Please ask him."

As the girl repeated her invitation, Joe cocked an eyebrow at Alix. "I'd love to join you."

Michael swiped at his mouth with the back of his hand. "What's for dinner?"

"Mom told you a while ago, Michael. Steak!" Kimberley seemed totally disgusted with her little brother.

"It doesn't smell like steak."

Alix finally entered the large room, walking toward its far end. In a quick stride, Joe made his way to the head of the table and pulled out the chair for her. "Allow me, please."

For a split second, Alix imagined that his hand lingered on the back of the chair. What she didn't imagine was the charge of electricity that shot through her body when her bare shoulder settled against his fingers and the quickening of her pulse when he touched her arm before backing away.

"Are you gonna help me, Mr. Joe?" Michael asked, trying to scoot his chair closer to the table.

"Now, Michael," Alix chimed in. "You told me you're a big boy now, remember? And big boys don't get people to help them with their chairs!"

"Female chauvinism at work," Joe remarked for her ears only.

Choosing to disregard his comment, Alix spread the linen napkin neatly across her lap. She took a sip of water while turning to look at the covered servers on the buffet. "I'm famished. Aren't you, Michael? Kimberley?"

"Ummm-hmmm," Michael agreed with a vigorous nod of his head.

Kimberley's upper lip curled in distaste. "That stuff smells funny."

Mentally, Alix concurred with her daughter.

Joe uncovered a bowl and brought it to Alix. "Mashed potatoes. I believe you suggested them?" He stood at her side, the serving bowl poised easily in his large hands.

"Yes, thank you." With shaking fingers, she took a spoonful. "Why don't we dispense with the formality of serving the meal, Joe, and eat family style?"

"Certainly, Alix." Joe removed the flower arrangement to make room for the bowls and platters. "For now, in the interest of efficiency, I'll hand each one to you first. In deference to your—" he grinned "—exalted position." At her sharp look of disapproval, he flexed his shoulders. "Sorry, just teasing. Bad choice of words."

"Mommy, are you mad again?" Michael helped himself to an overgenerous helping of potatoes and pushed the bowl back toward the center of the table. "Are you gonna throw your plate at Mr. Joe like you did at Daddy?"

"Michael! What in the world has gotten into you?"

The boy simply shrugged.

Alix flinched when she heard a lid clang as Joe placed it on the buffet, and she realized then how tense she was. She had never been as sharp-tongued with her children as she had since Joe arrived.

"Vegetables." With his announcement, he placed the server near enough to her nose to turn her stomach. "We have brussels sprouts and spinach."

Michael grimaced and stuck out his tongue. "Yuck!"

"I hate spinach!" her daughter added. "And I don't even know what those sprout things are—"

"Kimberley Smith, enough of that!" But, except for the fact that she knew what brussels sprouts were, Alix had to bite back the same pronouncement. Her blood was boiling! She had specifically asked him not to buy spinach. She opened her mouth to speak, but Joe's voice halted her.

"You're gonna love it, Mike. You too, Kim."

"But, Mommy, do I have to eat this gross stuff?"

Joe set the bowl on the table and, to Alix's annoyance, answered for her. "Yes, son. Two bites of each, if you want dessert."

"Where's my steak?"

With the flourish of a French headwaiter, Joe uncovered the meat platter and ceremoniously brought it to the table. As soon as the lid was raised, Alix knew they were headed for a showdown.

"My specialty!" He seemed proud as a peacock. The steaming platter was placed in the center of the table, and Joe quickly grabbed first the children's plates, then Alix's, and served each one a large portion of meat. "I know you'll love it."

At that moment, she would have given anything for the children to be out of earshot! It took more than a ton of effort to maintain her control. "I'm sure—"

"Ummm! It smells good," Little Benedict exclaimed, holding his fork under his nostrils. "But I never saw a steak with onions all over it before."

Joe set her plate in front of her and sliced a small portion of the foul-smelling liver. "Try one bite, Alix. As I said, it's my specialty."

Time seemed to be caught in slow motion as the fork moved closer to her mouth. She could almost hear the theme song from *Jaws* as she stared at the horrid brown goo. How could she possibly eat it?

"I-I'm not very hungry," she stammered.

"Sure you are, Alix. After that lunch, you need to eat something nutritious."

The chair legs scraped against the parquet floor as she scooted backward, dabbing at her lips with her napkin. Her stomach was churning from the smell of it.

"If you'll excuse me," she replied quickly, "I'm not feeling well. Children, stay here and eat your potatoes." To her utter disgust and revulsion, her son was chewing a large piece of the repugnant fare.

"Don't rush off, Alix."

Throwing the napkin on top of her plate, she grated out her words. "May I please see you outside?"

"Alix—"

She made for the front door, opened it with a yank and stepped out onto the wide veranda. Hugging her arms, she whirled to face him.

"How...dare...you! How dare you deliberately go against me like that!"

"Now, now. Settle down." He reached toward her, touching her arm, but she drew back as though she'd come into contact with the flat of a hot iron.

"Don't tell me to settle down! I want you to pack your belongings and get out of here. Now!"

"Alix, I apologize. I just wanted you and the kids to have a nourishing meal. Cereal's all right I guess, but growing children need something substantial in their tummies."

"Baloney! You're no doctor! You're just a ranch hand. Now, get out!"

"Settle down! I promise it won't happen again." The fading burnt orange of the sunset reflected the genuine remorse in his eyes. "I'm sorry."

With a trembling hand, she grabbed the porch swing's chain and bowed her head. "Why, why, must everyone try to run my life? Why won't people leave me alone and let me make my own decisions, whether they be good or bad?" She turned toward him. "And you. You're my employee, even if it is on a temporary basis! You have no right to interfere."

"You're right," he agreed quietly as he studied her face. "I don't. Look, Alix, I really didn't set out to offend you. It's just that I was always accustomed to... I guess I'm used to taking complete charge of whatever or whomever I'm responsible for."

She focused her eyes on the top button of Joe's shirt as he put his hands on her shoulders and continued. "I don't necessarily agree with you on what's right for Mike and Kim, and it's hard to teach an old dog new tricks. But if you're willing to give me a second chance, I'm willing to try to change some of my ways."

Her face shot upward, and she drank in each kind feature in turn. This man—this stranger—had spoken the words she had longed to hear first from her parents, then from her husband. How many times had she hoped they would say those words, and mean them? She wasn't so spoiled that she felt she had to have her way all the time. Life's compromises didn't frighten her, but she had always felt as if the total submission of her ideals was too much to ask.

"You'd do that?" she whispered.

"Yes." His big, gentle hand snaked into the hair at the nape of her neck. As he moved closer, he tilted her chin toward him with the crook of his forefinger. "We got off on the wrong foot, Alix. Why don't we wipe the slate clean and start all over again?"

"I suppose I overreacted. Yes, I'd appreciate it very much if you would stay."

As he whispered his acceptance, the evening breeze billowed her hair against her cheek and gently whipped the skirt of her dress around her legs and around the legs of his jeans, enveloping them in a powerful co-coon of closeness. Never in her life had she felt a man's strength in this way. It was the kind of strength that only gentleness could convey....

It seemed the most natural thing in the world to lean her head against the solid warmth of his shoulder, to bury her face against his broad chest. A mixture of the sweet essence of clear, unspoiled air and the clean, vitally male scent of Joe took her on a breathtaking sensory journey.

Would he realize how much she wanted his embrace? Would he kiss her? Alix tilted her head back, her lips grazing the light sandpapery stubble of his chin, and heard his sharp intake of breath. Her fingers slid up the hard sinew of his back, her body molding to his form.

"Alix," he groaned, his face lowering toward hers, and she felt the warmth of his breath on her lips. Nothing else existed, nothing else mattered now but—

Suddenly, without warning, he wrenched free and stepped back. His jaw clenched as he looked toward the house, nodding in the direction of the dining room. "We'd better go see about the kids."

The tenderness of the moment fell away like the petals of a rose, fading and wilting and dying. And a stab of agony pierced the wall of her heart. She had almost thrown herself at Joe, and he had rejected her. What would it take to pound some sense into her head? Would she never learn?

Alix nodded slowly, and a nervous laugh began to form in her throat. "By all means—"

## Chapter Three

Joe wheeled his pickup left onto the paved highway, glancing at the outside mirrors and the reflection of the empty horse trailer. He had already checked and double-checked it after hitching it to his truck, but all he needed was another senseless mistake like the one he'd brought on himself the previous night. If he hadn't been so damned irritated with Alix when he stormed off to town, he might not have bought the stupid liver to begin with.

Irritated wasn't exactly the right word, he thought as he shifted the truck's gears. He'd hired on as her employee, and she had every right to tell him their preference. No, it wasn't taking orders from her that bothered him.

Why not admit it? When he'd stalked out of that kitchen with her list, he'd been downright hungry—and it didn't have a thing to do with liver and onions! He

had watched her as she wrote that list, rattling on in a
fluster, and he had wanted to take her in his arms. He
had wanted to hold her body against his. He had wanted
to kiss her and run his fingers through her soft hair and
tell her she didn't have anything to worry about, that he
would never hurt her.

He'd been distracted to the point where he hadn't
anticipated how Alix might react to that ridiculous
meal. And he had regretted it the minute he saw that
aching look in her eyes, that tormented look on her
beautiful face. It had seemed so natural, holding her
and trying to comfort her. But in a split second he had
realized her vulnerability.

Hell, who was he kidding! His vulnerability! He
wouldn't have been able to stop at a kiss. Even then, he
probably wouldn't have come to his senses if he hadn't
heard Mike and Kim's voices from the house.

Pulling away from Alix had been one of the most
difficult things Joe had ever done. She had felt as good
in his arms as he had imagined she would, and he'd
wanted nothing more in that moment than to make her
his. But he couldn't let anything happen between them
yet. If they were ever going to make love, he wanted it
to be honest and unhurried, and without later regrets.

Slamming on the brakes for a sharp right turn, Joe
leaned forward and rubbed his eyes. Cursing himself for
two full hours before he had fallen asleep the previous
night hadn't helped matters at all. He'd been up with
the chickens this morning, reorganizing the kitchen and
fixing a big breakfast, and the rest of the day still
loomed ahead of him.

He unwound his lanky frame from the pickup and
adjusted his straw Stetson. Slamming the door shut, he
ambled toward the trailer. He had been looking for-

ward to getting the horses from the Davis place. He was eager to get back in the saddle, and the kids were beside themselves at the thought of learning to ride. They had waved goodbye to him as he'd left the Bar F a few minutes before, and he would be surprised if they weren't still standing on the front porch when he got back with the horses—

"Sam? Is that you, Sam?"

Turning at the sound of the male voice, Joe furrowed his brows. There was no mistaking the owner of that nasal twang. For years Henry Kastel had worked for the Sinclair family at the Double S Ranch near Johnsonville. But he'd been more than a mere employee. Henry was his friend, and it was good to see him.

"Sam Sinclair!" The wiry, bowlegged man trotted toward him.

It had been a long time since anyone had called him by his first name, and it seemed strange. "Hello, Henry."

"Well, I'll be doggoned! I ain't seen you since before you was sent up! Looks like you could stand to put a pound or two on them bones. But elsewise, prison life must nota treated ya too shabby. How ya doin', Sam?"

"I'm fine, Henry." Joe extended his hand, and the older man pumped it in a hearty handshake. "But I'm sure surprised to see you here."

"Yeah, me and Mama pulled up stakes a few months ago and come out here." Mama was Henry's pet name for his wife, Lillie Jewel.

"I wondered what happened to you. My new foreman said he didn't have any idea where you'd gone."

"Well, me and that young Dennis fella you hired to watch over the Double S didn't see eye to eye. No way that boy coulda filled your boots, Sam—you was the best boss any of us ever had. And I just didn't want to stay on after that judge came down so hard on ya." He shook his head and spit a stream of tobacco onto the hard ground. "I sure never figured he'd send ya up the river, you bein' a big-time rancher and such a hotshot horse doctor and all. Sure puts them rumors to sleep about rich people gettin' off easy nowadays."

"Yeah, I suppose." Joe rammed his fingertips into the pockets of his western-cut trousers and tried to change the subject. "How've you been, Henry? And Lillie?"

"Oh, just fine, I reckon. Mama ain't run me off yet. And Pretty Girl—" his chest swelled with obvious pride "—found her a fella who could run faster than her, and she whelped seven pups a few weeks ago!"

"I told you she'd come through for you someday." Joe fondly remembered Henry's beloved brown-and-white Heinz 57 as being anything but what her name implied. And he wondered if Henry had any idea how difficult it would be to find homes for all those mongrel pups. "I'll bet you and Lillie have your hands full."

"Yep." Henry leaned forward, cocking his head. "Say, Sam, you wouldn't mind lookin' in on Pretty Girl, would ya? That vet up to town said her and the little ones was okay, but I'd feel better if you'd take a look at 'em."

"I'll be happy to. Why don't I drop by this evening?"

"I'd be mighty beholdin' to ya."

"No problem. That's what friends are for."

"Then maybe as a friend you won't mind me askin' about somethin'. I know it ain't none of my business, Sam, but it's been gnawin' at my insides and I just gotta ask.'' He gave Joe a squinted look. ''Why didn't you stop and help that night insteada drivin' off? It was an accident, pure and simple. Hell, nobody coulda faulted ya for it! That Otis Brown weren't no great loss to the world anyhow. Ever'body in town knew he was nothin' but a drunk and a wife beater, not worth the gunpowder it'd take to shoot him!''

Henry took a careless sideways aim and spit on the ground again. ''Now don't you go lookin' at me that way, Sam. I didn't mean nothin' by that—''

''It's just that I've done my time, Henry. And I'd rather not dredge up the past.''

''I know ya feel bad about it, you bein' a doc and all. But ever'thing I said about Otis is the truth, and you know it. 'Course, you'da thought he was a deacon in the church or somethin' the way his missus was carryin' on. Wearin' them widow's weeds and all.''

''She had every right to grieve, Henry.''

''Well, dadburn it, she didn't grieve for long. It was enough to make a grown man sick. She took that money you give 'er and went through it like it was water. Got herself a fancy man, too.'' He shook his head with disgust. ''Just made a danged fool of herself, that's what she did!''

''When I gave her that money, there were no strings attached.'' No, the money and how the Widow Brown spent it meant nothing to Joe. What bothered him was being thought of as a killer by the people he'd known all his life.

''What are you doin' in these parts, Sam? You come to see the Ferrells?''

''Yeah, I needed to talk to them.''

''Fraid you're outta luck, then. They're out sailin' on some fancy boat—gonna be gone quite a spell.''

"I know. I'm here to pick up their horses."

"Sure thing, Sam. Sure thing." The older man's brows knitted as he ran his hand through his thatch of gray hair. "But I thought you and your missus was finished."

Joe opened the horse trailer and then turned to face Henry again. "We are."

"Then how come you're hangin' around the Bar F?" Henry eyed him knowingly, then shook his finger. "Come to think of it, I seen that high-stepper who's stayin' over there. That's what you're up to, ain't it, boy? You're after her!"

Joe's movement came to a halt, but he couldn't stop the irritation he felt at Henry's words. There was no denying the truth of the statement; he'd never wanted a woman more in his life than he wanted Alix. To some people, her attitude might seem uppity at times, but he could see right through it. And he didn't want to hear any derogatory remarks about her.

"Mind your own business, Henry."

"Uh-huh. I thought so." He chuckled, shaking his head in amusement.

"Listen, Henry." If he didn't want word to get back to Alix, he knew he'd better speak up now. "The woman who's running the Ferrell place doesn't know that I've been in prison, or that I was married to Tammi. And I don't want her hearing about it through the local grapevine, so I'd appreciate your keeping a lid on it until I get the chance to tell her myself." Joe lightly squeezed his friend's bony shoulder. "And ask Lillie to do the same for me, will you?"

"You can count on us, Sam. I'll talk to Mama as soon as I can get myself up to the main house."

"Thanks." Joe breathed a sigh of relief. Without a doubt, Henry Kastel was a man of his word.

"Dang it, boy" Henry grabbed a pocketknife from his pants and started cleaning a thumbnail. From past experience, Joe knew this to be the prelude to Henry's unsolicited advice, and he smiled as he readied himself for it. "When are you gonna wise up? You and that brother of yours always was saps for them highfalutin women."

The mention of his sibling sent Joe's mind racing, shutting out all other thoughts. "Henry, do you know where I can find Charlie?"

"Naw, ain't seen him in several months."

"Where'd you see him?"

"Did you say you wanted to pick up them horses? One's over to the stable and the other's grazin' by the creek—"

"Don't change the subject on me, Henry. Where did you see Charlie?"

"Sam, I'd rather take a whippin' than to tell you this." He exhaled loudly. "He was . . . with your missus."

"You're not telling me anything I don't already know." Yes, he knew that Tammi had taken up with his little brother. And that was only part of the reason why he was so worried. "Come on now. Where?"

"He was over to the Ferrell place. When I seen him, they was hightailin' it down the road in that fancy yella car of hers." He clucked his tongue. "Guess that boy ain't never gonna grow up. What is he now, about twenty-five?"

"Twenty-six." Joe hoped his only brother was safe, both from Charlie's own irresponsibility and from *her* clutches. Tammi's robbing of the Sinclair family cradle wasn't what was bothering him the most—she was capable of anything. The whole time he was in prison, he hadn't heard a word from his brother. Charlie had never gone back to the Double S; his foreman Dennis had attested to that. Joe still didn't have any idea where Charlie had been since the day of the accident.

He didn't even want to think about the sacrifice he had made to keep the boy out of trouble. He'd kept quiet about who had the car that night, assuring himself they'd convict a wild young kid but never a sterling citizen of the community. And regardless of the fact that his decision had backfired on him, he knew now he should have made Charlie face it. If his brother wasn't a man yet, it was about time he became one.

"Did he mention where he was going?"

"I never did talk to the boy. I just seen him. Mama's working part-time at the café in town, and all she heard was that he was on leave or somethin'."

"Leave?" he pressed. "What kind of leave?"

"Don't have any idea."

"Hmm.... Well, if you see or hear anything of him, will you let me know right away?"

"You bet."

"Thanks, Henry. Why don't we round up those horses now?" The gravel-packed road crunched under his worn boots as Joe walked with Henry toward the horse stalls.

On leave. That could mean Charlie was holding down a good job, Joe reasoned. He hoped so.

Maybe all Charlie needed was some time to pull himself together, to straighten out his life. There was no sense in chasing all over looking for the kid. He would stop at a pay phone in a few minutes and let his foreman know he'd be staying on at the Bar F for a while.

Reasoning told him to sit tight, that Charlie would eventually get in touch with Dennis and find out that Joe was in Bandera.

And reasoning also told him he'd better be honest with Alexandra. What if Charlie did come to Bandera, more specifically, to the Ferrells' ranch, looking for him and asking questions? Even though he felt certain Henry would keep his promise, he didn't want her to hear about his background from anyone else.

But common sense didn't stop him from dreading the inevitable. He would have to pick the right time to tell her, but he couldn't do it now—not after last night's stunt. Maybe if he was on his best behavior for the next few days, doing his job and making it a point not to collide with her emotions again, she would recognize his sense of responsibility and be more likely to trust him. Even then, he thought the chances of her understanding the circumstances and forgiving him seemed anywhere from slim to none.

If only he could take back the error in judgment that had sent him to the penitentiary, how different his life would be right now. And it hurt like hell to know that his past would forever haunt him.

Alix drained the last swallow from her fourth cup of black coffee, placing the mug on a small table covered with paint-smeared craft paper. She had set up her easel on the second floor in what she called the "studio," and it had proven the perfect place to work.

Located high atop the far north end of the house, the room was large and flooded with natural light. With three of its walls totally glassed from the wainscoting all the way up to the ceiling, it provided a magnificent bird's-eye view of the surrounding acreage. And the mirrored wet bar reflected the outside glory in another perspective.

It was very much like being outdoors, and yet it provided air-conditioned refuge from the June heat. In the two weeks she'd been here, the temperature hadn't wavered much from this day's ninety-eight degrees.

But her studio's most important feature was its seclusion from the noise and activity of the household. The area had its own private staircases—one from the outside and one from the far end of the kitchen—and it was totally isolated from the rest of the house.

Almost too isolated, Alix thought as she put down the brush and studied her nearly completed canvas. And far too quiet. She needed to learn how to operate the elaborate sound system, but the possibility of ruining it had kept her from experimenting with the many knobs and switches.

Alix crossed the room to pour herself one more cup of coffee. Pacing the floor, she tried to shake the odd restlessness that had been plaguing her all day. She couldn't have asked for a lovelier place to work, but for some reason all this privacy was beginning to grate on her nerves.

Vivian Ferrell had designed the secluded, self-contained area as a guest hideaway. At least that's what Alix's mother had said one time after returning from a weekend visit to the Bar F. And when Alix saw it for herself, she finally understood why Margaret Powell had blushed and said that the lodgings had provided a much-needed shot in the arm for her and "Uppie." Until that Monday afternoon a few years before, he had always been "Upton." And even now, Alix had to chew the inside of her cheek to keep from giggling when she

thought about her mother's use of the intimate nick-
name.

As soon as they had arrived at the ranch two weeks
before, Alix and her mother's housekeeper had made a
beeline to the much-touted guest area. Estelle had been
unimpressed by the huge, open room and its discreetly
tucked-away necessaries. Crossing her arms over her
ample bosom, she pursed her lips and said, "Hmmmph.
Now I've seen everything! Just imagine, making a nature call in the living room!" Estelle must have failed
Romance 101.

Alix, on the other hand, loved it. She decided right
then that Vivian Ferrell must be a romantic, since the
room had all the amenities for pleasure: a king-size bed,
a wet bar with a small refrigerator and icemaker, a fire-
wood crib, a quadraphonic stereo system. And gracing
one wall, an old-fashioned fainting couch of mauve and
gray.

If not for the fact that it seemed a waste to spend the
night alone and lonely in such a place, Alix would have
used the suite as her own sleeping accommodations. At
the same time, she had no such compunction when it
came to the L-shaped bath area. With its built-for-two
Jacuzzi, it was a haven designed for lovers.

Each evening, undeterred by convention or practi-
cality, she slipped into the circular sunken tub and lux-
uriated in gardenia-scented bath oil, while leisurely
sipping chilled champagne from a fluted glass. And
since Joe had arrived, she had let her fantasies go wild.
She'd imagined seductive music playing on the sound
system, and him slowly shedding his clothes. Then he
would build a fire...share the champagne...join her
in the swirling water....

Too much coffee, Alix reminded herself as she added a warm-up to the cold mug, was probably the major cause of the edginess she'd been feeling lately. She listened attentively, hoping for some small noise to break into the total quiet. But as she leaned her hip against the bar and sipped the dark liquid, she doubted that would happen. The children were napping, both of them exhausted after a combination of riding, swimming and the heat. And Joe was always busy.

Whoever it was who had coined the phrase "Good help is *so* hard to find nowadays" had obviously never met Joe Sinclair. In the seven short days since he'd arrived, Alix had never ceased to be amazed by his resourcefulness. The house was fastidiously clean, and the man was an absolute genius around the kitchen. He prepared three delicious, hot meals daily, always being sure to ask for her menu suggestions. And every afternoon, like clockwork, he took care of all the laundry. Well, with the exception of her lingerie. She couldn't bring herself to let him handle her sheer nightgowns, or her lacy bras and bikini panties.

She wasn't in the habit of watching the hired help, but with his close proximity—and the nagging fact that she found him wonderfully attractive and capable—it was impossible not to observe him. The children followed him as if he were the Pied Piper. And to Alix's astonishment, he never once lost patience with their constant chatter and endless questions.

The man was very nearly perfect, Alix mused as she went back to her easel. And in light of her own ineptitude around the house, she found it almost unnerving.

Even so, she didn't quite agree with him on some of his ideas about Kimberley and Michael. One minute, he would be overly concerned about their physical safety, and the next, he'd be assigning them household du- ties—making them pick up after themselves, make their own beds and help him with the dishes. But she had managed to hold her tongue; she wanted desperately to avoid another confrontation.

After all, she had left the bustle of Dallas for the sol- itude of the hill country in order to paint. Not to argue over the children, not to find a man, but to *paint*. To prove that she could make a living as an artist.

And away from the various distractions she'd en- countered in Dallas, paint she did. Alix was pleasantly surprised at the speed with which blank canvas took the form of cedar and oak, rock-ribbed hills, winding paths and sparkling streams.

Glancing toward the stables, she caught sight of Joe as he took off his blue chambray shirt. In stilled silence she watched him toss it over the top of the fence, then begin brushing down one of the horses. His strokes were firm and capable, but obviously gentle. And she re- membered how his hands felt when...

No, she lectured herself, I mustn't think about him! But color dotted her cheeks, just as it had each time the memory of their near-kiss crept back. She was being very careful around him, hoping he wouldn't see the effect he had on her senses.

Valiantly she had tried to put him out of her mind by burying her thoughts in her work. And unknowingly he'd made that task somewhat easier for her. He had treated her with cool detachment, basically ignoring her except for a few conversations about the children, the history and owners of the ranch and the running of the household.

He had been the epitome of the dutiful helper, al- ways bringing a lunch tray upstairs so that she could continue with her work instead of joining the rest of them in the kitchen. And once, he had caught the children in the studio and scooted them off, asking them not to bother their mother—when she would have loved nothing more than to accept Michael and Kimberley's private invitation to go riding with the three of them.

But how could she fault him for that? For probably the hundredth time, Alix reminded herself that he was only doing what he was hired to do. She picked up her brush, calling a halt to her afternoon break, and forced her attention back to the canvas.

"My third masterpiece," she teased herself out loud, adding a dot of ivory to a bluebonnet's crown. She might be unsure of herself in many areas, but she'd begun to believe in her artistic talent. She had to believe in it!

Her eyebrows furrowed at the shrill ringing of the telephone. "Now who could that be?" she asked the empty room. Realizing the children had only been asleep for about thirty minutes, she raced for the bedside phone and grabbed it before the next ring.

To her annoyance, it was her ex-husband. Wilt, the man who never called, never inquired. With visible effort, Alix kept her tone civil as she heard her ex-husband out. After a curt goodbye, she replaced the receiver in its cradle, fighting the urge to slam the telephone against the wall. In frustration, she wiped her hands and jerked off her smock. She needed fresh air, and fast.

She took the outside stairs and, in a near run, made for the creek. Settling on a large limestone boulder, she drew her knees up under her chin and hugged her legs. The mingled sounds of gurgling water and the chirping of a mockingbird were calming to her frazzled nerves.

Somewhat calming, anyway. Alix took a ragged breath, exhaling slowly, and watched a tiny yellow butterfly float away from a nearby bush. She didn't know how long she had been sitting there, five or ten minutes at the most, when she heard the sound of twigs snapping on the path behind her. But she didn't fear the intrusion. Incredibly she felt safe, and instinctively she knew it was Joe. Straightening her shoulders, Alix vowed to conceal her emotions.

"Taking a break?" he asked, his voice deep and soothing.

"Y-yes." She realized as he moved in front of her that the seemingly unmistakable sound had been more than the twigs. Working up from the bottom of his shirt, he was now fastening the third pearl snap.

"I saw you leave the house. You seemed to be in an awful big hurry."

Her eyes filled with the sight of him as he tilted her chin toward him, and she saw genuine concern in the depths of his dark cobalt-blue eyes. "I . . . needed some air." She tried her best to smile. "All that paint, you know. It was beginning to asphyxiate me—"

"What's wrong?"

She twisted her face away from his touch and bent to pick a blade of sun-dried grass from alongside the boulder. "Nothing. There's nothing wrong."

"Cut it out, Alix." Crouching down on his heels, Joe looked at her eye to eye. He took her hand, and the rough texture of his callused palms sent a tingling message of awareness through every cell of her body. "You don't have to put up a front for me. Something's bothering you, and if it helps to talk—"

"You don't want to hear my problems." No one ever had, she thought.

"Try me."

It couldn't hurt to talk to him, she thought; it might even help her deal with this irritating attack of self-pity, along with her sudden loss of objectivity concerning Wilt. "It's...it's the children. Their father wants to take them to Alabama for three weeks." A bitter laugh passed her throat. "For the first time in six months, he wants to see them."

"No offense, Alix, but you can't fault a guy for wanting to see his kids."

"You don't understand. He doesn't really want to see them. He only wants to stay in his mother's good graces by taking them to visit her. It's nothing but a show for his own benefit."

Joe scowled. "Then why are you letting him? Why don't you just tell him no and be done with it?"

"Because...I keep hoping for a miracle. I keep hoping that one day he'll wake up and realize that they're his flesh and blood." She looked away, pretending to study a pebble at her feet. "But that won't happen. And in the meantime, I keep letting him get the best of me."

"Has he spent any time with them since your divorce?"

"None whatsoever."

"I don't know the situation," he reasoned, "but since he wants to do it, why don't you give him the opportunity to be with them? I'd be willing to bet that if he spends a couple of weeks with Kim and Mike, he'll have a new attitude."

Tenderly, Joe swept a wayward lock of hair behind her ear. And she looked up into his kind eyes as he continued. "You've got two great kids, Alix. I've only been around them for a week, and they've already got me wrapped around their little fingers." He squeezed her hand. "The guy wouldn't be human if he couldn't respond to those two."

Alix laughed nervously. "And if he's not human?"

"Then at least you will have tried. And you can start accepting the fact and get on with your life." He lowered his chin, tilting his head in order to capture her gaze again. "But don't let it eat at you, honey. You won't get anywhere by worrying yourself sick over false expectations of other people. God knows, I've learned that the hard way."

Maybe he was right. Maybe she should give their father another chance, Alix decided. "Okay.... I'll give it a try."

She watched him, reveling in the wonderful feel of his palms and fingers as he rubbed her hand. There was so much she didn't know about this man, so much she wanted to know about him. His words had seemed helpful, possibly even wise. But from the pain that was etched in them, she knew he hadn't come to this point in his life unscathed.

"Have you ever been married before, Joe?" she asked.

"Yes." His hands stopped moving and he froze for a moment, his jaw muscles telling of his internal fight for control. He wrenched to his feet, wiping his forehead with the back of his arm. "But I didn't come out here to talk about me."

"A nice man I know told me that sometimes it's good to talk." The tenseness of her face relaxed slightly, and she smiled up at him. "What was she like?"

Joe didn't want to discuss Tammi. Not really. He had thought about her some when he was cooling his heels in the slammer. But he had never talked about her to anyone, and it probably wouldn't be a good idea to start by spilling his guts to Alix. "Let's just say we came from different backgrounds and weren't exactly suited for each other."

"I take it you're divorced then. How long ago was it?"

"It was final almost two years ago."

"Do you have any children?"

He couldn't tell her about the baby; the wound was still too fresh. In fact, he wondered if he would ever be able to forget, or forgive, Tammi's abortion. To her, having purpose in life meant striving for the perfect tan, the perfect tennis game. And, no doubt, the ultimate disgrace would have been to lose her precious figure!

"No," he answered slowly, gazing out toward the rushing water of the creek. "We didn't have any children."

"You're not over her."

"I'm over her, all right. I guess I'm still not over some of the things she did to us, though." He hesitated for a minute, trying to forget how similar the two women's backgrounds might be, and then reached into his breast pocket for a cigarette. "As far as she was concerned, I was just a temporary distraction. Someone to keep her amused for a while."

"You sound very bitter."

"Yeah, I'm a little bitter." Joe cupped the match's flame, taking a long drag from the filtered tip. He didn't like to think about that part of his past. It was best forgotten. Like a fool, he had never stopped to ask Tammi why she was interested in him, why she married him— until that day when he had come home early and found her in bed with her tennis instructor. After kicking the guy out, he had asked her. And for the first time he had

gotten it through his thick skull that she didn't give a
damn about him. "She only married me because she
was bored with the other men she'd known. Bored!"

"You're being too hard on yourself...and maybe on
her, too." Briefly, Alix wondered if Wilt had made
vague excuses about their marriage, or blamed her for
all their problems. "Did you ever try to understand
her?"

"Why are you taking up for her?" Forgetting his
pledge to be gentle with Alix, to give her time, his eyes
turned to brilliant steel. "Are you that kind of woman,
Alix? Is your existence based on social one-upmanship?
Do you have to have the showiest parties, the finest
clothes, the best figure?"

Alix could feel the blood draining from her face as he
went on.

"Hell, there are people who don't even have the
money for a decent Christmas dinner, much less any
gifts to give their kids." He threw down the half-
finished cigarette, grinding it under his boot heel, and
then glared at her again. "And on Christmas Day, she
had the cook throw out five pounds of beluga caviar
that her plastic-coated friends didn't eat! Is that what
it's like with you too, Alix?"

She watched him intently, shaking her head and
trying to stay calm in the face of his uncharacteristic,
uncontrolled anger. He had just described a nameless
woman, a woman who could have been any one of a
dozen of her acquaintances. He had described a life-
style she had known, and for the most part enjoyed, all
of her life. But she wasn't like that.

Suddenly, Alix wondered what had made him give up
the easy life. He was no ordinary ranch hand, so why

had he offered to fill in as her housekeeper? A hundred dollars a week was a far cry from beluga caviar.

"No," she answered, "I wouldn't do something like that, Joe. But we're not talking about me. You still love her, don't you?"

"No." He shook his head. "But does a person ever really get over their first broken heart?"

"I don't know."

"What do you mean, you don't know? Haven't you been in love before?"

"No," she whispered hesitantly.

His eyes concealed any signs of emotion. "Not even with your children's father?"

Alix sat motionless. "N-no." All of a sudden, his stony gaze reminded her of the calm before a storm.

Leaning forward, Joe planted his palms on the rock, his thumbs digging into the tender flesh of her hips. He scrutinized her with a look that bordered on fury, and she felt his hot breath on her mouth. "How could you marry a man and not love him? Did you marry him for his money, Alix?"

"No."

"How could you lie in bed with him and let him make love to you night after night if you didn't love him?" Not waiting for her answer, he continued his barrage. "How could he accept that from you?" His hands gripped her upper arms tightly, pulling her to her feet. "If you were my wife, I wouldn't accept anything less. I'd want you whispering my name and telling me you loved me, and I'd want you to mean every word!"

"Stop it!" He didn't know the pain she'd suffered! He didn't know about her empty arms, the lonely nights when she would have happily given all her worldly possessions to turn to her husband, to love and be loved by him. This was the most private of her anguish, and she would share it with no one—especially not with Joe! Angrily she pushed her palms against his chest, wedging a space between them. "You have no right!"

"I have to know, Alix!" His hold on her tightened. "Why did you marry him?"

"Because I had to!" She wrenched free of him and rubbed her aching arms. "Because I was pregnant!"

"You could've gotten rid of it."

"How dare you!" She backed away, almost choking on her angry words. "I loved my baby from the beginning. I wanted her! And it's none of your business, but I thought my relationship with my husband *was* love!"

Alix lowered her voice, fighting to control her tears after a single drop rolled down each cheek. "But as it turned out, he didn't want me." Her fists were clenched at her sides, her fingernails digging into her palms as she continued. "Now! Does that satisfy your curiosity?"

"No, not exactly," Joe answered as he studied her. "But it confirms one fact."

He closed the distance between them, the rage in his expression suddenly replaced by the gentleness she had detected so many times before. After wiping her tears away with his knuckles, he held her face between his large palms. "The guy can't possibly be human," he added huskily. "I want you, Alix."

"How can you say that? You don't know me, Joe. You don't know what—"

"Shhh," he soothed, his breath warm against the corner of her mouth. "Oh, Alix. My sweet, sweet Alexandra. I know what's important. I know that I need you more than—"

"Please don't tease me like this," she pleaded, quivering as his fingers caressed her scalp, his thumbs grazing the pleasure points of her ears.

"But I'm not teasing." Lowering his face to hers, he captured her lips in a kiss of frenzied need, his mouth at first blistering and insistent, then tender and seductive as his tongue parted her lips. His arms circled her waist, crushing her breasts against the solid warmth of his chest. And the clean, male scent of him enveloped her senses.

As he unleashed the dam of her pent-up emotions, Alix slid her hands up the hard wall of his back, her fingers raking through the hair at the base of his neck. For a wild, sweet instant, it was possible to forget everything but the ecstasy of the moment. A moment when every fiber of her being was awakened to the exquisite taste of undeniable need for Joe, a need like she'd never known existed. She drew him nearer as she moaned his name, fading into the breathless heat of their passion.

His mouth left hers, leaving a trail of soft, searing kisses along her cheek before he whispered hoarsely into her ear. "We're both human, Alix. I know that I want you, that I can't get you out of my mind." His hands cupped the curve of her hips, fusing her to him, and he searched her eyes. "You want me too, Alix. You can't deny that."

Yes, she wanted him! She wanted to give in to her feelings, to accept the rising tide of passion that was cresting in her body. But he had rejected her once, and if he did it again, it would tear her heart to shreds.

Her hands suddenly released him. "Don't do this to me, Joe! Please," she begged, pushing against his chest. "Just leave me alone!"

"I can't, Alix. There's no sense in fighting it...."

"Don't touch me!" Whirling away from him, trembling, Alix ran up the path toward the house.

She had had no choice but to lie to him. She couldn't tell him that she did want him to touch her just as much as she wanted to touch him! She couldn't tell him that she didn't dare trust her own emotions. And that she was frightened—because he was beginning to mean much, too much to her!

## Chapter Four

"Alix, we have to talk." Joe stood in the doorway of her bedroom, one palm pressed against the frame, watching her as she rubbed her cheek across the pillow.

"I don't want to talk," she whispered in reply, pulling the sheet up from her neck to cover her face.

"Well, I do." Twelve months ago, he would have said to hell with it, his pride was involved here. But he had changed a lot in that one year in prison, and he wouldn't let the shackles of the past ruin his chances for the future. He had pushed her too far, and he had to make things right with her. Not later, not tomorrow. Now. "And if you aren't going to ask me in, Alexandra, I'll come in uninvited."

"Don't you dare!" Her voice, muffled by the sheet, held a note of desperation.

He walked across the room, pausing on the way to collect her discarded blouse and jeans from the floor.

Realizing her state of undress, and suddenly curious about the extent of it, he swallowed hard and fixed his gaze on her shapely form. The thin sheet outlined every curve, leaving little to his imagination, and he inched closer to the woman who occupied so many of his thoughts lately.

Feeling his body heat rising steadily, Joe took a series of deep breaths. He had to push aside his raging desire for her. If she were ever going to trust him, he would have to give her the time she needed. "All I want to do is talk. And if you don't look at me, I'll peel that damned sheet off you myself."

"You wouldn't!" Alix clutched the fabric tighter. She could hear his ragged breathing, could feel the mattress sway under his weight, and her pulse quickened.

"I assure you, I would. Now look at me," he demanded.

"All right," she said at last, slowly drawing the sheet down to her chin.

"That's better." His voice was too husky to be normal.

She watched his intent gaze, then squeezed her eyes shut as he reached to comb her hair back from her temple. His touch rekindled the fire still smoldering inside her body. Her lips still felt swollen from his kiss, and she ached for him to stretch out beside her, to keep on kissing her and then... Dear Lord, how could she keep denying what she felt for him, what she'd felt for him since that first day?

"Alix, I had no right to make comparisons between you and...her. If that's why you're upset, rest assured it'll never happen again. She doesn't mean a thing to me anymore."

If only she could tell him why she was upset, she thought despondently. If only she could give in to her instincts and emotions, throw herself into his arms right now and make love with him. But if she did, she would fail him miserably. And that was the one thing she couldn't bear.

"Joe," she pleaded, "we can't continue like this. Out by the creek, we said and did things that go far beyond what our relationship ought to be."

"I'm attracted to you. That's no secret." He reached over her body, pulling the sheet tight across her hips as he placed his hand on the other side of the bed.

Alix fought unsuccessfully to control her racing heartbeat. "Is that why you agreed to take this job?"

"Partially," he answered hoarsely.

There were so many unanswered questions about this man. "What's going on, Joe? For the life of me, I can't understand why you offered to stay and work here. You're not an ordinary ranch hand, and no matter how well you've done the job, you simply don't fit the picture of a housekeeper. And—" she tried desperately to make her words sound casual "—I don't believe for a minute that it was your interest in me that influenced you to work here. I'm certain that finding a woman to share your bed is the least of your problems."

He paused, grimacing as he rubbed his firm jaw. "I'm here because I want to be. Because, at this point in my life, I need you and the kids as much as you need me. I'll admit that I don't need the money you're paying me—"

"What did you do on your last job?"

Time seemed to be suspended as he studied her, his dark eyes serious and unwavering. Finally he answered. "I'm a veterinarian, but I'm not in practice right now. And I own a ranch near Johnsonville, the Double S, since my full name is Samuel Joseph Sinclair. I've been called 'Sam' most of my life."

He watched her for a long moment before he continued. "I've got a competent man running the ranch for me right now. So, for the time being, I'm free to do what I want to do."

"Sam . . ." She stared at him as she tried out the new name. "Who—or what—are you running from, Sam Sinclair?"

"I'm not running from anything. I've just put a bad time in my life behind me, and I want to do what makes me happy. I don't care to discuss it—except to say that I've spent a year in hell. It has no bearing on my ability to do my work for you. Can you accept that?"

Joe had been good to her and her children, and that was all that mattered. "I suppose I can," she conceded, curious about his ex-wife, the faceless, nameless woman who had hurt him so badly, the woman who had probably caused him to give up his veterinary practice. But whatever was bothering him, he had a right to his secrets, just as she did. Without a doubt, his "year in hell" was something that would be terribly painful for him to discuss, but perhaps someday he would feel comfortable enough to confide in her.

"Thank you," he said softly. He rubbed her arm, his hand warming the once-cool percale and sending persuasive jolts of current through her veins. "And I want to apologize for my actions down by the creek. I won't deny that I want you. Hell, I won't deny that it's taking every ounce of willpower I've got to keep from crawling under that sheet with you." He slid his thumb underneath her bra strap, his nail lightly skimming her shoulder. "For both our sakes, I should probably get out of this room now."

"Yes," she whispered. Involuntarily, her hand moved up to his face, her finger gently tracing the scar that cut through the edge of his eyebrow. She knew she was playing with fire. But she needed to touch him just this once. "That might be for the best."

Their gazes met and held, and Alix couldn't breathe, couldn't look away from his penetrating cobalt-blue eyes. "Joe?" she murmured, her fingers wrapping around his wrist, bringing his roughened palm to the warmth of her cheek. "What have you done to me?"

"Sweetheart, it doesn't take a genius to see that you've been hurt by life. We both have." Tenderly, provocatively, his fingers outlined her ear and the slender column of her throat. "But we can't look back, only forward. We'll take one day at a time." His body slipped into alignment with hers, and he cupped her face between his palms. "One minute at a time. And if I don't kiss you right this minute I think I'll die."

A tentative smile touched the corners of her mouth. "Then... kiss me," she finally said breathlessly.

He groaned as his lips came down on hers, searing, dissolving what little was left of her reserves. She met his embrace, her arms circling his neck, and the sheet slid low on her rounded, lace-covered breasts. She buried her hands in his hair and basked in the feel of his aroused body, the wonderful, salty taste of him, the musky scent of him. And when he whispered her name, she wanted to melt into his body....

*"I hate you!"*

Alix jumped to a sitting position, and Joe's arms fell away from her as he sprang to his feet. Kim, her eyes filled with tears, raced across the bedroom and pounded her fists against Joe's stomach.

He reached for her, holding her by the shoulders. "Kim! What's wrong?"

"I hate you!" Kim screamed at him.

"Kimberley—" Alix clutched the sheet tighter under her arms.

Joe released the girl, and she spun to face her mother. "I hate you, too! Why did you let him kiss you?"

"Oh, angel," she tried to soothe. "I was upset. And Joe was trying to make me feel better." The words sounded so trite....

"You never kissed my daddy," she cried. "Mommies and daddies are supposed to kiss each other, and you hardly ever did. So why are you kissing him?" She stepped back and whirled away. In a near run, she shouted over her shoulder. "Make him go away!"

"Wait, Kimberley," she pleaded. "Please wait!"

"Let her go, honey. Give her a chance to cool down." Joe's viselike fingers restrained her. "She needs to learn that you have a right to a life of your own."

"That may be true, but you have no right to tell me what to do about her! Can't you see why she's upset? Now please, let go of my arm!"

He dropped his hand and watched her as she pulled on her robe. "I think you're making a mistake."

"It's my problem. Stay out of it!" She cringed at the wounded look on his face, but her children had to come first. Wilt's rejection had been too much for them, and she couldn't let them be hurt any more! They were simply too young. She couldn't expect them to understand the relationship—or lack of relationship—between her and Wilton.

With that, she turned and ran after Kim. And her heart sank as she realized what she had to do. No matter what she felt for Joe, she would have to find someone to replace him.

Sadie Metzger glanced around the den, eyeing each one of the Ferrells' possessions in turn as she continued to talk a mile a minute. Alix was trying, quite unsuccessfully, to devote her full attention to the woman who had already irritated her by showing up half an hour late for their interview.

She nodded at one of Sadie's comments, then rubbed the muscles at the back of her neck in a futile attempt to ease the tension—tension that had grown steadily worse over the past five days. Her frustrating search for a new employee had turned up only one applicant, a team, as it turned out: Mrs. Metzger and her son Zeke, who hadn't uttered a single word since they arrived. Kimberley and Michael hadn't said a word either, for that matter. They'd been too busy studying the young man, who appeared to be in his mid-twenties and was as thin as a rail.

"...and, Mrs. Smith, you can be sure that my boy and I would do right by you." Sadie's cap of short white curls bobbed up and down as she spoke. "Why, Zeke's been working horses since he was knee-high to a grasshopper. And I've been keeping house for folks around here ever since my late husband, God rest his soul, departed this life."

"Yes, Mrs. Metzger. I'm sure your references are impeccable." Alix's eyes moved to the man who sat next to his mother on the sofa. His feet were crossed at the ankles, and he was grinning from ear to ear. One chapped hand, showing numerous scrapes and scars, drummed the red cap that rested on his knee. Involuntarily, Alix pictured him in overalls, pitchfork in hand, posing for the cover of a feed and seed catalog.

"Now, understand," Sadie went on, her sober, demanding voice breaking into Alix's musing, "I don't do any mopping or heavy work. I've got the arthritis real bad. And we can't live in, we have our own place to look after. Our workdays are strictly eight-to-five."

"I see." Who *was* going to do the heavy work? Alix wondered with alarm. She could see Joe out of the corner of her eye, his long, lean body propped against the frame of the door that led to the kitchen. But as she prepared for the all-important question, she forced herself to concentrate on Mrs. Metzger. "And how much salary are you asking?"

"My gracious, let's see," the woman deliberated, tapping her index finger against the edge of her trifocals. "I think eight hundred a month is fair. For each of us, mind you."

Alix's eyes widened. Sixteen hundred dollars a month? Joe cleared his throat, and she looked in his direction just in time to see his hand move up to stroke his jaw. She was almost certain that was a grin he was hiding! He had been so maddeningly agreeable and understanding when she told him about her decision to look for someone else, and this was probably the reason. No doubt, he knew it would be next to impossible to find a replacement.

What was she going to do? Even if these people deserved sixteen hundred dollars a month, Brad Ferrell's stipend wouldn't stretch that far. And she could ill afford the difference. She could also ill afford the chaos that had come into her life over the past five unbelievably long days. She was going slowly insane trying to avoid Joe, trying to get some work done. Trying to stop thinking about the sound of his voice when he whispered her name, the feel of his hard body when he held her against him.

"Mrs. Smith?" Sadie persisted. "That sounds about right to you, doesn't it?"

"I, uhh... Well, to be quite frank, I'll have to give it some thought. My financial situation is such that I can't afford that much money."

"It never ceases to amaze me the way you rich folks are always poor-mouthing about money. Surely you don't expect us to work for nothing!"

"No, of course not, Mrs. Metzger," she answered, struggling to ignore Joe's quickly stifled laugh. "But I'll have to let you know."

"Well, you better not think too long. We do have several other job offers, you know."

"I'll certainly keep that in mind," Alix replied, not at all impressed by the woman's obvious bluff. If Sadie Metzger did have another job offer, she decided, it was probably to sell used cars.

Kimberley, sitting angelically on a straight-backed chair at Mrs. Metzger's side, started swinging her legs. Alix watched her as she slanted a disdainful look at Zeke. Clearly, Kim was wary of another man on the premises to take away her mother's attention. Squelching a grin, Alix fought the urge to pull her daughter aside and assure her that, when it came to Zeke, she had absolutely nothing to worry about.

Sadie reached over to pat Kimberley's chestnut-brown hair. "You have such nice little children, Mrs. Smith. They're both so well behaved!"

"Thank you." Maybe she'd been wrong about the used cars. Maybe it was for some diplomatic post.

"And by the way, our church's Vacation Bible School starts tomorrow. I'm in charge of registration, and we'd love to include your little dears. The bus comes right by your property."

"Oh, Mother! Can we?" It was the first bright smile to light Kimberley's face in days.

"What's a Vacation Bible School?" Michael asked with a baffled frown.

"My gracious! What kind of training have you children had?" Not waiting for an answer, Sadie straightened righteously. "It's a way for children to learn more about the right way to live, little boy. You city children need to have your life put on the right course!"

The nerve of the woman! What did she think Alix had been doing with their lives? Dragging them around to cocktail parties? "We attend church regularly, Mrs. Metzger." For the children's sake, she tried to control her voice, and her tongue. "But Michael didn't recognize the term 'Vacation Bible School' because we refer to it as 'Summer Church School' at our...church in the city."

"I'm sorry, Mrs. Smith. I didn't mean—"

"Can we go, Mother? Please?"

"Well..." She supposed Mrs. Metzger's intentions were good. And why should she deny her children one of their favorite summer activities, and the chance to meet some of the neighboring children, just because she didn't especially care for the woman? Every church was entitled to at least one person like Sadie on its rolls. "I don't see why not. Thank you for inviting them, Mrs. Metzger. I'm sure they'll enjoy it."

Sadie quickly explained all the details, including the bus schedule. And Kimberley and Michael, satisfied that they were going to have the time of their lives, scampered outside to play hide-and-seek as their mother stood up to say her goodbyes to the Metzger duo.

"Miz Smith," Zeke blurted without warning, displaying a gap-toothed smile. "You sure are purty." As Alix colored at his offhand remark, he went on, "If anybody ever tells you any different, you just kick 'em."

"Zeke Metzger!" his mother admonished. "You keep your comments to yourself."

Alix spied Joe, and as she watched the amused grin that traced his rugged features, she wondered why he didn't go into the other room or something. The Metzgers were doing a beautiful job of unnerving her. They certainly didn't need any help from him. She turned her head, but not before catching Joe as he motioned toward Zeke and mouthed "Good taste!"

Sadie's eyes drilled a hole through Alix, as though she had invited Zeke's candor. "I must admit, Zeke's only acting like any red-blooded male." Her mouth pursed as she looked at Joe with distrust. "We women can never be too careful about our reputations!"

"You're absolutely right, I'm sure," Alix agreed as she steered them closer to the door. "And I'll have to get back to you about the—"

"Don't take too long, though!" Sadie's finger wagged. "Remember now, we do have those other offers."

"Oh, please," she commented, ushering the Metzgers out the front door as quickly as possible. "By all means, don't let my indecision stand in the way of a good opportunity."

Alix leaned back against the safely shut door, only to see Joe standing there shaking his head and laughing. She buried her face in her hands. Now that the ordeal was finally over, she could appreciate the humor in it, but she wasn't about to let him enjoy the situation any more than he already had!

Straightening, she forced her hands down to her sides and tried to look serious. "You certainly didn't make that absurd interview any easier!"

Holding up his palms in a gesture of surrender, he managed to stop chuckling long enough to ask, "What can I say? I'm sorry, but—"

He was still in the doorway, and Alix brushed past him. "I've got to get back to work," she mumbled, racing through the kitchen and up the stairs to her studio.

Ignoring her canvas, she threw herself facedown across the bed and fought the urge to laugh and cry at the same time. What was she going to do? It would be a cold day in hell before she'd hire those two. Sadie Metzger would try to bulldoze the household, and Zeke's cow eyes and "compliments" would drive her batty!

Alix rolled over and stared at the chandelier overhead, taking a series of deep, calming breaths. There were two problems she had to face: her money situation...and Joe. Without a doubt, he was the best thing that had happened to her, to them, in a long time. And he had said he needed them, too.

She smiled and got up from the bed, heading enthusiastically toward her easel. Even though her heart hadn't been in her work lately, she'd felt compelled to start on this painting a few days ago. Somehow, she knew this one was going to be special.

Yes, Alix thought as she picked up her brush and gazed out the window. If Joe would consider staying on

for a while longer, she would view his help with re-
newed gratitude.

Surely she could find a way to deal with Kimberley's
jealousy. After all, it would only be a short time before
Wilton picked them up for their visit with his mother.
Her entire future, and the children's, depended on her
being able to support them. She had to be practical!

There was no alternative. She would talk to her
daughter that night, she decided, and make her understand that Joe Sinclair was an employee—a very good
employee—and nothing more.

Straddling a kitchen stool, Joe poured himself a glass
of iced tea and watched Alix's prospective employees as
they drove away. Yeah, ol' Zeke had practically sali-
vated while looking at her. Not that he blamed the guy;
he'd been guilty of the same on more than one occasion.

Although visibly uncomfortable about the interview,
Alix had looked gorgeous. She had worn an apricot-
colored linen dress and matching high-heeled sandals.
Joe knew her clothes were expensive; Tammi had spent
enough of his money for him to have an idea of prices.
But the cost of her clothes had nothing to do with the
fact that she always looked like a million dollars. Alix
had the ability to make a pair of jeans and an ordinary
blouse look elegant, as if they'd been designed especially for her.

But he preferred seeing her in dresses, like the ones
she wore to dinner each evening. She had a habit of
never wearing nylons, maybe because of the June heat.
The sight of her bare legs, long, sleek and shapely,
drove him to distraction. When he watched her walk
across the room, all he could think about was running

his hand along the smooth length of those perfect legs, up to her thighs. He could visualize her stretched out beside him in bed, then underneath him....

God, he was becoming more obsessed with her by the day, by the minute. An all-too-familiar rush of warmth shot through his body as he remembered the way she had responded to his kisses. He thought of her silky chestnut hair, her gold-flecked emerald eyes, those lips that seemed to have been created for his. And her soft, throaty voice, which made his one-syllable name sound like a caress.

Listening to the echo of her light footsteps as she moved around upstairs, Joe stood up and started pacing the kitchen floor. It was all he could do to keep himself from joining her when she bathed up there in that hideaway his former mother-in-law had built. He wondered if she had any idea how much strength it took on his part not to fold her into his arms when she came back downstairs after her nightly soaks. He had used every excuse imaginable to get close to her, to smell the gardenia scent of her skin.

It was stupid to torture himself like this, he knew. He wanted her, and she wanted him, even if she wasn't ready to admit it yet. Before Kim had walked in on them, Alix had let down some of those stubborn defenses, and he knew that, given time, she would open up to him even more. Her body and her spirit were mysteries to him now, but he was determined to know all of her. No, by damn, he wasn't going to let her get rid of him so easily!

Lucky for him, Sadie and her son Zeke had played right into his hands. "Purty Alix," he crooned under his breath, a broad smile lifting the corners of his mouth as he bounded up the stairs to her studio.

In the three days that had passed since Alix interviewed the Metzgers and promptly asked Joe to stay on, she had made a pointed effort to spend more time with Michael and Kimberley—especially Kimberley. Before, Alix hadn't wanted to burden the children with the realities of their financial straits. But after having a no-punches-pulled talk with her daughter, Alix was pleased that Kimberley seemed to understand and had agreed, somewhat grudgingly, to accept Joe as their employee.

Humming a cheerful tune, Alix squeezed a thick dollop of white into forest green and, with a stir of her palette knife, mixed the oils. The household was running as smoothly as ever, the children were enjoying Vacation Bible School and, once again, her work was coming along well. Now, if she were to hear from her mentor at the art gallery, everything would be rosy.

"Alix," Joe called from the stairway, breaking into her preoccupation. "The mail's here."

"Wonderful!" A smile lit her face, and her eyes lingered on the man who was striding toward her. He had acquired a tan since arriving at the Bar F, and it gave his rugged face even more character. He must have just showered, she mused. Dampness made his dark hair slightly wavy, and it glistened as it caught the morning light. The sleeves of his faded work shirt were rolled up, exposing the whipcord strength of his forearms. The fabric's softness only served to emphasize his broad shoulders and the muscular expanse of his chest. Her eyes lowered for a split second to the front of his tight jeans....

Unnerved, Alix tore her gaze away from him. Over the past few days, she had found it increasingly difficult to control her perusal of him, to ignore his physical presence. He was indeed a rare specimen of man.

She'd thought him virilely attractive that first day; he was even more so now.

"Here you go." He handed her the small stack of mail, then dropped onto an oversize chair and studied her as she thumbed through it. "Judging by that look, I'd say you didn't get whatever it was you were expecting."

She couldn't help but smile. Her facial expressions had never been an open book to anyone but him. And strangely enough, she had decided she liked that quality in him. Even though she didn't understand why, the fact that he could read her so well seemed to give her an odd sense of security.

"Exactly," she answered with a sigh, holding up one fat blue envelope. "Here we have my bank statement, which I don't even care to open." Frowning, she picked up a large white envelope. "This one's from my ex-husband's clever attorney, probably advising me of the latest excuse for holding up the sale of the house. And this—" she gestured toward a newsletter "—is a truly delightful piece of mail when you're expecting something important. It's the latest issue of *Septic Tank Today*." Alix shook her head and rolled her eyes. "Let's hope the title isn't some sort of an omen."

"Hey," Joe laughed, "who put a burr under your saddle?"

"No one." It might not be prudent to tell him about her hopes and dreams, but she desperately wanted to share them with someone. And, she admitted to herself, she didn't want him to leave. "When I told you I was an artist, I left out one important fact: I'm only a beginner. To be quite honest with you, I'm trying to get my career started. A friend of mine, Hamilton Fischer, owns a gallery in Dallas, and he's promised me a showing if I can complete six landscapes before the middle of July. I mailed him the first one last week, and I've been waiting to hear his feedback."

"What are you worried about?" His eyes were intense, never leaving hers. "I'm no art critic, but I've seen your work and it's very good."

"Do you really think so?"

"Absolutely."

"I appreciate your vote of confidence, Joe. It means a lot to me." He had a wonderful way of making her feel good about herself. "But it remains to be seen whether Hamilton will agree."

"What makes you think this Hamilton fella won't like your work?" He eased back, stretching his long, muscular legs out in front of him. "Didn't he see a sample before he offered to show your paintings?"

"No, none of my oils. I—" she colored slightly "—showed him a few pencil sketches. Really, he's only giving me this opportunity in the name of friendship. But he's a businessman and if my work isn't good enough, I'm sure he'll be the first to tell me. All he knows with any certainty is that I used to dabble in oils before I was married and that I have a degree in fine art."

He studied her for a long moment. "Why didn't you paint while you were married?"

"Well, I suppose I was busy with other aspects of my life—having the children, social responsibilities and such." That was all true, but she couldn't bring herself to tell him about Wilton and his open disdain for her talents.

Joe didn't miss the stark shadowing of Alix's haunted green eyes. He had obviously delved into an agonizing part of her past. There was something there she needed time to sort out, and he decided to change the topic to matters of the present. "Why did you start painting again?"

"Necessities of life, you might say. Financially, my ex-husband came out the big winner in our divorce." She laughed unconvincingly. "If my dad found out about the slice Wilton took out of my trust fund, I'm afraid he wouldn't think I was too old to take a switch to my legs!"

He sensed that she was making light of a subject that brought her abject pain. Always before, Alix had guarded her private thoughts with the fierceness of a she-cat protecting her cubs. And it gave him a distinct feeling of satisfaction to know that she was finally beginning to trust him with her inner self.

"I'm not sure that I'm doing the right thing, trying to make a living as an artist," Alix continued with a shrug. "My parents aren't . . . overly enthusiastic about my work. I suspect that my father would prefer I quit before I fail. And my mother simply pats me on the head and says, 'Oh, how nice. Now why don't you call one of your friends and go have lunch in the Village?'"

"That sounds rather coldhearted."

"Oh, I don't know." She paused and glanced out the window. "You can't expect people who own a Rembrandt and a Picasso to get excited over a few amateurish landscapes."

He had had a hunch that a lot of people had let her down, and she had just confirmed his suspicions. But he also had a hunch that she was tougher than she realized. "Don't sell yourself short, Alix."

"I'm trying not to," she said, her gaze drifting back to him. "My older sister Roberta encouraged me to take a stab at this. I've always looked up to her. She's a big-time real estate agent in Dallas and the brain of we three Powell girls. But she's the only person who's given me any moral support."

"You see? Things are already looking up. You have two of us to give you moral support now." His eyes held hers, refusing to let them go. "I'm proud of you, Alix. You're doing what you want to do, and you've gone with your gut instincts."

Joe stopped himself before he could add what he wanted to say in warning: *Don't ever let anyone else make your decisions for you, Alexandra. Take it from me; you'll be sorry if you do.*

"That's true, I guess." She smiled at him, the shadows lifting from her eyes and leaving them clear and bright. "But I'll feel better when I hear from Hamilton. This is my one chance to prove myself."

"Don't worry. I'm sure you'll do just fine." He would venture that there was a lot more than a career riding on this "one chance" of hers. She had to prove something to herself, and he would do everything in his power to make that happen... even if it meant buying the whole damned gallery and every one of her paintings.

She tilted her head toward her easel. "What do you think of this one? Honest opinion, now."

Joe stood up, anxious to get a glimpse of her latest effort. Moving his head first toward one side of the canvas, then the other, he appraised her work-in-progress. "As I said before, I'm no art critic. But I think you've done a great job of capturing the creek's aura." It was the scene of their first kiss. He knew right then that he wanted this painting, wanted a reminder of that first taste of her lips, and of the desire he felt welling up from deep inside her when he pressed his body against the softness of hers.

"This is my fourth. And I must admit, it's also my favorite—" Alix clamped her mouth shut, turning her face back toward the painting, and Joe smiled inwardly as he noticed the blush that had suddenly risen to her cheeks.

"Do you think the colors are complementary?" she added, her voice trembling.

"The colors are perfect." He didn't know how she would react to his constructive criticism, but he had to give it a try. "My only suggestion would be to give less emphasis to the trees and more to the water. What do you think?"

Joe watched her carefully. He could almost detect her self-defense mechanism registering in the warning zone, but then she cast a critical eye on the canvas.

"I think you're absolutely right," she said, grinning appreciatively. "Maybe you *should* be an art critic." As she picked up a brush and touched the point into aquamarine blue, her tongue moistened the curve of her upper lip.

"I shouldn't hold up progress, and I need to feed the horses," Joe blurted out. Didn't she know she was driving him crazy by moving her tongue that way? "I'd better get out of here and let the artist work on her masterpiece."

What he wanted to do was haul her into his arms and tell her everything would be okay. And then haul her into bed and make everything okay. Instead he turned, intent on leaving before he lost control of his senses and did just that.

"Joe," she called, stopping him. "Thank you."

She was gliding toward him, her hands extended. When he lowered his face toward her regal, uptilted chin, Joe felt her warm breath against his neck. He inhaled the flowery scent of her, and as his thumb brushed a smear of paint from her cheek, he went rigid with desire.

The kids were in town at church school. They were alone…with no distractions…and he wanted her with a fierceness that knew no boundaries.

## Chapter Five

Alix had meant to clasp Joe's hand, to let him know she appreciated his faith in her work. But when he touched her cheek, the courage of her convictions fell away, and a tremor of delicious anticipation raced through her body. He was standing near, very near, as he slowly wiped the smear of pale yellow paint down the leg of his jeans. Her eyes filled with the sight of his face, his presence.

Caught up in the breathlessness of the moment, her knees felt weak, as if they couldn't support her weight, and every inch of her body ached for his touch. He had a way of throwing her into a state of physical and emotional chaos, a glorious state that she didn't understand and didn't even want to question.

Her arms went up to him, circling his neck at the precise moment he reached for her. His strong hands drew her closer, the heels of his palms caressing the sides of her breasts as he pulled her body against his. Her eyes were lost in his, and she found herself helpless... reveling in both the strength and the gentleness of his touch as he took her breast, his hand slow but firm as it moved in a circular pattern of sweet, seductive torture.

He slanted his head to hers, his lips parting slightly, and his breath fanned her mouth. With ease, he lifted her until her bare feet were almost off the floor. And she welcomed the intimate pressure of his lips, invited the warmth of his tongue as he explored her mouth.

Alix moaned, her body trembling as his hands moved with agonizing slowness around her waist. She fought the urge to take his palm and put it back on her breast, to tell him not to stop, to beg him to make her his. She gasped with pleasure as he continued his unhurried, rapturous journey, caressing the base of her spine and then cupping her hips to pull her hard against his aroused body.

His pelvis moved sensuously against hers. "Alexandra," he whispered, his voice husky. "Oh, sweetheart, this is what you do to me. I'm going crazy wanting you."

Even though she could feel the blatant evidence of his need for her, even though she wanted him more than anything else in the world, she knew she couldn't go through with it. He would never be satisfied with her. He wanted the warm, responsive woman he believed she was, and she couldn't bear the thought of seeing him disappointed. She was torturing herself and Joe. Somehow, someway, she had to control her desperate craving for him.

"Please, Joe," she groaned, turning her mouth away from his. "We can't—"

"Why not?" he asked, capturing her hand and moving it dangerously close to his lower body. "We're alone. There's no one to stop us."

Warmth blazed from her hand to every nerve in her body. It would be so easy to give in to her desire, to reach out and rub her palm along the denim. But she knew that if she touched him, she wouldn't be able to say no. And then she would have nothing left, not even her pride.

Trembling, she yanked her fingers out of his grasp. "It just wouldn't work."

"Work! Hell, woman, I guarantee it works."

She pulled away from him, unable to confront the anger in his eyes.

"Why do you constantly fight what we feel for each other? Look at me, Alix! Don't stand there hugging your arms when you know you'd rather be hugging me."

"I'm sorry, Joe. I—"

"Look at me," he repeated, his voice leveling off to its usual deep baritone. "I don't want you to be sorry, darlin'. What I want you to do is stop fighting me. I'm a man, and you're a woman…a very desirable woman."

Alix willed her tone to be calm, struggled for a way to make him understand her inner turmoil without opening a wound that was too painful to face. "Joe, please listen to me. I've told you before that we shouldn't get involved with each other. I'm here in Bandera to work—I mean to paint. And it wouldn't be wise, considering the circumstances, to start anything."

"Because of Kimberley?"

"Yes, because of Kimberley, and because of us. At this point in my life, I can't allow myself to get into a relationship. It wouldn't be fair to either of us. And if you can't accept that, then it's time for you to pack up and go back to Johnsonville." She cringed at her own words, knowing they were cutting him to the quick. But she had to convince him. If she didn't, they would both suffer. "If you can't accept that, then..."

The blue of his eyes hardened to tempered steel. "Okay, boss lady. I get the picture."

"No!" She started to reach for his arm, but caught herself. "I didn't mean it like that. I stopped thinking of you as an employee a long time ago. Can't we be friends?"

"We're already friends," he stated bluntly. "Both of us want more than that, and you know it."

"Just friends, Joe." She ached to tell him that her words were hollow, but for her own protection, she couldn't. "Please?"

For what seemed like several minutes, he paced the floor and rubbed his jaw.

"All right, Alix," he said, finally stopping to face her. "Since you insist, we'll just be friends." His statement completed, he turned abruptly and left the studio.

Alix stood in front of the wide expanse of windows, watching him take the outside stairs and stride directly toward the stable. She leaned her forehead against the cool glass...hating herself for what she'd told him, for the way she had hurt him.

It was for the best, though, she thought as she lifted her head and sighed. Hopefully she had convinced him that she meant what she said. And now, she decided as she watched him fling open the doors and enter the stable, all she had to do was convince herself.

"Mommy," Michael called later that afternoon, interrupting Alix's work. "Joe wants you to come downstairs. Come on! He needs your help."

"Not now, Michael," she hedged. "I'm busy."

He tugged at her arm, his eyes as bright as two shining stars. "Please, Mommy. He said to hurry!"

Even though she had decided earlier to avoid Joe for the rest of the day, she didn't want to disappoint her son. With an "Okay, sugar," she let herself be steered to the kitchen. Joe was bending over the table, a cloth cake-decorating bag balanced precariously in his large hands.

Kimberley sat on a stool close by, near enough to watch but not to participate. "Joe's making a fancy cake." Her small voice held a hint of anticipation. "And he says he's got a surprise for us."

Michael raced to Joe's side, then ran a chubby finger around the frosting bowl's rim. The big man, wearing a white ruffled apron that looked ludicrous against his masculine western attire, calmly reprimanded the boy with an "Ahh, ahh!" He straightened, grinning proudly, and beckoned Alix forward.

"What's going on here?" she inquired lightly, warmed by the sheer domesticity of the scene, and relieved that Joe seemed to be his usual self again. The gleam was back in his eyes, and he was smiling that slow, lazy smile she had grown to love....

"Joe's got a big surprise for us, Mommy," Michael explained, his eyes now as round as saucers. "We'll get it tomorrow if we're good and eat all our vegetables at dinner tonight."

"I see." He was no doubt paving the way for spinach and brussels sprouts again, Alix surmised dryly. Pulling out a chair, she sat down and propped her chin on her hand. "I thought sweets were against your principles."

"Hey! This is a special occasion, woman."

She lifted her brow quizzically. "What's the special occasion?"

"If I told you, it wouldn't be a surprise. Right?" He looked down at her, capturing her gaze as he went on. "Now, what will we put on this cake? 'Surprise' or 'Tomorrow'?"

"Let's make it 'Surprise,'" she answered decisively. 'Tomorrow' sounds like something Scarlett O'Hara would put on a cake."

Kimberley eased away from the stool and stepped closer to the table. "May I help, sir?"

"Sure, honey."

"Joe?" Kimberley asked after finishing a crooked *S*. "When do we get our surprise?"

"Tomorrow, like I promised. Probably in the morning."

Alix marveled at the patience Joe showed with Kimberley as they labored over the lettering. "That's good, Kim." His voice was gentle and sincere as he knelt behind her, offering encouragement but no adult assistance. "I didn't realize an eight-year-old could write that well."

"My teacher said I print better than anyone else in the whole second grade," she said, beaming, and then frowned in exasperation. "Most of those kids just scribble-scrabble."

Joe laughed behind his hand at Kim's personally coined term, which she managed to pronounce as if it were only one word. And Michael, under the impression that no one was looking, dipped his fingers into the bowl of leftover white icing. But Joe saw him from the corner of his eye, and he slapped the little boy's hand playfully. Kimberley giggled, and it warmed Alix's heart when she detected the small sign of improvement in her daughter's attitude toward him.

After their somewhat lopsided creation was finished, the children proudly carried the cake into the dining room. As soon as she and Joe were alone, Alix whispered, "What's the surprise?"

"You're as bad as the kids," he scolded with a grin, offering her a dollop of frosting from the tip of his finger.

"No," she muttered, wanting nothing more than to lick the sweet, tempting icing that he held directly in front of her lips. "No, thanks."

Alix stared at him as he brought the frosting to his own mouth with what seemed like deliberate slowness. Good grief, she thought as he finally turned to rinse the cake-decorating paraphernalia, she was letting her imagination run away with her.

"Why did you call me down here?" she asked warily.

"Because 'friends' don't avoid each other all day." There was no accusation in his tone, only a pleased smile on his face. "And I knew the only way I could get you out of that studio was to use the kids as co-conspirators."

Michael ducked his blond head through the doorway. "Mommy, Mr. Joe told us it's okay to feed Spirit and Redwing some sugar cubes, so me and Kim are gonna go to the stable." He seemed to ponder a thought, then quizzed Joe. "Are you sure that sugar won't choke those horses?"

Joe shook his head and laughed. "No, Mike. When I said 'enough sugar to choke a horse,' I was just using an old expression. Don't worry, a couple of sugar cubes won't hurt them. All it'll do is keep you and Kim on their good side.''

"Then is it okay, Mommy?''

"Of course it is.'' Did Michael ever forget anything? she wondered, leaning over to let him give her neck a quick squeeze before he ran off to meet his sister.

She turned to Joe, rolling her eyes at his broadening smile of self-satisfaction. "You are a devil, Joe Sinclair!''

"Who, me?'' he asked innocently.

"Yes, you.'' Alix stood up and pushed the chair under the table. She needed to get back to work and away from Joe's unsettling presence.

"Don't go, Alix,'' he urged. "You can't work all the time. Why don't you take a break? Maybe give me a hand with dinner?'' He grinned again as he eyed her questioningly. "I thought we could eat a little early tonight, but I'm running behind schedule. I could sure use some help.''

She had to start learning how to manage around the kitchen; maybe she could get a cooking lesson without his even being aware of it. And a break would be a welcome treat, she admitted to herself. And if she had to be totally honest with herself, she would also have to admit that she relished the thought of having a few more minutes with Joe.

"All right,'' she agreed. "What's for dinner?''

"Meat loaf, salad, fresh green beans and mashed potatoes. Sound good to you?''

"Wonderful. Where do we start?'' She looked past him to the butcher block counter, where he had already set out a can of tomato sauce, a package of saltine crackers, an onion and some seasonings.

"Grab the ground meat and a couple of eggs from the refrigerator," he told her. "And keep your mouth shut."

"I beg your pardon!"

"I said, keep your mouth shut." He laughed and gestured toward the onion. "They don't bother me, but if they make you cry, breathe through your nostrils instead of your mouth and you won't have any problem."

"Very interesting," she commented, then clamped her lips together in an exaggerated fashion.

Joe chopped the onion while she silently found a large bowl and mixed—according to his careful instructions—the meat, cracker crumbs and whipped eggs. He dumped a handful of the pungent onions into the concoction, seasoned it with herbs and then got her started on her next project.

Trying to pay attention to everything he was doing, Alix stopped snapping the beans long enough to watch him grease a pan and shape the meat mixture into a loaf. "What else did you put in that?" she asked nonchalantly.

"Just the tomato sauce and a little sweet milk."

"Sweet milk? That sounds horrible."

"Yes, sweet milk." He popped the pan into the oven and dusted one palm against the other. "Now finish up there, or we'll be eating at midnight!"

She did as he bade, then tore the salad greens while he peeled the potatoes. "I don't know very much about cooking," she found herself confessing. "But you make it look easier than I imagined."

"Life is easier than you imagine, Alix," he replied quietly. "If you'll just enjoy the present and stop worrying about the past."

His eyes, she thought, seemed to be reaching inside her. "I think I'll set the table," she offered, anxious to get away from him . . . before she made further confessions that she would regret later.

Once settled at the table, Michael talked excitedly about the upcoming "surprise" and about a chili cook-off he'd heard about from his friends at church school. "They have it every year," he spouted, "on the Fourth of July, but it can't be on the Fourth of July this year, 'cause it has to be on a Saturday and that's July the first. It's a fun-raiser for the fire department, so can we go?"

"That's a *fund*-raiser, Michael," his older sister corrected, not bothering to hide her impatience with him.

"Same thing," he commented. "It's the day after tomorrow, Mommy. Can we go?"

"Why not?" she answered, laughing. "It sounds wonderful."

Joe listened with rapt attention as Kimberley recounted an incident that had happened earlier that day. But whenever Alix and Joe spoke to each other, the child's face would set in defiance.

After they had all polished off slices of the rich chocolate cake, Joe leaned back and patted his stomach. "Well, kiddos, help me clear the table and then I've got to run. We'll leave the dishes until tomorrow morning. I was expected somewhere thirty minutes ago."

Michael squirmed against his chair. "Are you gonna go see Willie?"

"Willie?" Joe asked, sounding confused.

"Yes, Willie. You were talking on the phone a while ago and you said, 'I'll see ya at six, Willie.' "

"Ohhh, you mean Lillie." The chair legs scraped as Joe stood up and thumped Michael lightly on the arm. "No more eavesdropping, young man. Now let's get this table cleared."

"Oh...damn!" Alix muttered, tossing the biography off her lap and dropping her head against the back of the sofa. She'd leafed through the thick volume twice—and she still didn't know one thing more about Vincent Van Gogh than she had before.

She checked her wristwatch. It had been well over two hours before when Joe had sauntered cheerfully into the den to tell her goodbye. She could hardly have missed the fact that he was dressed to kill, outfitted in tailored western-cut trousers, a long-sleeved shirt—with three snaps unfastened at the top!—and his best dress Stetson. He had stooped down to wipe a speck of dust off his right boot, and she hadn't missed those, either. She could spot an outrageously expensive pair of hand-tooled ostrich skin boots when she saw them, and she'd never seen them on him before tonight!

The nebulous "somewhere" he'd mentioned at dinner was undoubtedly a date with Lillie. And why not? she asked herself as she glanced at her watch again. He was a man, with a man's needs. She had repeatedly spurned his advances, and she had no right to feel possessive toward him.

But she did. And each tick of the grandfather clock grated on her nerves. She could visualize that...that floozy curling her arms around his wide shoulders and whispering sweet nothings into his ear. Green-eyed fury overtook her every time she imagined him kissing Lillie the way he had kissed *her*, every time she thought about Joe making love to the willing woman.

She wanted to be that woman. She wanted to learn the mysteries of his body. Would he be a forceful lover? Tender and considerate? Or would he be like Wilton?

Their college and courtship days seemed so long ago. Alix shuddered, realizing now that Wilt had known all the right words to say, all the right things to do. She'd been mesmerized by his charm and movie-star looks... and excited over the prospect of learning the joys of intimacy. But as she thought back on it, their lovemaking had seemed hurried and clinical.

After they married, the few times she had timidly suggested that he was rushing her, Wilt had sneered and told her she was being ridiculous. Before her, he was quick to point out, no woman had ever complained about his lovemaking!

Gradually, as time wore on, their infrequent attempts had dwindled to nothing. And Alix had been relieved. She had certainly never experienced what a normal woman was supposed to experience when she was with a man, the kind of rapturous abandon that a man like Joe would expect from a woman.

Yes, Joe Sinclair would need a woman who... The nerve of that man! she fumed as it suddenly dawned on her. He had asked her to help him with dinner so that he could hurry off to Lillie's waiting arms! "Going crazy wanting you," she mimicked, remembering his words for the hundredth time that day. "Like the devil!"

Jumping up from the sofa, Alix slammed the book down on the coffee table and stomped into the kitchen. All her fanciful thoughts about Joe were getting her nowhere—there was no way she was going to get involved in another hopeless situation.

She had to stop behaving like a smitten teenager. All that talk of his about not looking back, about living for the present and not dwelling on the past was pure bunk! Didn't he know that people learn from their mistakes?

Banging cabinets, Alix set about fixing herself a cup of hot tea. She cast a disdainful look at the dirty dishes that lined the countertop and curled her lip.

"You could have at least washed the dishes," she muttered, glaring at the stack of plates, "before you rushed off to meet that . . . that wanton hussy!"

"I said I'd do the dishes in the morning."

Red dotting her cheeks, Alix whirled around to face the object of her anger.

"And I wouldn't exactly call Lillie a wanton hussy," he added, smiling. "In fact, she gave me something really special tonight."

*I'll just bet she did,* Alix thought as he breezed past her.

"Hey, Kim. Mike," he called. "Come down here. I've got the surprise."

Raising her chin, Alix abandoned her tea and marched back into the den to bury her nose in the story of Van Gogh. She heard the children's feet as they descended the stairs and tried to decipher their mingled voices as they followed Joe's easy baritone into the kitchen. The back door slammed, and she listened to Michael and Kimberley giggling with anticipation. Again the door opened and shut, and she heard excited squeals of delight.

Curiosity propelled her into the kitchen. Her eyes widened, and she planted her fists on her hips. "What in blue blazes is that?"

A satisfied smirk played across Joe's features as he nodded toward the floor. "Correct me if I'm wrong, but it looks like an animal of the canine variety."

She moved toward the children. They were sprawled on the floor, each vying for the attention of a lop-eared pup with overlong legs and paws the size of small apples.

"Isn't she pretty, Mommy?" Michael asked reverently.

"Michael, this dog is not a girl. He's a boy," Kim corrected with all the arrogance of her three superior years. She turned the pup over on his back, pointing in the general vicinity of his fat belly. "Don't you know anything?!"

"Isn't he pretty, Mommy?"

"Simply gorgeous." How dare Joe Sinclair bring a pet into the house without her permission? She was going to have a terrible time explaining to the children that they couldn't keep the puppy, she thought as she glared at Joe. "You might have warned me," she said through clenched teeth.

He chose to ignore her as he hunkered down to pat the brown, black and white fur on the dog's back. "Don't squeeze his neck too hard, Mike. You'll have to remember he's just a baby."

"What's his name?" Michael asked, his eyes big and round as he pulled the puppy onto his lap.

"He doesn't have a name yet, son. You and Kim will have to decide on one."

"Let's call him Fred," Kimberley suggested.

"No! I don't like that." Michael hugged the dog protectively. "I wanna call him Spot."

Kimberley reached for the animal. "That's a stupid name, Michael."

"You don't have to make up your minds right now, kids," Joe intervened. "Let's get this little fella something to eat. I'll bet he's hungry."

Kim and Mike nodded, watching attentively while Joe prepared a dish of dog food that had materialized from a paper bag. As the gangly pup wolfed down the mixture, Kim ran her finger along the length of his back. "Look, Mike. He has a *T* on his back. Why don't we call him T-Bone?"

"Yeah," Michael agreed. "That's a good name for him. He prob'ly likes steak, too!"

"No doubt." Exhaling loudly, Alix crossed her arms over her chest. "It looks as if I've just acquired another mouth to feed."

"He won't eat very much, Mom." Kimberley's eyes were serious, her voice solemn. "He can have part of my food."

"Oh, angel." Alix's heart tightened. Perhaps she'd gone too far in her warnings about their money situation.

"Mine too, Mommy."

"I'm sure we'll be able to manage without that," Alix told them, glancing from their excited faces to Joe. "Well, I suppose we won't have to worry about what to do with the leftover liver and onions from now on," she stated, inching closer to the puppy. He licked his chops, then wagged his tail enthusiastically as Alix reached to pat his head. "You know, T-Bone, if nothing else, you're so ugly, you're cute!"

T-Bone's soulful brown eyes settled on Alix, and then he licked her hand. "And who," she asked, "is going to take care of T-Bone? He'll need to be fed and—"

"No problem, Alix," Joe interrupted. "I wouldn't have brought Kim and Mike a dog if I hadn't felt sure they could handle the responsibility." He looked at the kids. "We'll work out a schedule, and I'll teach you how to take good care of your puppy all by yourselves. Okay?"

"Yes, sir," the two young voices chorused.

Joe stood back, enjoying the looks of pleasure on the kids' faces. He'd made up his mind to accept the pup last week when Henry Kastel had been upset over what would become of Pretty Girl's last whelp. He had originally planned to pick up the animal the following day, after he'd had the opportunity to buy inoculation supplies, but when he visited with the Kastels earlier in the evening, the kid in him had been anxious to bring the puppy to Kim and Mike.

He'd known that he was inviting Alix's ire by bringing the dog back to the Bar F. But he could handle her anger—he had proved that on more than one occasion. Beyond that, it didn't take much reasoning on his part; he knew that Alix was a softhearted woman who wouldn't deny her kids the pup.

He smiled as he watched her. She was taking to T-Bone as fast as the kids were. It was ironic. He had accepted this animal in the hopes of helping Kim work out her feelings of jealousy. And in doing so, he'd inadvertently brought out a bit of healthy jealousy in Alix. Even though he hadn't planned it that way, he decided it wouldn't hurt his cause to let her stew about him and his "wanton hussy" for a while. She'd meet Lillie soon enough, and in the meantime, a little jealousy on her part was a good sign.

Yes, he congratulated himself as he watched all four of them playing in the middle of the kitchen floor, it was just the sign he'd been waiting for.

## Chapter Six

Alix's mid-morning walk had been tiring, considering the added weight of her supplies. But a rain shower had cooled the incessant late-June heat, and the thought of painting in natural surroundings had gotten her adrenaline flowing. As she had made her way to the juncture of Pipe Creek and Red Bluff Creek, she spied a fawn running through the cedars and decided to make it the focus of another painting—probably her sixth and final one. For now, though, she needed to concentrate on finishing her fourth.

But concentrating wasn't the easiest thing to do at the moment; she couldn't remember feeling this good in a long, long time. To her somewhat reluctant delight, Michael and Kimberley were ecstatic over T-Bone's arrival the night before, and on Monday, only three days from now, Wilton would be taking the children to visit their grandmother. As much as she dreaded seeing them leave, the idea of having unlimited time to devote to her work was beginning to sound better and better—especially since she'd finally heard from Hamilton.

Willing herself to get back to her work, Alix studied a pair of redbirds as they flitted back and forth between two sycamore trees. In the hopes of capturing their in-flight likenesses on canvas, she removed a thin sable brush from a jar. Yes, she decided as she turned toward the unmistakable sound of approaching hoofbeats, this was just the touch she needed—

Sitting tall in the saddle, Joe tipped his straw cowboy hat and reined in the horse. "Morning, Alix."

Her heart skipped a beat as she smiled back at him, and a comfortable warmth raced through her body. "Good morning to you, too." Of course she was happy to see him, she told herself. They were friends, and she was anxious to share her good news with him.

"I'm glad to see you're taking advantage of the break in heat." The saddle groaned as he leaned forward to run his palm down the stallion's sleek black neck. "But why didn't you tell me you wanted to work outdoors? I could have carried those things for you." He gestured toward her easel and paints.

"I looked for you, but—" She stopped herself. "It was no problem."

"Next time, let me know." Joe swung his long, trim legs to the ground. He looped the reins around a tree limb and moved closer to Alix.

"It's perfect," he commented as he surveyed her work. Raising an eyebrow, he turned to face her. "You took my suggestions, didn't you?"

"Yes, I did. And I'm grateful to you." It was true, in more ways than one. He was a good man; kind and decent. He'd done so much for her, and she hoped some-day to repay his kindness.

"And what, may I ask, has you in such a good mood this morning?"

"Rest assured it isn't that dog," she teased. "I will never forgive you for giving that beast to my children!"

"I didn't figure you would." His even teeth flashed white against the deep tan of his face. "From your otherwise jovial mood, I take it something good's happened. What's up?"

"I heard from Hamilton Fischer. He loves the painting I sent him!"

"That's wonderful," he congratulated, hugging her tightly before taking a step back. "I can't say I'm surprised. I knew he'd be impressed."

"Thanks."

In long, even strides, Joe crossed to the creekbank and lowered himself to the ground. "Spirit needs a chance to cool down a bit, but don't let me interrupt you." He took off his hat and ran his hand through his dark hair. After tossing his Stetson onto the grass, he stretched his legs out in front of him, crossing one booted foot over the other. "I'll stay a while and watch you work, if that's okay." Not waiting for an answer, he threaded his fingers together behind his neck and leaned back against the sycamore trunk.

God, she's more beautiful today than ever, Joe thought as he studied her profile. It was wonderful to see her eyes alight, that look of wounded resignation gone from them. Watching her as she glanced from the creek to her canvas, he couldn't help thinking how carefree and happy she looked, how comfortable she seemed to be with her newfound confidence in her abilities. Again, he found himself wondering what, or who, had caused her to lose faith in herself.

Her hair was caught up in a ponytail, with wispy curls framing her face. She was engrossed in her work, allowing his eyes the luxury of roaming her body at leisure, giving him the opportunity to further commit every inch of it to memory. The jeans she wore hugged her hips in the most tempting of ways, and every time she turned just so, he could see a hint of her ample cleavage peeking out of the V of her red blouse.

His gaze shifted upward, and he couldn't stop the tightening in his groin. Watching her ponytail swish back and forth every time she moved her head, he had to admit to himself that friendship was the last thing on his mind. Instead, the way she looked now, fresh and natural and innocent, reminded him of being young again, and it felt good.

Until now, he hadn't realized just how old he had felt for the past couple of years. He hadn't thought about it in ages, but he suddenly remembered his first car. It had been ancient and in disrepair when he had bought it during his senior year of high school, and he'd owned plenty of new, expensive models since then. But right now, he had an irrepressible urge to drag her into the back seat of that '57 Chevy for some good old-fashioned, serious necking....

Yeah, getting to know Alix—literally as well as figuratively—was more important to him now than ever. And it was simply a matter of time before she admitted that she wanted the same thing. Regardless of what she kept saying, kept denying, the way she reacted every time he touched her told him all he needed to know.

If time was what she needed, then he would give it to her. But not too much. His patience was wearing mighty thin.

"Alix?" he asked, flexing his shoulders. "Why don't I take you and the kids to the chili cook-off tomorrow? You don't want to go alone, do you?"

"I don't suppose I want to brave it on my own," she finally answered. "Yes, I'd be honored to accept your invitation."

Joe continued to watch her as she turned and picked out another paintbrush. Satisfied with her reply, he settled back against the tree trunk again. His libido problems aside, he felt good. Damned good. Kim was speaking to him again, if only about T-Bone. And Alix was feeling better about herself. That was real damned good.

He had telephoned Dennis, and the Double S was running like clockwork. With all the time Joe was spending with Alix and the kids, he hadn't been able to look for his brother. But after giving it a lot of thought, he had hired a detective to sniff out Charlie's trail. He'd already given up a year of his life for him, and if that year had taught him nothing else, it had taught him that he needed to get on with his own life. So why not let some two-hundred-dollar-a-day Dick Tracy do the legwork? The man was highly recommended and knew what he was doing, and ever since Joe laid eyes on Alix Smith, he hadn't had the zeal he once had for finding Charlie himself. He had bent over backward to fulfill his obligation to his brother, he reasoned, and it was high time he fulfilled his obligation to himself.

Joe broke off a blade of grass and stuck it between his teeth. "I almost forgot, Alix. Your mom phoned a few minutes ago. She wants you to call her back when you get the chance.''

"My mother?'' she asked, her brows knitting. "Did she say why she was calling?''

"No, but it didn't sound urgent.''

"You don't know my mother! She could be in the midst of a tidal wave and still sound cool as a cucumber.'' Glancing toward the long path to the house, then back to her easel and supplies, Alix frowned. "I'll come back for these things later, Joe. Do you mind giving me a ride back to the house?''

"Well...'' He hesitated.

"Please?''

Great, Joe thought as he hoisted himself to his feet. As soon as he swung into the saddle behind her, she'd know damned good and well his mind wasn't on friendship.

Alix, caught up in anxiety over her mother's call, noticed Joe was taking an inordinate amount of time retrieving Spirit's reins and answering her. "I don't want to spoil your ride, but—''

"No, no problem. Let's go.'' His voice was rough, almost gravelly. Adjusting the crown of his hat, he then led the horse a few feet into the clearing. "Come around this way. Be careful now, stallions can be pretty finicky at times.''

"It's okay, Joe. I'm a good rider.''

"That may be true, Alix, but don't forget I'm a veterinarian. And I specialized in horses. Take it from me. Stallions can be skittish around certain people.''

She took a step back, eyeing him questioningly. "What do you mean, 'certain people'?''

Staring at her point-blank, he crossed his arms in front of his chest. "*Female*-type people, Alexandra.''

"Oh." She glanced away from him, trying to think of something to say. "Well, I'll be careful, then. I just didn't realize they were so sensitive."

"Sensitive, huh?" Joe laughed. "I guess that's as good a word as any. Yeah, you women do tend to have that effect on us males."

Trying to avoid his arresting gaze, Alix adjusted the legs of her jeans and then reached for the saddle horn. It was a long stretch to the stirrup, and she hopped a few times as she tried to get a toe in it.

"Here." Joe moved behind her, cupping her hips before she could manage to mount the horse without help. "Let me give you a boost," he offered, his hands moving lower.

"Sensitive" was not the best word, she thought as she threw her right leg over the saddle. But whatever the proper word was for it, it worked both ways. Exactly what kind of an effect did Joe think he was having on *her* right now?

Swinging easily into the saddle, he aligned himself with her backside—and as soon as he did, she knew she should have walked the distance to the house. None of the cowboy movies she'd seen had ever pointed out this aspect of riding two to a saddle!

"Ready?" she asked shakily, and then wanted to bite her tongue when she realized how the question could be taken.

Joe bent his mouth to her ear. "I'm ready."

Wrapping his arm protectively around her waist, his grasp tightened as they headed up the path. Spirit moved along at an agonizingly slow gait, each jostle propelling her harder against Joe's pelvis. "Can't," she asked, trying to breath normally, "can't this horse go any faster?"

"You smell good," he ventured, ignoring her question. She could feel his warm breath stirring her hair, his splayed fingers rubbing against her ribs.

"Liar," she finally answered, willing herself to look straight ahead instead of turning her face toward his. "I smell like oil paint and turpentine."

"No way. You smell like gardenias."

Caught between the saddle horn and Joe's arousal, she fought the warmth that was spreading deliciously through her veins. "You're a flatterer."

"No. Just being honest."

"Joe?" As they started up the hill to the house, the curiosity she'd been trying to squelch since the previous night got the best of her. "Who's Lillie?"

"She's a friend of mine."

*Darn him!* "Like we're friends?"

"Uh huh."

"Did she give you the dog?"

"Uh huh."

"Why do I suddenly have the urge to wring that monster's neck?"

"Lillie's not a monster—"

"I didn't mean her. I meant that dog!"

"Oh." He laughed easily. "I thought you meant Lillie."

Even though she didn't want to know, she had to ask. "Why don't you tell me about her?"

"Lillie's a fine woman, a wonderful cook."

He seemed to be deliberating every word, and it was driving her insane.

"She's got great legs, too, and—"

Her head jerked to the side, and she glared up at him. "I don't need to know everything, thank you."

"If I didn't know better, I'd think you were jealous."

"Well, I'm not jealous." His chuckle was almost as infuriating as the lazy smile on his face, and she tried to sound nonchalant. "I was simply curious."

"Here we are," Joe announced, tugging gently on Spirit's reins and then dismounting in one swift, coordinated move. He reached for her, helping her down.

Alix lifted her chin and forced a light smile. "Thanks for the ride," she stated calmly, brushing past him toward the house.

Darn that man! she thought, closing the front door and stomping up the stairs. He'd gotten to her and he knew it! Just because he was handsome and sexy and could read her every thought and was always so... infernally right! First he'd wormed his way into her heart, and now he was driving her crazy with jealousy.

"Lillie's a fine woman," she mimicked, slamming her bedroom door. "A wonderful cook!"

Exhaling a deep breath, Alix snatched the telephone's receiver from its cradle. Joe Sinclair, she admitted to herself as she jabbed the buttons on the phone, had the nerve-racking ability to bring out the best and the worst in her.

"Lillie's got great legs!" she muttered, peering outside and watching as Joe rode back down the hill.

"What?" Alix's grip tightened around the receiver, and she turned away from the window. "No, I'm sorry, Mother. I wasn't talking to you. I was...thinking about a horse."

Better to be here, Alix thought as she gazed up at the sky, than sulking all alone back at the house. The normally relentless central Texas heat had abated in favor of billowy clouds, and the sky appeared to be promising perfect weather for the annual chili cook-off.

After yesterday's confrontation about Lillie, topped off by the disappointing news from her mother, Alix had thought about staying home. But when she overheard Joe telling the children that a couple of his friends might be at the fund-raiser, she knew she had to come along, just in case one of those friends happened to be...that woman.

"Hey, dreamy eyes." Joe's fingers laced with hers, his free hand gently nudging her cheek. "Penny for your thoughts."

Her gaze filled with his angular face, his dark-fringed blue eyes. Controlling her emotions when she was around this rugged man, she had decided after hours of tossing and turning last night, was a near impossibility. Her nerves were so on edge, she could barely think straight....

Grinning, Joe turned her wrist to drop a copper coin into her palm. "I'm waiting."

"I wasn't thinking about anything in particular," she fibbed. What she was actually thinking about at that very moment was how good, how natural and warm and good it felt to be walking close beside him, her hand in his.

The loose-packed gravel crunched under her sandals as she stepped into pace with Joe's boots. She studied a large group of apparent free spirits, spectators assembled around a pavilion where a raucous lemon-rolling contest was in progress. "I'm not sure I like the idea of Michael and Kimberley wandering around on their own."

"They're within earshot, and I gave them the usual warnings about what to avoid." Joe smiled his assurance. "Don't worry, toots. The crowd's safe here."

*Toots!* The name tore into her already raw nerves. "Don't *ever* call me that!"

Alix jerked her hand out of his grasp, her self-defense mechanism surging into full swing as she turned to face him. "Whether you think this crowd is safe or not," she accused, "Michael and Kimberley are only children! Why do you insist on giving them so much responsibility?"

"Because they'll be adults some day, Alix, and they need to be prepared for the real world." His eyes flamed as he went on. "A sense of responsibility isn't something you can wrap up and give them at their twenty-first birthday party, you know! It just doesn't work that way."

"I'm sure it doesn't," she shot back, "but that's not the point. Don't you think you're stepping out of bounds with your parental-style advice?"

"I meant no offense." Obviously trying to control his temper, Joe folded his arms over his chest. "Correct me if I'm wrong, but I thought you hired me as a glorified nanny. If you want me to be responsible for them, you can't fight me at every turn. It's counterproductive."

She might not have much else, but she still had her pride. "I hired you to cook and clean for them." She raised her chin. "Not to take my place."

"I'll keep that in mind, Ms. Smith." After studying her for an indeterminate amount of time, his expression softened. "Hey, let's not argue." He reached out, his hand caressing her shoulder. "You tell me what to do, and I'll do it."

*Why are you so forgiving?* her mind screamed. And then remorse settled through her. Not able to face him squarely, she stared at his chest and his green western shirt. His words made sense, as always! It was only natural that her children would look to him as an authority figure, and she had no right to treat him this way.

"I'm sorry," Alix whispered. "I apologize for being defensive." She spun on her heel and raced toward the ladies' rest room, but he grabbed her arm before she could get through the door. Pulling her behind the building, he backed her up to the wall.

"I'm not going to let you run away from me, Alix," he stated flatly, still holding her arms.

"I won't," she murmured, still unable to look up into his eyes. "It's just that I was upset, but I was wrong to take it out on you. My parents are flying off to Paris with my younger sister, and they aren't going to be at my gallery showing after all." Her words came out in a rush. "I was disappointed when my mother told me, but I shouldn't be taking my frustrations out on you. I'm sorry, Joe."

"Apology accepted." He released her arms, then pressing his palm against the building, he leaned toward her. "Now. Let's talk about what's really bothering you."

"I told you." Her eyes shot up to his. "It's important to me that my parents have faith in my work, and—"

"That's a bunch of bull!" His eyes pinned her to the wall. "*You* have faith in your work. That's all that matters, and you know it."

"Okay. You're right." Her hands flew to her hips. "I'll tell you what's really bothering me. You're right about everything!" She tried to keep a scream suppressed to a whisper. "I have this foolish, stubborn sense of pride, and the fact that you're always right seems to keep rubbing it the wrong way. And what really drives me to distraction is that I love...I love that quality in you, but at the same time it irritates me that you're so perfect!"

"That's also a bunch of bull." Ramming his fingers into his pockets, he turned and stared into the distance. "I've made my share of mistakes, Alix. I'm far from perfect."

"Well, I'm convinced that you're perfect."

He moved around to face her again. "You don't know what you're talking about, Alix. I—"

"I know exactly what I'm talking about." In the past few minutes, her emotions had run the gamut from happiness to confusion to unwarranted anger. All of a sudden, though, for some odd reason, she felt content. "And I feel better now," she proclaimed, smiling up at him. "I got it off my chest, and I've found one thing you're wrong about." Seeing his puzzled look, she went on to explain. "You don't think you're perfect, but I know you are."

Joe put his arm around her shoulder, shaking his head in mock bewilderment, and pulled her close. "Come on. There's someone I want you to meet."

Hoping he hadn't felt her flinch, Alix reminded herself that she was the one who had set up the rules about their relationship. Joe was a normal, healthy male, and if he had a woman in town, then she would simply have to accept it. But she didn't have to like it!

She wanted to meet Lillie, and yet she didn't. She had drawn her own mental picture of the woman—petite and young, with the body of a centerfold and long, painted fingernails—but it was senseless to dwell on a ridiculously stereotyped figment of her imagination. Senseless and torturous, she repeated inwardly.

As Joe led her through the crowd, Alix forced herself to put the svelte, blond image out of her mind. She had never before seen an event like this one, and she wasn't about to let her niggling thoughts of jealousy ruin an otherwise beautiful day.

She loved chili, the spicier the better, and signs touted the virtues of "Wild West Wonder," "Orville's Five Alarm" and other such concoctions. Numerous and varied caldrons of chili were being prepared by teams of cooks, and Joe explained that each group had staked out its own territory early that morning. A tantalizing aroma wafted through the air, and she inhaled appreciatively, her stomach growling in anticipation of the piquant sustenance.

Joe peered through the noisy crowd. "There he is!"

A glorious wave of relief washed over Alix as the word "he" registered. Her line of sight was drawn to a grizzled man of about sixty who was dressed to resemble a trailride cook. The man had a ladle in one hand and a child's cap gun in the other, and it seemed humorous that this was exactly what she had expected her summer helper to look like.

"Step right up, folks," he bellowed. "Step right up! 'Henry's Hotter'n a Firecracker' is gar-un-teed to put hair on yer chest!"

"Henry," Joe called.

"Whoopee!" The cap gun fired twice. "Sam Sinclair! Git over here, boy."

"Alix," Joe said, after greeting the man, "I want you to meet a good friend of mine. This is Henry Kastel."

He turned to the older man. "Henry, I believe you've heard me mention Alix Smith."

"Glad to meet ya, ma'am." Henry gave her a playful wink as he took her hand, shaking it vigorously. "I do believe I recall Sam bringin' up yer name a time or two."

"Where's your better half, Henry?" Joe asked.

"Oh, you know Mama," he answered. "She's flittin' around here somewhere, busy as a game warden the first day-a huntin' season."

"Sam! I'd about given up on you."

Alix watched as a pretty woman, probably in her forties, appeared seemingly from out of nowhere. Dressed in a blue gingham skirt and blouse, she rushed over and threw her arms around Joe. He gave the woman a bear hug, then planted a big kiss on her rosy cheek and asked, "How you doing, doll?"

His arm still wrapped around the woman's waist, he turned to Alix. "Alix Smith, this is Mrs. Kastel, Henry's wife and a very dear friend of mine."

"Pleased to meet you, Alix." Mrs. Kastel moved toward her. "Why, Sam's told me so much about you, I feel like we already know each other. And I won't hear of you callin' me Mrs. Kastel. Most of my friends call me Lillie Jewel—" she extended her hand "—or just plain Lillie."

## Chapter Seven

I'm so happy to meet you, Lillie!"

As soon as Alix realized she was pumping the woman's hand a bit too enthusiastically and smiling a bit too broadly, she released her grip. "And I want to thank you for giving us the puppy. My children absolutely adore him."

As she talked to Lillie, she ignored the knowing, satisfied grin on Joe's face. There was something about the woman, an aura of friendliness, that made Alix like her immediately. She was a short brunette with a natural, ready smile, and her luminous blue eyes literally sparkled.

"Mama," Henry exclaimed, "get Miss Alix a chair, will ya? I want her in my camp to pretty up the place."

Alix laughed easily as she took the offered seat. She cast a glance at Joe, who was poking Henry on the shoulder. "Henry, don't you start flirting with my woman."

*My woman.* Her eyes widened, and she gaped at Joe.

"Now, boy, don't get yer dander up. You know Mama takes real good care-a me." Henry squeezed his wife's waist to drive home his point. "Don't ya, Mama?"

"You better know it!" Lillie simpered tartly, then turned to the younger couple. "Ain't he a card?"

"I wouldn't say he's a card, Lillie." Standing beside Alix's chair, Joe rested his hand on her shoulder as he laughed. "I'd say he's more like a full deck."

Alix smiled up at him, enjoying their easy camaraderie. "Excuse me, but I'm curious," she said, trying to concentrate on forming a coherent sentence instead of on Joe's light touch. "How do you know one another?"

"Oh, my husband and I used to work for the Sinclairs at the Double S Ranch," Lillie answered. "Henry worked the livestock, and I cooked for Sam and his—"

"I'm ready for some of that secret recipe of yours, Henry," Joe interrupted quickly. "How about you, Alix? Are you ready for some chili?"

"I'd love some," she remarked. How unlike Joe to interrupt a person in midsentence, she thought. Apparently Lillie had known him for a long time. Long enough, probably, to know about the "year in hell" that he was so closemouthed about.

Henry ladled out the thick concoction, and Lillie handed them each a Styrofoam cup filled to the brim. Alix blew the steam from a spoonful. "This smells delicious." Her taste buds fired to life from jalapeño peppers as she tasted the reddish-brown chili. "This is delicious, Henry!"

"Why, thank ya, Miss Alix. I aim to please." With two more pops of the cap gun, he winked at his wife. "Right, Mama?"

Lillie slapped his arm playfully, and warmth filled Alix's soul. How refreshing to see the obvious love shared by the two, a love that was tender and secure and open to teasing. It touched those around them, drawing them into a circle of familial togetherness, and she felt at ease, as if she'd known the couple for years.

For several minutes, she took in the modern-day Wild West atmosphere and savored the taste of Henry's creation. Henry was putting on a show worthy of Jesse James, and Alix and Joe laughed with him at his antics.

"I'm new at this," she told Joe. "How does a chili cook-off work? Do we taste all the entries and then vote on the one we like best?"

"Not exactly. You taste all the entries, if you want to, but a panel of judges selects the winner."

"Oh. Well, I hope Henry's chili wins." She nudged Joe's lean thigh. "I wonder what he puts in it?"

He leaned down, smiling devilishly, and his breath against her ear drew a quiver. "If I were you, I wouldn't ask."

She made a face at him, then turned toward the chef. "Henry, what ingredients are in this chili?"

"Oh, Lordy. That's a trade secret, but seeing as how you're so doggone pretty, I'll let you in on it." He squinted his eyes and stage-whispered, "Rattlesnake."

Alix's stomach turned upside down, and she almost choked. "What!"

She felt green all of a sudden. Trying to ignore their round of laughter, she watched as Henry moved back to his cast-iron kettle and served samples to a new group of unsuspecting tasters.

Joe took her hand, guiding her to a standing position. "Are you okay?" he asked softly.

"Ask me when I'm over the shock," she answered. "You warned me, but I didn't think you were serious!"

"You look like you could use a walk, Alix," Lillie commented. "I'm working the next shift in the concession stand. Why don't you come along and keep me company?"

"Thanks, Lillie, but I think I should check on the children first."

"I'll make sure they're okay," Joe volunteered. "You two go ahead. I'll meet you there later."

As soon as they were behind the drink counter, Lillie taught her the prices, tied a carpenter's apron around her waist and promptly put her to work.

After a few minutes in the concessions building, Alix found herself enjoying the hustle and bustle going on around her. Lillie seemed to know almost everyone, especially the children who ran in and out, and it soon became apparent that she ran a tight ship. "Here's your soda water, P.J.," she told a teenager. "But I'm not selling you a beer. You tell your daddy if he wants one, he can come and get it himself."

Alix made change for customers and, when there was a temporary lull in business, started clearing and wiping off the three small tables. She listened as Lillie greeted the townspeople and chatted with them, offering advice on everything from the treatment of bunions to the best recipe for homemade ice cream. In the midst of visiting with their parents, she reminded children of their eating manners, scooted them away when they tried to reach into the pickle jar and generally kept them in line. The kids did exactly what they were asked to, and—to Alix's surprise—none of the parents seemed to take offense. They were like one big, happy family.

This small town and its friendly citizens were a whole new world for her. This was Joe's world, she thought, laid-back and unpretentious. And she felt oddly at home. Only a month ago, if anyone had told her she would feel this way, she would have denied it to the hilt. But now...

"Our relief's here, Alix." A tall bottle of beer in each hand, Lillie gestured toward the far table. "Now that we're off duty, let's sit down and relax a spell."

Noticing that there were no glasses to drink out of, Alix copied the woman's lead, sipping the cold beer straight from the bottle.

"I sure am glad to see Sam lookin' so happy," Lillie announced. "It's about time he started living his life again. Why, I was just tellin' Henry the other day that I hoped Sam would find himself a good woman. Lord knows he deserves to be happy."

"Yes. He's a wonderful man, Lillie." Alix took another sip. "But I think you've misjudged our relationship. We're just friends."

Lillie smiled knowingly and patted Alix's hand. "You're all that man talks about when he's with me and Henry. If you want him, girl, go after him. He's yours for the takin'."

She knew Joe wanted her physically. But she also knew—better than anyone—that an ongoing relationship encompassed much, much more than an initial spark of chemistry.

"I think . . ." She looked up as Joe entered the building and stopped at the counter to buy himself a beer. "Well, as I said before, we're just friends."

"Fiddlesticks!" Lillie leaned forward as she whispered conspiratorially. "Anyway, friendship is the best basis for love. I know I'm sticking my nose in your business, but I'll bet that handsome cowboy would do everything in his power to make you happy."

"Ladies?" Joe asked, striding toward their table. "Is this what you call 'working' the concession stand?"

"It's a dirty job, Sam," Lillie answered. "But somebody's gotta do it!" She stood up and gave Joe a quick hug. "I'll see you two later. I've got to go make sure Henry's behaving himself!"

As soon as Lillie was gone, Joe helped Alix to her feet. "I'd better get you out of here, too."

"Why?" she asked as he moved behind her, untying her apron.

"Because," he answered, smiling as he turned her around to face him, "I don't want some handsome cowboy strolling in here and offering to buy the barmaid another longneck."

"Don't worry." Laughing at his use of the term "handsome cowboy," which Lillie had used to describe *him*, Alix gestured toward the beer. "One longneck is my limit, and you're the only handsome cowboy who's approached me today."

"I find that hard to believe." He picked up the two bottles, clasping their tall, slender necks with one hand. "You'll be glad to know I've done my scouting," he said as he guided her toward the door. "I found the kids and they're fine, playing safely and having a great time with their friends, and then I discovered a nice shady spot where we can finish these in private."

Leaving the building, they walked through the crowd in companionable silence. Within a few minutes, they reached a beautiful, secluded spot on the edge of the grounds.

"You were right again, you know," Alix told him as he led her past a clump of live oaks and toward an old covered wagon.

"Oh, no," he groaned, pretending disgust. "What was it this time?"

"Lillie's a fine woman," she answered, smiling up at him sheepishly. "And she does have great legs."

"I wouldn't lie about a thing like that." He glanced down, beyond the hem of her dress, and kept talking. "I know a great pair of legs when I see them."

"I'm not surprised," she teased, laughing. "After all, you're a doctor. A doctor who specializes in horses, no less!"

"It's good to hear you laugh, Alix," he murmured, his dark cobalt eyes exploring her face. "Are you having a good time?"

"Ummmm." She nodded slowly, her gaze locking with his. "It's been a wonderful day. I can't remember ever having this much fun."

He wanted her to like his way of life, he reminded himself as he set their near-empty bottles in the wagon. But she was Junior League and champagne...and he was hometown rodeos and beer. Past experience had taught him that if life-styles couldn't be blended, then all the sexual chemistry and affection and friendship in the world still wouldn't be enough. Not that Tammi had ever been his friend—far from it. But she'd taught him well, and he wouldn't make the same mistake again.

"I'm glad," he finally said. "You're a city girl, Alexandra, and I'm just a country boy. It means a lot to me to see you so accepting."

"I've lived in Dallas almost all my life, but I love the country."

He eased his back against the wagon and anchored her between his spread thighs, his hands locking behind her waist. The arousing scent of his after-shave assailed her, and she could feel the denim against her lightweight dress, could feel his muscled inner thighs and his blazing evidence of maleness.

"Put your arms around me," Joe said, his tone low and husky.

He was a narcotic to her defenses. Tentatively touching his chest, she fought the intoxicated desire to melt into his embrace. "Why?" she asked, her voice no more than a whisper.

"Because, Alix," he said, electricity seeming to vibrate between them as he slowly tilted his head to hers, his lips parting ever so slightly, "I intend to kiss you."

The force of his passion held in check, he pulled her body harder against him and began to explore the feel and texture and taste of her lips...each corner, and then the hollow at the curve of her upper lip. It was slow, erotic, like nothing she had ever felt before. And the unaccustomed act caused her to shiver in anticipation.

As liquid heaviness settled between her limbs, her nails dug deeper, and the unspoken invitation was all he needed. Wildfire raged between them as his demanding mouth seared his personal brand onto her lips. Her arms went around him, holding him, stroking him, wanting to take him into her very soul.

"Mommy, Mommy!" She felt Michael tugging at her arm, and Joe loosened his hold on her. "I saw an almond dillo race!"

Trying to control her ragged breathing, she hesitated for a moment before stepping out of Joe's arms. In a way she was glad for the interruption, she rationalized. In a way. "An almond dillo—? A what, Michael?"

Clearing his throat, Joe reached down and ruffled the boy's blond curls. "I think he means an armadillo race, city girl."

Kimberley came bounding up, a cone of cotton candy in her hand and traces of the sticky sweet all around her mouth. "May I have a dollar, Mom? My friend Jennifer and I want a Coke."

"A dollar for the little lady and her friend." Joe handed her the money, then lifted her up into his arms and kissed her cheek. "Are you having fun, Kim?"

"Yes, sir," she answered, her eyes wary. "Thank you for the dollar. Would you . . . would you please put me down now?"

"Sure." Joe lowered her to the ground, a look of sadness flickering in his eyes. Taking a handkerchief out of his back pocket, he wiped pink residue from his jaw and called after her. "Stay close, Kim."

Alix watched the hurt expression in his eyes, knowing that it was just as much for Kimberley as it was for himself. He was always setting aside his own feelings, watching out for her welfare, even her children's welfare, instead of his own.

Suddenly she realized how much she cared for him, and it frightened her. It was as if he had the ability to reach deep inside her, to touch her emotions, to tug at her heart—and she was afraid she might not be able to give him what he needed in return.

She had been telling herself the same things over and over again for the past month. It read like a negative mental checklist: their relationship, whatever else it might become, was temporary...all too soon, summer would be over...they would go their separate ways... and she simply couldn't allow herself to be hurt and disappointed by love again.

But now she knew that, more than anything, she couldn't allow herself to disappoint *him*. Joe Sinclair was a wonderful man; a wonderful, healthy, virile man, and he deserved far more than she could ever give him.

"I think we should call it a day, Joe." Alix's voice was shaky. "I'll catch Kimberley."

Even the children were unusually quiet on the short trip home. Tired and dirty, the four of them had piled into the cab of Joe's truck. Michael was curled up on his mother's lap, leaning comfortably against her, and Alix rested her chin on the top of his head. Out of the corner of her eye, she could see the thoughtful looks Joe kept giving her as he sped down the road.

"Oh, no!" she moaned, her back stiffening as she caught sight of the familiar white car that was parked in front of the house. Wilton wasn't expected for another two days! And right now her ex-husband was the last person in the world she wanted to see.

"Look, Mike!" Kimberley shrieked. "Daddy's here!"

Wilton, dressed to the nines in casual yet elegant clothing, stepped out of his Mercedes and gave a lazy salute as the truck pulled up next to him. He opened Alix's door and ducked his perfectly styled head into the cab.

"Well, what have we here?" he asked, sneering at Joe. Not waiting for a reply, he glanced at his children as they jumped to their feet. "Hello, kids."

"Daddy!" they squealed in unison, scrambling over Alix's lap and trying to throw themselves into his arms.

"Whoa, there." Raising his hands skyward, Wilton stepped back. "Don't touch my clothes. You two are filthy!"

"Yes, sir." Kimberley shrank back, and Alix climbed down from the truck, putting her arm around her daughter in the hopes of alleviating some of her crushed feelings. At that particular moment, she couldn't help comparing Wilton to Joe. *He* hadn't been repelled by Kim's cotton-candied face, she told herself.

"Daddy," Michael gushed, undaunted, "we went to a chili cook-off today!"

"Out slumming, Alexandra?"

"Good afternoon to you, too, Wilton." She heard Joe's door slam and turned to watch him as he came around the back of the truck. He shoved the keys into his front pocket and then, doffing his hat, ran his fingers through his dark hair.

Wilton moved forward. "Wilt Smith," he stated. "And who, might I ask, are you?"

"I'm Joe Sinclair. I work for Ms. Smith."

"Ahhh," he commented, raising a brow and finally meeting the handshake Joe offered.

"Daddy, we saw an almond dillo race. And we've got a puppy now!" Michael rambled on excitedly. "And those people who used to live here have two horses that are real big, and Joe taught us how to ride. Daddy, when are we gonna go see Gramma?"

"That's nice, Michael," Wilt stated offhandedly. Obviously he hadn't heard a word the boy had said, and Michael's face registered confusion, then hurt.

"If you'll excuse me, I've got chores to do," Joe said. "Why don't you kids run on inside and wash up?"

"Please do." Wilt gestured toward the house. "And use a little soap."

After Alix hugged the children and sent them off with Joe, Wilt turned to her. "Well—" he dusted imaginary soil from his sleeve "—so this is your little hideaway."

"This is my summer home," she corrected, putting emphasis on the last word. "What are you doing here? You said you'd be picking them up on Monday, not today."

"I wanted to get an early start." He smoothed his blond hair, even though it didn't need smoothing. "I notice you've got a nice pool. Why don't we go around and sit out back? I want to ask you a couple of things before we leave."

"Fine," Alix said, her arms swinging at her sides as she headed for the pool deck. Anything to get him on his way.... He'd only been here five minutes, she thought ruefully, and already she was anxious for him to take his pompous looks and his snide remarks and get out! Thank goodness the couple who worked for his mother would be watching out for the children. If she hadn't been absolutely sure of that, and if they hadn't been wonderful people that she'd known for years, she would have never agreed to let Kim and Mike go to Alabama with him.

Joe braced his heel on the fence railing and took a long drag from his cigarette. He had used chores as an excuse to get away from Wilt Smith before he did something he might regret later. To hell with the fact that he was once married to Alix. It wasn't so much that as it was the man's entire attitude. He hadn't seen his kids in ages, and yet he wouldn't let them come close to him for fear of getting a speck of dirt on his precious clothes!

Alix's voice floated from behind a thick hedge of ligustrum. Joe knew he should move, but he felt compelled to stay.

"You could have kissed them! For heaven's sake, Wilton, can't you see how much it hurts them when you—"

"Get off it. They were filthy. I realize you're on holiday, toots—and you've never been a candidate for 'Mother of the Year'—but you could at least make an effort to keep them presentable."

*Toots!* Joe groaned inwardly, wishing he'd never used the term. If only he'd known...

"I am not on holiday!" Alix was saying. "And, what's more... Forget it, Wilton. Just forget it! I don't have to defend my actions to you anymore."

"By the way, who's your ranch hand Romeo? He seems awfully chummy with the three of you." Smith paused. "Are you shacking up with him, Alix?"

"How dare you!"

Joe threw his cigarette to the grass, grinding his heel into the stub as if it were Wilt Smith's face.

"No, probably not," Wilton answered for her. "If he knew what an iceberg you are, he'd make tracks real quick, wouldn't he? Smart move on your parts, toots. Keep him guessing."

A pained cry tore from Alix's throat, and Joe heard her running away. It took every ounce of his willpower not to go after her, and then go after Smith, but he knew better than to follow his instincts. Defending

Alix's honor by beating her ex-husband to a pulp would do nothing but further traumatize her and the kids. Beyond that, and disregarding the chances he'd be taking with a parole violation, he knew it wouldn't solve anything.

But finally, unmistakably, he understood the reason for Alix's insecurities. Smith had spent years undermining her confidence in herself as a woman.

Why hadn't he seen it before? He'd purposely given her time and understanding and friendship, when what she needed was a man to appreciate her. And by damn, he was going to be the appreciator!

Deciding it would be best for everyone if he made himself scarce for a while, Joe crossed to the stable. Yeah, he told himself again, he'd see to it that Alix got what she needed. Tonight.

"Kimberley!"

Alix was frantic. Racing outside in a near stumble, she screamed, "Kimberley! Where are you?" Her eyes scanned the area, and she caught sight of Joe as he rushed out of the stable. "Joe, have you seen Kim?"

"No. What's wrong?"

"She . . . she's gone! I told her to stay in the den with her father, but she's not there. She's not anywhere in the house. Oh, Joe, she was awfully upset about her dad. Where could she have gone?"

"Calm down, honey," he tried to soothe. "We'll find her. She's probably down by the creek. She loves it there."

"But you told her never to take T-Bone out of the yard and he's gone, too!"

"Damn!" Joe sprang into action, racing to his pickup, and Alix followed behind him. Without another word, he opened the passenger door, grabbed his rifle from the gun rack and reached into the glove compartment for ammunition.

"What are you doing?" she wailed, her fingers pressing against her face.

"Let me handle this," he ordered. Inserting a clip, he worked the bolt to put a shell in the chamber. "You get back to the house. Wait outside in case she comes back while I'm out looking for her."

Joe planted the .306 under his arm, with the safety on and the barrel pointed down, and cut a trail toward the water. He had warned Kim time and time again about taking that dog out into the open spaces. He just hoped . . .

His field of vision swept the creeks and their juncture. Just then he heard the puppy's piercing bark from the distance, and his feet didn't seem to touch the ground as he followed the noise. Cresting the slope of a hill, he spied Kim throwing sticks for the dog to fetch.

At the same time, he caught sight of a wild hog about thirty yards behind her. Judging by the length of the tusk curling up from the bottom of its mouth, it was a full-grown boar. The beast rooted the ground and spewed saliva as it snorted its vicious warning. Joe moved fast, running to get within better range, and yelled at Kim—hoping she would obey and that he'd be able to coax the hog's attention away from her. "Climb the tree, Kim. Hurry!"

Instead, she turned to the mammoth Russian boar, and Joe heard her terrified scream. T-Bone jumped in front of her. Growling and yapping, he sprang back and forth in an effort to protect her. "Climb the tree, Kim!" he yelled again as he stopped short and raised his rifle. "Get away from T-Bone! Now!"

"It's gonna get me!" Kim shrieked. She scrambled for a tree just as the boar started to charge.

Knowing his first shot had to count, Joe centered the rifle scope on the ferocious hog as he released the safety. He squeezed the trigger, and the air exploded with the sound of the bullet tearing from the barrel. He quickly lowered the scope, the breath leaving his lungs as he watched the huge animal teeter...and then hit the ground, a stream of dark blood tainting its bristly coat.

"Joe!" Kim cried, clinging to a tree limb. "Help me, Joe!"

"It's okay, honey," he called, dropping the rifle as he sprinted toward her. "He won't hurt you now. He's dead."

He pulled her into his arms, and she hugged him tightly as she sobbed. "I was so scared. He was so big and ugly!"

"I know. I know." He held her firmly, trying to kiss away her tears. "You're okay now, honey. I won't let anything hurt you."

Crying and gasping and choking, she tried to talk, pouring her heart out about some special doll her dad had promised her. Her tiny body shook uncontrollably, and Joe rubbed her back and rocked her, not understanding half of what she said, only enough to conclude that her father had let her down. "There, there," he soothed, holding her tight, waiting as she tried to catch her breath. He heard and felt the racking sobs that always precede the calm, and then she went limp against his chest, her body jerking occasionally as she took a series of deep but uneven breaths.

At last she turned her head to look up at him, her arms tightening around his neck. "I'm sorry I've been mean to you, Joe." Fresh tears rolled down her cheeks, and her voice was small, sorrowful. "I wish...I wish you were my daddy."

"Oh, Kim...." Joe held her close, pressing a gentle kiss against her temple. She was scared and upset and disappointed, and he knew he couldn't tell her that he felt the same way. Instead, he whispered, "I love you, honey. Shhh.... Don't worry, now. Everything's going to be okay."

He heard Alix calling first his name, then Kim's. Turning toward the sound, he watched her face register horror as she took in the scene.

"Oh, no," she cried. "No!"

"Everything's under control," he called to her as she raced toward them, and then he had both Kim and Alix in his arms. "She's fine."

"She could have been killed," Alix said between relieved kisses, her trembling voice barely audible. "You saved her life...."

Hugging them tighter, Joe glanced at the fallen boar. He knew it had to weigh close to three hundred pounds, and he shuddered to think what could have happened. "Let's get back to the house," he finally suggested, releasing his hold on Alix. "I'll come back later and get rid of the hog."

T-Bone was dancing circles around the huge animal. His tail wagging and his tongue lolling, he looked extremely pleased with himself—as if the victory were totally canine.

"Here, boy." Joe whistled for the dog but to no avail. "Grab the pup, Alix."

Kim in his arms, T-Bone squirming in Alix's, they started toward the house. When they reached the spot where Joe had dropped his rifle, he set Kim down momentarily, picked up the rifle and then lifted her back up with his free arm.

"I don't understand," Alix said, her words coming out in a shaky rush. "How did you know to take a gun? How did you know she was in danger?"

"Because of T-Bone. That giant hog back there," he said, smiling softly at Kim, not wanting to frighten her any further, "is called a Russian boar. I want you to understand this, Kim. There are quite a few wild hogs around here, but you don't need to worry about them. It wasn't you who tempted old porky. He wouldn't have come after you if you'd been alone. It was the puppy who got him excited. Understand?"

"Yes, Joe." Her voice was still quivering. "I promise I won't take T-Bone out of the yard anymore. Never, ever!"

"Good girl." His tone lightened. "Now, why don't you and I go to the stable? I'll let you take one quick ride around the pen before you leave for your grandma's house."

Alix slammed the French doors behind her. Disgusted, she glared at Wilton as he reposed on the sofa, his loafered feet propped on the armrest, his attention riveted to a televised golf tournament.

He looked up and yawned. "Why aren't you getting their stuff ready, Alix? Michael's already in the car."

She dropped T-Bone onto a chair. "No thanks to you, Kim's alive!"

"What are you talking about?"

"While you weren't watching her, she took her dog out there—" Alix's finger jabbed in the general direction "—and she was nearly attacked by a wild boar!"

"She's okay, isn't she?" He didn't look the least bit concerned.

"Yes!"

"Great. Then don't try to lay the blame on me for something that's your fault, toots. You're the one who wanted to bring them to this godforsaken place, not me." He sat up, his elbows resting on his knees. "Just hurry up and get their things. We've got a plane to catch."

Alix stood rock-still, trying to control her jagged breathing, and stared at him as he went back to watching the television. Why? she asked herself. Why, for so many years, had she closed her eyes and refused to see this man for what he really was?

It suddenly dawned on her that, until this very minute, she had never even asked herself that question. And yet the answer came to her now—as quickly and as easily as the question had—and a strange calmness settled over her. She had never wanted to admit to anyone, especially to herself, that she had been a fool.

But she had. She'd been a silly, foolish girl who'd fallen in love with an egotistical man. An egotistical, insensitive man who didn't deserve to be loved. She had put too much faith in Wilton and none in herself, and her own pride had worked against her as surely as his phony charm had.

But she smiled to herself as she realized that none of it mattered any longer, because she was a woman now—not that foolish young girl—and she didn't have to believe his lies anymore.

Walking toward the hall, Alix reminded herself that her children would be well taken care of in Alabama; she knew Wilton well enough to know that, beyond a shadow of a doubt, he wouldn't have them alone for a minute. Canceling the trip would only hurt Michael and Kimberley even more. Good, bad or indifferent, he was their father, and they deserved this vacation.

"I never thought I'd hear myself say this, Wilton." Turning on her heel, Alix calmly picked up the children's packed bags and threw them in the direction of the doorway. "But I'm glad you divorced me."

She looked him in the eye, her gaze unwavering, her voice clear, strong and steady. "Get out."

## Chapter Eight

The first traces of twilight were beginning to soften the hilly terrain, and cold chills ran up and down Alix's spine as she skirted around the clearing where the fallen boar had been only an hour or two before. She held her arms, trying to rub away the shivery sensation, and watched Joe as he skipped pebbles across the clear, rushing water.

"I hoped I'd find you here," she said.

Joe hunkered down on his heels, picking out several of the smaller rocks, and then hoisted himself back to his feet. Thank goodness he didn't turn to face her, or reach out and touch her, she thought. If he had, she would have gone to pieces.

"I'm going to miss the kids," he finally said.

"Me too," she whispered in reply, boosting herself up onto a huge boulder and hugging her legs to her chest. "Thank you . . . for saving Kim's life today."

"Don't mention it."

"But she could have been killed! You could have both been killed, and it would have been my fault."

"No one was hurt. We're both fine." He dropped the handful of pebbles. "And it wasn't your fault, so stop blaming yourself."

"No! Don't try to spare my feelings, Joe. That incident with the boar would never have happened if I had made Kim listen to you, if I had ever reinforced your instructions." Her voice held a quiet note of regret. "Instead I fought your attempts to have any control over them. I guess I resented the way they've always seemed to look up to you as an authority figure."

She lowered her lashes, unable to look at him while she swallowed her pride and confessed her failures. "I've never been very good at disciplining Kim and Mike. And every time I saw them mind you so easily, so unquestioningly, it made me realize my shortcomings as a mother—"

"Stop it, Alix! You've got two terrific kids, and they wouldn't be good kids if they didn't have a good mother, so stop putting yourself down like that. You're doing your best, and that's all anyone can do." Moving toward her, he placed his big palm on her shoulder and squeezed it reassuringly. "Do your best, and don't look back."

"I . . . I don't think that's enough."

"Sure it is. I may not have any children of my own—" she watched as a look of sadness shadowed his eyes "—but I've been around long enough to realize how hard it is to raise them."

"But I was wrong to try to protect them from life and its responsibilities. You told me that yourself."

"I told you that because I've been guilty of it, too. I finally learned my lesson the hard way and I don't want to see the same thing happen to you." He leaned against the edge of the boulder. "Do you remember me telling you I had something to do with raising my little brother?"

"Yes."

"Well, today's episode with Kim was minor compared to the mistakes I made with Charlie."

"Somehow I can't imagine that."

"It's true. My mother overprotected him for years, and after she died, I kept right on pampering him when I should have been helping him grow up and face reality."

"It's obvious your mother didn't overprotect you. Why did she treat Charlie so differently?" All of a sudden, Alix realized that this was the first time Joe had volunteered anything about his past. And at the same time, she realized she wanted to know everything there was to know. "Unless you'd rather not talk about it."

"No. I want to tell you." Resting his hip against the huge rock, he shoved his fingers into his pockets. "When I was a kid, my dad used to take me on overnight hunting and fishing trips all the time, right there on our ranch. Charlie's ten years younger than I am, and it used to drive him crazy that he couldn't go with us."

An easy smile touched his face, a smile filled with happy childhood memories, and she studied it as he went on. "Dad kept promising him that he could go with us as soon as he turned seven. So on the night of his birthday, the three of us took off on a hunting trip. Oh, Charlie didn't actually take part in any of it, ex-

cept to tag along, but we stayed out for four days, and
the kid was happy as a lark the whole time."

His voice became quiet, and the smile faded. "Charlie had a low-grade fever the last day we were out, and
none of us thought anything about it. But after we got
back home, it developed into a full-blown case of
pneumonia, and he almost died from it.

"My dad passed away the following year, and Charlie got pneumonia several more times during his childhood. With each bout of illness, my mother protected
him more and more." His voice took on a grim tone,
one she had never heard in it before. "I was away from
home by then, so there was no one there to balance
Mom's pampering. And truthfully, it probably
wouldn't have made any difference if I had been there."

Joe paused for a long moment before continuing.

"Anyway, before Mom died three years ago, she
made me promise her that I'd protect him, that I'd
make sure nothing ever happened to him.

"Charlie was twenty-three by then, and I guess I
knew deep down that he was too old to be getting into
teenage-type scrapes with the law, but I kept thinking
about my promise and bailing him out. He'd always
been kind of a wild, impulsive kid, and the trouble he
got into seemed innocent enough—you know, disturbing the peace a time or two, a bunch of speeding tick-
ets, that sort of thing."

Joe laughed, a faint, humorless snicker that was filled
with pain and bitterness and cynicism. She had never
seen him with his emotions so raw, and she wanted to
hold him, to try to make everything better.

He turned away from her as he went on. "I was just
beginning to realize the seriousness of the situation

when he did something really bad. And then he took off."

"Where did he go?"

"I don't know. He's been gone ever since." He turned back around to face her, and the pain she saw in his eyes tore at her heart. "I haven't heard from him in well over a year."

"Then, he's your—" she started. "Charlie's your 'year in hell,' isn't he?"

Joe nodded slowly. "Yes."

The only time she had ever seen him lose his temper was that day when he had talked about his ex-wife, and Alix had simply assumed... She felt a clear sense of relief, followed rapidly by a twinge of shame, and sorrow.

"I don't even know whether he's dead or alive, and that wouldn't be the case if I'd handled things differently. So you see, I know firsthand what can happen—"

"I'm sure he's fine, Joe," she interrupted. Her voice was a gentle caress as she reached out, taking his large hand between both of hers. "Maybe he simply needed some time alone to straighten out his life. After all, he's had Joe Sinclair for a role model." She tilted her head and smiled up into his eyes. "I'm sure he'll be back," she whispered.

"I hope so."

"He will. Keep telling yourself that, and in the meantime, I want you to practice what you preach!" At his puzzled look, she explained herself. "You did what you felt was best at the time. Isn't that what you just told me to do?"

"Yeah, I guess I did." His tone lightened as he squeezed her hand.

"I know you did. In fact, Dr. Sinclair, I remember your exact prescription: 'Do your best, and don't look back.'"

"Giving me some of my own medicine, huh?" He smiled, pulling her to a standing position and lifting her off the boulder. "Come on, Ms. Smith." He laughed and put his arm around her as they started walking. "I want to get you back to the house before you start rattling off all the old clichés. I have a feeling that 'Physician, heal thyself' is right on the tip of your tongue."

Alix wrapped her arm around his waist, nudging him playfully. "Amazing!" she commented dryly. "That's exactly what I was going to say next."

"Well, I've got another prescription for you. You've had a big day, and I want you to relax and take it easy while I run into town for a while. Maybe take a nice, long, leisurely soak with no kids to interrupt you."

"Doctor's orders?" she asked.

"Doctor's orders."

"And then do I take two aspirins and call you in the morning?"

"You can take two aspirins if you want to, but I don't think you'll need them tonight."

He held her close beside him, her soft curves nestled perfectly against the hard angles of his body as they walked in silence toward the house. His spiritual warmth, his gentle strength, was something she had never known before him, and she had never felt closer to anyone than she did to Joe at that moment.

No, she told herself as she looked up at him, she wouldn't need aspirins tonight. No medicine in the world could cure the tender, loving fever she felt for this man. And even if there were a cure, she wouldn't dream of taking it.

Alix sank into the fragrant water of the Jacuzzi, letting the oily swirls envelop her body. Leaning her head against the tub's edge, she closed her eyes while her tired muscles finally began to relax. With a long, calming sigh, she recounted the events they'd been through and survived all in one day.

A serene smile touched her lips as she thought of Joe. He was strong, yet gentle; authoritative, yet understanding; handsome, yet totally unaffected by his obvious appeal. And she knew that, even if he hadn't saved her daughter's life earlier that day, he would always be her hero. In her mind's eye, he would always ride a white horse and wear a white hat—

Her thoughts were interrupted by the ringing of the telephone. Grabbing a towel, she raced to answer it.

"Evening, Alix." Joe's mellow voice floated over the line. "I'm in a bind. My pickup's got carburetor problems, and I'm stranded in town. Will you rescue me?"

"Of course," she answered, smiling softly. "But I'm just getting out of the tub—doctor's orders, you know—so it'll probably take me about thirty minutes to get there."

"Great. Take your time. I'll go to the Silver Dollar and have a drink while I'm waiting for you."

Taking more time than was probably prudent, and never once asking herself why, she slipped into a lace-edged dress that matched the green of her eyes. For jewelry, she opted for a delicate gold bracelet. Its matching necklace was the perfect accent, and the scoop-necked bodice of her dress exposed just the right amount of cleavage.

Alix freshened her makeup, adding a touch of mascara and lip gloss, and brushed her hair into shining waves that fell naturally around her shoulders. Deciding to go bare-legged, she chose a pair of medium-heeled sandals, grabbed her clutch bag and car keys and hurried off to rescue her hero in distress.

Within minutes, she descended the worn wooden stairs that led into the cozy tavern. The walls were covered with rough-hewn logs, and horizontal ribbons of cigarette smoke drifted past signs advertising various brands of beer.

Her heart missed a beat when she spotted Joe, who was advancing toward her in long, even strides. Dressed in dark brown, western-cut trousers and a yoked white cowboy shirt, as well as a Stetson and ostrich skin riding boots, he was the quintessential Texas rancher.

"Well, hello," he murmured appreciatively, taking her arm. "Care to stay awhile and enjoy the music?"

It didn't take her long to consider his question. "Yes," she answered, smiling up at him. "I'd like that."

With his warm hand at the small of her back, Joe led her to a table. Seating her in a chair, he then slid his palms up and down her bare arms, sending tingly jolts along the length of her spine. His face tilted toward her neck. "You smell good," he whispered in a smooth drawl. "Like soap and flowers and woman all mixed together."

He smelled wonderful, too, she thought. Clean and masculine and distinctively Joe. Her head felt light from his scent . . . and his nearness. "So do you," she admitted huskily.

"I do?" he asked, his eyes teasing her as he sat down, moving his thigh into alignment with hers. "What kind of flowers?"

"Oh, no!" Her cheeks flamed as she realized how she had returned his compliment. "I didn't mean like flowers and woman and..." He had her totally flustered. "I meant—"

"I know," he said gently, smiling as he reached up to trace her flushed cheek with the back of his fingers. "And thank you."

The waitress came by, and as Joe ordered their drinks, Alix realized she didn't know what to do with her hands. If she were more forward, she would have liked to cover his hair-splattered knuckles with her palm. Instead, she laced her fingers together and placed them in her lap. But she didn't fail to notice that his arm had stolen across the chair back. His hand went around her shoulder, and the intimate pressure was wreaking havoc with her senses.

How many times had she wondered, fantasized, about the mysteries of being his lover? She had imagined him slowly discarding his clothes, piece by piece, and then reaching out for her, holding her, kissing her—

"Looks like we've got company."

Alix looked up to see who Joe was talking about just as Henry and Lillie cut across the edge of the crowded dance floor. Happy to see them again, she waved them over.

Seated across from them, the Kastels filled them in on Henry's first-place win at the cook-off, and they toasted his good fortune. "Say, Miss Alix," said Henry, adjusting the crown of his hat, "you wanta struggle? If Sam don't mind, of course."

"Struggle?"

"That's country talk, Alix," Joe explained, smiling broadly. "He means, 'would you do me the honor of this dance?'"

"Oh. Well, of course, Henry," she said, intrigued by the warm atmosphere around her, and by the marvelous sounding country and western music the band was playing. "Let's . . . struggle."

They joined the couples who were crowding the dance floor to two-step through a light coating of sawdust. "I've got a lot to learn about this kind of life, Henry," she told him as he led her easily around the floor. "For instance, why do all these people still have their hats on? I thought you were supposed to take your hat off when you went into—"

"Never when ya go into a dancehall, Miss Alix. But always when ya go into someone's home," he stated. "And you never, ever put your hat on or take it off by the brim like those TV cowboys do. A real cowboy don't mess with the brim of his hat!"

"I had no idea there were so many rules about hats."

"Those're the only hard-an'-fast ones," he said as the music stopped. They clapped, and Henry swung her back into his arms as Arkey Blue and his band went into a tune about the "back streets of Bandera."

Joe shifted in his chair, leaning it back on two legs. If he knew Henry—and he definitely knew Henry—Alix was getting an earful of sage enlightenment.

"Quit gawking at her," Lillie complained with a smile. "You're giving me a complex!"

"Come on now!" he teased. "No one could ever take your place in my heart, and you know it."

"Don't give me that, Sam. You don't have me fooled for a minute. You're in love with that woman."

"Got it all figured out, have you?"

"Yes, sir. And she's in love with you, too!"

"Uhmmm." He shook his head. "I'm not too sure about that, but I'm working on it."

"Oh, pooh! Wake up and smell the coffee, Sam. Can't you see the way her eyes light up like candles every time she looks at you?"

Joe couldn't help laughing at the blunt statement that was so typical of Lillie. She had never been anything less than candid. "I guess I hadn't noticed."

"Men!" She leaned forward in her chair, her eyes twinkling. "Listen. You always had quite a reputation around Johnsonville as a ladies' man. And if half of what I've heard is true, you won't have any trouble getting her to admit her feelings."

"How about another drink?"

"I'm doing just fine, and stop trying to change the subject. It's time you got on with your life, Sam. You've done your time, and—"

"That's something I'd rather not talk about, Lillie."

"Well, maybe it's something you should talk about." Her voice became serious, sorrow coloring her words. "When you were in prison, Henry and I were hurt that you didn't put us on your visitor list. We couldn't even write to you."

"I...I didn't want you to see me behind bars."

"Did you think we'd love you less if we saw you at your worst?" she asked. "Well, you were wrong! It's about time you put your faith in the people who love you, Sam. 'Four walls do not a prison make,' as the saying goes. So get on with your life and quit lettin' the grass grow under your feet as far as that woman of yours is concerned!"

"Yes, ma'am!" he told her as she stood up and, with a "so there" shake of her head, flounced off toward the ladies' room. He didn't dare tell Lillie that, as of tonight, that was exactly what he'd decided to do.

*That woman of yours,* he thought as he watched the sexy sway of Alix's hips. He liked the sound of it....

Alix's curiosity surfaced as she looked beyond Henry's shoulder and watched Joe cup a match over a cigarette and then stretch out his long legs. His blatant virility was apparent in every move, every action.

"Henry?" she asked. "How long have you known Joe—I mean, Sam?"

"Pretty near all his life. I hired on at his dad's spread when Sam was still wet behind the ears."

"What was he like? As a boy, I mean."

"He was a fine little fella, sorta quiet, but real responsible-like, ya know? Kept himself busy with the horses and cattle." Henry went on talking as he sashayed her to the sounds of a lying-and-crying song. "After me and Mama got married, he was always up to our place listening to my stories. And he loved Mama's cookin'." His voice took on a tender quality. "Course, after ol' Sam Senior went to his greater reward, we didn't see too much of the boy. Not too long after that, he went off to vet school, and then he was busy startin'- his practice. But Sam was like a son to us, since we never could have any of our own."

"I can tell you and Lillie mean a lot to him, too."

"He's a fine man, Miss Alix. And you're a fine woman. Why, I bet you two'd make a powerful good team."

She darted another glance at Joe, who was watching them intently. "Yes, Henry. He's a fine man...." Somehow, she couldn't imagine him ever being young and vulnerable and scared, as little boys tend to be, even though they profess to be big.

But whatever he might have been at one time, he was a man now...with a man's desires. His intense blue eyes were staring at her with the promise of something no boy could ever give. And she wondered why, until today, it had never dawned on her that her...sexual problem...might have actually been Wilton's problem and not hers.

Joe certainly thought of her as a woman, she mused, and every time he touched her, every time he even came close to her, she responded to him like a woman. Not for the first time that day, Lillie's words echoed in her mind: "If you want him, go after him. He's yours for the taking."

The music changed to a different, even slower tempo, and Henry kept on talking, but Alix's eyes stayed on Joe. He was tipping a Coke bottle to his lips, his corded throat working as he swallowed. He set the bottle down on the table and then he winked at her. And her legs felt weak.

Henry swung her around, steering her to the other side of the floor. When she looked up, Joe was tapping Henry on the shoulder. He stood in front of her, looking directly into her eyes as his friend excused himself.

"Dance with me?" His soft-spoken question was more like a statement, and he pulled her against him. "I was watching you," he breathed close to her ear. "What were you thinking about?"

"I was thinking about you," she answered, her body melting against him.

He dropped his chin, and his hat brushed against her hair. The slight sandpaper roughness of his jaw moved along her brow as they swayed to the slow ballad. The barrier of clothing was no match for the heat of his body, and she could feel the undeniable evidence of his arousal against her flesh.

Her hand was circling his neck, her fingers raking softly through the hair at his nape as she reveled in the scent of him, the feel of his hard body. She tightened her hold, but it seemed as if she couldn't bring him close enough, couldn't get enough of him.

"Joe?" she asked softly.

"What?" he whispered, his hand caressing the small of her back, then moving below her waist.

She raised her head, and her eyes held his. "Could we go home now?"

The scent of wood smoke gave the upstairs haven an aura of winter. Joe was stretched out beside her on the rug, the dancing flames of the firelight casting his features in golden relief. The soft strains of Rachmaninoff filled the room's vastness with an air of romantic solitude. They were alone, shut off in a world that belonged only to the two of them.

"Do you like the fire?" he asked, his voice low and inviting. Balancing his long form on one elbow, he sipped from a balloon glass of brandy they'd been sharing, never taking his eyes from her.

"Mmmmm, yes. The fire's wonderful." With the air conditioner turned up to its highest setting, it didn't matter that the month was July. Nothing mattered except that they were together.

His fingers began to comb through her chestnut tresses, spreading them against the floor pillow. "Your hair is beautiful. Have I ever told you that?"

"No."

"I should have." He traced her cheek with his thumb. "And your eyes are beautiful. I love those flecks of gold." His nail skimmed the curve of her lower lip. "I keep remembering the way your kisses taste...."

He dipped his head, his lips moving to the sensitive skin on the side of her neck and to the hollow of her throat. Then the movement stilled, and he looked deeply into her eyes. "You don't know how many times I've dreamed of being in this room with you, Alix. Have you ever thought about me when you were up here?"

"Yes," she admitted, her voice barely audible as she studied his eyes, fascinated as she watched the cobalt blue turn to deepest indigo. "I've thought about you...a lot."

A purr of anticipation escaped her throat as he stroked her cheek and lowered his face to hers. Her hand slipped under his arm, her fingers caressing his thick biceps as his lips touched hers. The kiss was at first tender, hesitant, almost excruciating in its slowness. But suddenly, with a groan, he grew aggressive. His brandied tongue parted her lips, exploring the recesses of her mouth.

She felt his hand sliding down the length of her body. Brushing aside the hem of her dress, he caressed her thigh, and she didn't want him to stop.... But as he pulled her against him, she felt his hardness and drew in a sharp breath.

"Don't be embarrassed, sweetheart. It's a natural reaction." He smiled softly, huskiness giving his voice a sand-smooth quality as he whispered. "I'm not ashamed of what you do to me, what you've always done to me."

"No, it's—" She reached for him, her fingers outlining the faded scar that ran through his eyebrow. "It's just that...it would hurt me terribly if I didn't make you happy."

"You always make me happy." He swept her hair back, and she shivered from the light, airy touch of his lips against her ear. "Just being with you makes me happy."

His large hand cradled her neck as he held her only inches from his face. "I love you, Alexandra." His dark gaze locked with hers. "But you know that, don't you? I think I've loved you since that first day I saw you. You were so beautiful, so vulnerable. And you were trying to be so brave."

"And I love you, Joe," she whispered, her heart racing. "I never let myself admit it until today. But I do."

"Then let me love you, sweetheart." His lips moved closer to hers. "I want you so bad, I'm aching."

"I want you too, darling. I can't keep denying it—"

"I'm not going to let you deny it. Not any more." She felt a storm trembling through him, and her heart was singing with the knowledge that she caused it. "Say it again, Alix," he murmured.

"I love you," she breathed softly, taking his face between her hands. "I love you." Hungry for the taste of his lips, she kissed him passionately. Her lips moved down from his jaw to his throat with an urgency that she had never known existed. Her nails explored the slope of his neck, and she stopped to knead the taut cords of his shoulders.

Joe's fingers seemed to tremble as they slid beneath the cloth at her bodice, smoothing it away, drawing it to her waist. In a single, easy motion, he unfastened the front clasp of her bra. "You're perfect," he whispered, his hand taking one of her breasts. "Absolutely perfect."

Gently he urged her onto her back, and a tight thread of desire wound through her. Her nipples hardened as the heels of his palms grazed them. Then slowly, his

mouth descended to her shoulder, then to the round-
ness of her breast. His lips and his tongue drew first on
one tight, sensitive nipple, then the other, and she
moaned as she held him to her.

The pressure of his mouth eased, the tip of his tongue
skimming her midriff. He guided the dress past her hips,
and she lifted herself as his fingers peeled the lacy barrier of her panties down her legs.

Alix watched him as his eyes took in every inch of her
naked body. Basking in his adoring, worshipful gaze,
she suddenly wanted to know what her mind had only
dreamed of.

"Would you . . . undress for me?" she asked timidly.

A smile played across his lean, rugged features. "I
think that could be arranged."

Spellbound, she watched him shift to his feet and, in
slow, deliberate movements, release each of the pearl
snaps on his shirt. As he loosened his shirttail, her eyes
worked to memorize his solid upper torso and the dark
pattern of hair that veed provocatively into his trousers.

"Everything okay?" he asked, his voice teasing but
seductive as he dropped his shirt to the floor.

"Very 'okay.'" In fact, he was magnificent.

He freed the fastener at his waist, and slowly, ever so
slowly, his fingers slid the zipper lower. She watched as
if hypnotized, while he drew the material down his well-
toned thighs.

Her eyes widened as she saw him standing before her,
his feet planted firmly apart, wearing bikini briefs that
were as dark as the hair on his body. His back was to the
fire, and the flickering light behind him made it all seem
like a dream—a glorious vision of masculinity that, if
she reached out, might disappear before her eyes.

She ached to touch him, to hold him and know that he was hers, to twine her fingers into the curly mat on his hair-roughened chest. And when he stepped out of his briefs, she saw that he was...more of a man than she had ever hoped he would be.

Alix stood up as if in a trance and walked toward him. He pulled her against him, her breasts crushing into the wondrous pelt, and she took a series of deep, ragged breaths. Savoring the musky essence of his skin, she gloried in the knowledge that he was real and that she was in his arms.

Combing his fingers through the back of her hair, he gently pulled on it to force her face up toward him. With his forearm bracing her nape, he brought her lips to his. His demanding tongue probed, then explored the intimate darkness of her mouth as she floated with him to the rug.

Her eager fingers traveled over his broad back, his shoulders, and then between their hot flesh to rake through the hair on his chest. A primal groan vibrated in his throat as his palm moved past her waist, past her hips, charting a rapturous course for the warmth that beckoned him. His tender, rhythmic strokes awakened a pagan thrill within her, spreading sweet, delicious heat through her veins.

"I want you now, Joe," she pleaded, half out of her mind with her need for him.

"Not yet, sweetheart," he whispered. "Not yet." He was above her, his eyes dark with longing, and once more, her breasts felt the urging of his lips. "You taste so good, so right," he murmured. His fingers clasped the curve of her hips as he rested his faintly stubbled cheek against her stomach. "I want to know all of you...."

Sensing his intentions, she was afraid to move, afraid to breathe, afraid the spell would be broken. And then, as if the words were coming from someone else's throat, she heard herself moaning his name. His caresses were rapid-fire, yet gentle...slow, erotic torture that seemed to be driving her to the edge of consciousness and sanity.

"My sweet, beautiful Alix," he whispered. Covering her body with his, he captured her mouth in a drugging kiss. Then, surging hard into her softness, he filled her swiftly, fully. She gasped, her nails digging into his buttocks. And she cried out against him, over and over, as the force of his lovemaking awakened responses she'd never dreamed were inside her, waiting to be unleashed.

She felt every muscle in his body tense, and held him tight against her as he groaned her name. Wordlessly they clung to each other, for what seemed an eternity, until their uneven gasps slowed to deep, synchronized breathing. Reaching up, she ran her fingers through his hair.

Joe braced his palm against the floor, balancing himself above her. "Alix?" he whispered. And when he saw the tears that filled her eyes, a worried look of concern came over his face. "My God, sweetheart. Have I hurt you?"

"No! Oh, no." Her voice was a strangled murmur as she tried to control her sobs. "You've made me so happy! I...I never knew it could be this wonderful. I've never—" He was smiling softly, his thumb trying to brush away her tears. "Please, Joe. Just stay here and hold me." She pulled him closer, as close as she could get him to her. "I want you to stay here...on top of me, inside me—"

"My sweet, sweet baby." The tone of his voice was infinitely gentle, more tender than a caress. "I'm not going anywhere. I'm yours now...and you're mine." He pressed his lips against her ear, his hot breath fanning her hair as he whispered. "I'll take care of you from now on, sweetheart. It will always be this wonderful."

Joe held her, trying to adjust his heavy weight to keep from crushing her. With his hands and his body and not another word, he soothed her as she cried softly, spilling all the tears of pent-up frustration—and passion— that she'd been holding in for so long.

He had wanted to be honest with her before they ever made love for the first time. But as he felt her warm tears against his shoulder, and listened to the gentle sobs that were finally beginning to subside, he knew he'd been right in not telling her.

This night was for her. After what she had been through, for years and especially today, she didn't need the problems of his past piled on top of her own....

As Alix drifted into a blissful, heavenly sleep under the calming weight of Joe's body, she felt him rolling them both over, snuggling her up close against him. Sometime later, she awoke to his hungry kisses. Then, with a new golden dawn breaking over the hills in the distance, he made slow, beautiful love to her again. And it was even more wonderful than before.

## Chapter Nine

Joe stirred, shutting his eyes against the bright sunlight that flooded the studio, and reached across the bed for Alix. For the past six days, they hadn't been able to get enough of each other. And yet, he reminded himself as he smiled and ran his palm along her cool pillow, it wasn't as if they hadn't tried....

Instead of stroking her silky hair and her warm, smooth skin—a natural reflex that had easily become habit, and that never failed to arouse him—his fingers curled around a piece of paper. He forced his eyelids open, trying to adjust to the light and focus his vision on the card. What started as a red-on-white blur became a heart, surrounded by floating cupids, with an arrow piercing its center and the inscription A.S. J.S. within its hand-drawn boundaries.

He stretched lazily, expelling a long groan of contentment, and opened the card to see what she'd written inside.

*You're wicked, insatiable...and I love you for it! But I've got to WORK.*

Glancing toward the bedside table, he noticed that her wristwatch was gone for the first time in days. Before, she had always been so conscious of time. But she had taken off her gold watch on Sunday morning, and he'd been secretly keeping tabs ever since, smiling inwardly when he saw it in that exact spot day after day.

It never ceased to amaze him the way she reacted to their lovemaking. She had been like a virgin, like a fresh and innocent child-woman who had never been touched by a man. And she'd made him happier than he had ever been in his life.

He held the card, reading and rereading it, his mind reeling as he thought of the way her hungry responses to him almost seemed to shock her. Every time they touched each other, it was as if she had just started opening a surprise package and couldn't wait to see what was inside. And her eagerness left no room at all for being hesitant or shy.

They had each confessed their fantasies of the past few weeks, and then they had transformed them into realities: taking champagne baths in the Jacuzzi, going for long walks and moonlight swims, riding the horses over every acre of the property and making love endlessly... as if each time were the joyous, new discovery of a singular mind, body and spirit.

Still smiling and clutching the note, Joe headed downstairs. An hour later, after showering, shaving and packing a lunch, he found Alix by the creeks—where he knew she would be. He reined in the black stallion and dismounted, watching her face light up when she turned toward him.

He set down the picnic basket, taking his time as he secured Spirit's reins, and then sauntered over to her. She raised her paintbrush high in the air as he reached for her, wrapping his arm around her waist.

"Wicked and insatiable, am I?" he teased, his voice low and throaty as he brushed aside the collar of her soft, pale peach blouse.

"Yes," she whispered, her breath escaping in raspy waves. "You're terrible!"

His mouth searched out and found the sensitive spot where her neck joined her shoulder, and she realized she would never get used to the flip-flops her stomach started doing every time he touched her. She would never *want* to get used to them.

"And what about you, sweetheart?" Joe asked. "In less than a week's time, you've turned into—" he paused, his hand moving below her waist to cup her hips "—a wanton hussy."

Laughing at his use of her own words for Lillie, before she'd met the woman, Alix poked him playfully in the ribs.

"It's hot as the devil out here," he murmured, his palm rubbing up and down the dark fabric of her designer jeans. "Why aren't you wearing shorts?"

"Because—" she stretched the word into three syllables "—I thought about what you told me... about the effect my bare legs seem to have on you... and I don't want to be accused of encouraging you!" She feathered a kiss against the edge of his firm jaw, then pasted a sober look across her face. "I'm a serious artist, you know, and my day of reckoning is only a little over a week away. I'm determined not to let you distract me from my work today."

"I won't distract you, honey. I promise." He took the paintbrush from her, placing it in a jar, and then ran his fingers through the soft tendrils that had fallen loose from her ponytail. A gentleness touched the corners of his mouth as he pulled her tightly against him. "Are you worried? About the showing, I mean?"

Wordlessly Alix nodded her head against his chest, happy that he always seemed to know what was bothering her. As she held on to him, her cheek brushing against the softness of his blue chambray work shirt, she found herself hoping that his ever-present strength would seep into her and comfort her as it had so many times before.

"Don't worry about a thing, sweetheart," he said soothingly, rubbing her back. "You've worked hard, up until the past few days, anyway, and your paintings are beautiful. Everything's going to be fine."

"But look at this one." Raising her head, she turned slightly and pointed toward her easel. "It's anything but beautiful!"

"That one's not supposed to be beautiful yet. It's not finished!" He grabbed her hand, directing her toward the shade of a sycamore tree. "Come on. We'll have lunch, and then I'll leave you alone to work. I've got to go into Bandera to wash my truck and pick up a few supplies, and while I'm gone you can make it beautiful."

He opened a thermos, poured icy lemonade into its cap and handed it to her after they sat down on the ground. Alix hadn't realized how hungry she was until he unwrapped the ham sandwiches he'd made.

"Joe," she finally said, finishing the last bite of her sandwich. "Why am I deluding myself that I can make a living at this? All I've got are a few measly landscapes, and I'm staking my entire future on them. Even if they do sell, they won't bring enough for a month's utility bills!"

Smiling devilishly, he took a long swallow of lemonade. "I'll bet they would if we'd make a solemn vow not to use the fireplace for the rest of the summer."

"Cute," she answered dryly. "Now stop trying to humor me out of my black mood! I want to enjoy it a while longer."

"Come here, then." He pulled her into his arms. "And let me enjoy it with you."

"Joe!" She put up what seemed like a halfway decent fight and then snuggled against him. "You promised!"

"Okay, okay." He gestured overhead toward the sleek, black horse and handed Alix a few sugar cubes before he closed the picnic basket. "Spirit and I will leave you to your work. But first, give him some sugar."

Alix smiled warily, rolling her eyes skyward. She stretched to reach Spirit's nudging mouth, and when she did, she felt Joe's palm as he gently captured the fullness of her breast.

"You're impossible" she murmured, her hand moving to cradle his.

"I know," he whispered, his lips and his hot breath on her throat, his fingers working at the buttons of her blouse. "Now . . . give *me* some sugar."

Alix stepped back several feet, trying to assess the canvas objectively. A proud smile flashed across her face as she tilted her head first one way, then the other.

In the few hours since Joe had left her, she had made it beautiful!

She had stood up when he left, putting her hair back up into a ponytail and retying the ribbon he'd pulled loose. She knew she had to return to her painting, even if her legs were still wobbly and her mind was still dwelling on him, not on her work. And as she watched him ride up the rocky path toward the house, she also knew what was wrong with her fifth landscape.

She had hastened to her easel, barely able to capture the likeness of horse and rider in the far distance before they disappeared completely from her view. Then she had filled in what was missing, making the upward slope of the rock-laden path the focal point of the scene. Monopolizing the foreground was the sycamore. Their sycamore, she would call it from now on.

But the painting reached its zenith at the crest of the hill, as the narrowing path became almost nonexistent. Joe, sitting tall and majestic in the jet-black stallion's saddle, lifted his face to the sky. In that precise moment, it was as if he were a part of the heavens, reaching out and taking them, making them his own... waiting at the pinnacle to share the vastness of them, as always, with her.

A single, salty tear of happiness rolled down her cheek. Maybe no one at the showing would grasp this landscape's message, she told herself as she wiped her cheek, but it didn't matter; she understood its meaning—and Joe would, too. Holding that thought, she took the completed canvas off the easel and started her climb to the house.

With the painting deposited safely in her studio, Alix felt glorious. No, she decided, that wasn't the most suitable term. Actually her mood bordered on daring.

She stood in the middle of the kitchen, giving the large room a once-over. With childlike enthusiasm—and a womanly wish to please—she put her plan into action. She, Alexandra Smith, was going to fix a surprise dinner for Joe!

"Let's see," she pondered aloud, her hands on her hips. "What did he put in that meat loaf?" She mentally ticked off the ingredients and then rifled through the refrigerator and pantry to find them.

She turned the oven temperature to... Was it two-fifty? That sounded right. Humming one of the songs they'd danced to Saturday night, she assembled the meat dish, grimacing as she added the milk. She popped the pan into the warm oven, then turned to the sink. Two large, scrubbed potatoes were soon alongside the meat loaf, and she stood for a moment, peeking through the oven's glass panel, amazed at how simple it had been.

Realizing she needed to hurry, Alix raced up the stairs. She bathed in gardenia-scented water, Joe's favorite, slipped into a long, tawny-colored nightgown, again, Joe's favorite, and went back downstairs to fix a vegetable. Finding a box of broccoli spears in the freezer, she followed the microwave oven instructions to the letter, setting the kitchen table while the short cooking time elapsed.

"Wow!"

She turned at the sound of Joe's smooth baritone and the long, low whistle that filled the room.

"What's going on here?" he asked, setting a brown grocery bag on the counter.

"I've got dinner ready!" she stated, her face alight with a smile of self-satisfaction. "I hope you're hungry."

"Starved," he drawled seductively, his eyes devouring the satiny length of her body. "Looks delicious...."

"I'm dessert, you cad!" She slipped into his arms, rejoicing in the warmth of him, in the distinctively male aroma of his skin. "And not until after you've finished all your vegetables," she whispered next to his ear.

"What are we waiting for, then?" He let go of her abruptly, rushing around the kitchen to put his purchases away. "Hurry up, woman! Let's get dinner on the table."

He finished his own task as she proudly placed the food on the small table. The meat loaf looked a little gray around the edges, but surely it was done, she thought. She had baked it exactly an hour; she remembered the prescribed time specifically.

"I was beginning to worry about you, darling," Alix said, casting Joe a knowing look as he seated her. "You were gone so long, I thought maybe you were having carburetor problems again."

"No," he answered innocently. "The truck's been running fine since we picked it up Monday afternoon." Leisurely spreading his napkin across his lap, Joe returned her knowing glance. "Oddly enough, the trouble seems to have cleared itself up."

"That is odd," she agreed, "but I guess we shouldn't question it."

Grinning, Alix reached to pass him the butter. But her hand froze in midair when he sliced through the potato. A loud noise shattered the room's quiet as his knife made contact with the plate—and the potato fell into two neat, undone pieces.

"This looks good," he assured her, smiling brightly. "You didn't cook all the vitamins out of it."

That rule might apply to broccoli, maybe, but to potatoes? Swallowing a forkful of the green vegetable, she felt it stick in her throat as she watched him delve into the pink-centered meat loaf.

"It's raw!" she wailed, nearly choking as her self-confidence took a swift nosedive.

"No, it's fine," he told her quickly. "I like my meat on the rare side." To prove his point, he chewed another large portion.

"Well it seems you're in luck," she stated dismally, taking a bite of the meat loaf. Nausea overwhelmed her, and she spit the atrocious fare into her napkin. "It's awful! Why didn't you say something?"

"Tastes good to me. In fact," he said as he reached for the serving dish, "I think I'll have a second helping."

"Please don't." Her chin quivered, and she grabbed his wrist. "You're just trying to be nice. I appreciate the gesture, but please don't."

"Come here, baby." His voice held all the gentleness of a father soothing a hurt child. He wrapped his large hand around hers, pulling her onto his lap. "It'll be okay," he murmured, smiling down at her as he held her head against his broad shoulder.

"I don't know what happened! I was sure I remembered how we made it before."

"Honey, because you fixed it, it's the finest meal I've ever been served." His thumbnail outlined her collarbone. "Uhmm, tell me, what did you put in it?"

Alix began to name the ingredients in sequence. "... and sweetened milk."

"You mean, as in sweetened condensed milk?" He was obviously stifling a chuckle. "Honey, you misunderstood me. I said sweet milk. That's what country-type people call regular milk—as opposed to sour milk or buttermilk."

"Oh, for Pete's sake. I feel like a fool!" Watching the way he was trying to contain his amusement, she couldn't help but laugh at herself. She recalled how she had known instinctively, the first day she'd seen him, that he would be able to make her laugh. And he had. She couldn't ever remember being this happy....

"It was my mistake," he said as he laughed with her. "In the future, I'll be more careful when I teach you to cook. I'll have to keep in mind that you're my city girl—"

"You're an absolute saint for putting up with me." Her lips nuzzled his cheek. "You know it?"

"Let's not get started on that again," he warned playfully.

"All right, if you insist." She reached around to the back of his neck, her fingers raking through his dark hair. "What will we eat?"

"Liver and onions?"

"Joe!" She shot him a mischievous glare. "Be serious, now."

"Okay." He raised his scarred eyebrow in a questioning leer. "Why don't we skip dinner? Go straight into dessert?"

"But I'm hungry!"

"I know," he whispered. "You're always hungry."

"Darling," she said coyly. "I'm talking about real food now. Not the fruits of love—"

"I've got an idea, then." He lifted her up from his lap. "Why don't you slip into one of your dynamite sexy dresses? Something a bit less revealing than this, but not *too much* less." His eyes and hands moved like a silky caress along her nightgown. "And I'll take you into San Antonio for dinner."

"You mean a real, honest-to-goodness date?"

"The real thing," he answered, turning her around and swatting her bottom. "I'll put on my Sunday-go-to-meetin' clothes," he called after her as she rushed away with overdramatic enthusiasm, "and we'll go someplace nice. Some fancy spot right on the river."

Watching her leave the room, Joe felt like the cad she had jokingly called him only a few minutes before. He knew a lot of people in San Antonio, but he'd just have to take his chances on being recognized.

He had been wanting to take her out for ages. And under normal circumstances, it would be a simple thing to do—the kind of thing an ordinary man would do for the woman he loves. But it was beginning to look as though nothing in his future would be normal, simple or ordinary ever again.

He had thought about telling her that day; telling her that he would be a marked man for the rest of his life and then begging her to forgive him. But then he had seen how worried she was about her showing, and the timing wasn't right. The timing never seemed to be right.

Now he had no choice about where they would go for dinner. He didn't dare take her into Bandera, not when someone might inadvertently spill the beans about seeing him there with his parole officer that afternoon...while he was in town for such a long time, "washing his truck and picking up a few supplies."

Turning on his heel, Joe headed toward his quarters to get his three-piece suit.

"A saint!" he muttered disgustedly, almost choking on the words as he slammed the back door behind him.

"Darling?" Alix slipped her hand over his, stopping him before he could unlock the front door. "You seemed so fidgety at dinner. Are you sure you're all right?"

"I'm fine, honey, really." Joe turned to her on the dark porch, pulling her toward him as he wrapped his arms around her waist. "I'm just glad to have you alone again." He feathered the softest of kisses against her hair and then pressed his cheek to the top of her head. "To be back home."

Her arms went instinctively around his shoulders, circling his neck, and they stood on the front porch in silence, clinging to each other under the moonless, starless sky. "It's strange," she said at last. "This isn't really my home, or yours either. But it feels like home, doesn't it?"

"Yes," he murmured against her hair. "Ever since I held you in my arms out here that first night, it's felt like home to me."

She laughed, a soft, small laugh of newfound joy and security. "I ached for you to kiss me that night. But I thought you didn't want me."

"I've always wanted you." His lips were almost touching hers, and she closed her eyes, hoping the precious moment with him would stay with her forever. "My sweet, beautiful Alix," he whispered. "I'll never stop wanting you."

Despite the darkness that enveloped them, she could feel his gaze on her. "I never dreamed it was possible," she murmured, "to want a man the way I want you. I don't think I'll ever understand it, but—" It didn't matter if she was with him or not. Everything inside her seemed to cry out for his touch—his physical touch and the tender yet turbulent contact she would always feel with his soul. "Oh, darling, you've taught me to laugh again, to love as I've never loved before. I never knew this kind of happiness existed."

"Neither did I." His voice was hushed, his hot breath caressing her when he spoke, and a heaviness settled deep inside her as he cradled her against him. "But it does...."

Her hands tightened around his neck, and he lifted her off the porch as his mouth came down, his lips making slow, tender love to hers. And then she felt him move, heard him draw in a deep lungful of air before he buried his face against the rapid pulse of her throat.

The sound of a car's engine suddenly sliced through the quiet, and their bodies were bathed in the harsh glow of its headlights. Joe pivoted away from her, unlocking the front door and reaching inside to flip on the porch light.

Shielding her eyes, Alix peered toward the vehicle intruding on their privacy.

"It's the kids!" she said with motherly excitement. "And my sister Roberta. What on earth—?"

Kim and Mike raced into her arms, both of them talking a mile a minute.

"I'm so glad you're home!" Alix said as she hugged them. "But why aren't you in Alabama?" She looked up as her sister started toward the porch. "And why is Aunt Roberta with you?"

"Don't I get a hello?" Joe asked.

The hushed tone of his voice warmed Alix's heart, and all at once, both of her children rushed from her arms into Joe's.

"Hey, you two!" he said, crouching down to meet their eager hugs and kisses. "We sure missed you around here."

"Roberta?" Alix asked as she embraced her sister enthusiastically. "This is a wonderful surprise, but what are you doing here?"

"I'll explain later—" she gestured toward the children "—when we're alone."

"Aunt Roberta!" Michael's words came out in an almost breathless jumble. "This is Mr. Joe. 'Member? I told you how Kim used to like him but then she got mad at him 'cause she saw him in Mommy's bed kissing her, right on the mouth—but she's not mad at him anymore 'cause he—"

"Michael," Joe interrupted, "it's almost eleven o'clock. You two run upstairs and get ready for bed." He opened the front door and scooted the kids inside. "Your mom will be up later to tuck you in. And if you get a good night's sleep, I'll take you riding first thing in the morning."

He left the door ajar, listening as they squealed and ran up the stairs, and then adjusted his necktie before he turned to Alix's sister. Roberta's hair was a shade or two darker than her younger sister's, and he couldn't tell the color of her eyes under the porch light, but she had Alix's regal looks.

"I'm Joe," he said, smiling and extending his hand. "But I guess you know that. I'm happy to meet you. Is it 'Miss Powell'?"

"Yes." She met his handshake. "But please call me Roberta. I've heard such glowing reports, I feel as if I already know you."

"About Mike's glowing reports," Joe said, ushering the two women inside the house and then shrugging off his suit's summer jacket. "Maybe I should explain—"

"Please don't bother. Mike's always had a horrible case of foot-in-mouth disease," Roberta commented dryly as she and Alix sat down on the sofa. "In fact, it could someday prove to be terminal. Several times lately, I've thought about encouraging the child to print out his last will and testament."

Alix watched Joe as he laughed, straightening his waistcoat and then taking a seat on the massive rocking chair across from them. She gazed his way for a brief moment, thinking about their glorious evenings alone together. Every night that week, after dinner, he had pulled her onto his lap in that big, old-fashioned oak rocker....

The sound of Roberta's laughter brought her thoughts back to the present. Thankful that her sister had a sense of humor, Alix relaxed and kicked off her high heels, smoothing the skirt of her cocktail dress as she tucked her feet underneath her legs. "Kim and Mike haven't been with you this whole time, have they?" she asked.

"No," Roberta answered. "Poor little things. They were miserable in Alabama, and evidently their father was pretty miserable, too. He called me two days ago, saying that he'd tried to reach you repeatedly, which probably means once or twice." She rolled her hazel eyes. "Anyway, he put them on a plane for Dallas. I knew you had work to do, so I kept them for a couple of days. But now I've got to get back to work, and Mom and Dad are gone. I would have kept them longer, but I didn't have anyone to leave them with during the day."

"It was sweet of you to keep them as long as you did." Alix reached over and rubbed her sister's shoulder. "But why didn't you let me know? We could have driven up to get them, instead of you going to all this trouble."

"No trouble," Roberta assured her. "But I apologize for showing up like this, in the middle of the night. I tried to reach you before we left Dallas. And then I decided we'd just come and take our chances that you'd be here when we arrived. I'm actually here as your sister and your real estate agent. The kids have raved about this place until I simply had to see it, and I've been dying to tell you— There's been another bite on your house, and this time, it looks like the deal's going to go through without a hitch!"

"Oh!" Alix almost squealed as she hugged her sister again. "You don't know how relieved I am to hear that!"

"I think I do," she said, a genuine smile on her face.

"You'll stay for the weekend, won't you?" Alix asked excitedly.

"I'd love to, but I can't. As usual, I've got my fingers in too many residential and commercial pies." She laughed as she squeezed Alix's hand. "If you've got a bed for me, though, I'd love to stay overnight and see your landscapes before I leave tomorrow."

"Of course! You can have my old room. I'm sleeping up in the studio now." Realizing that her explanation was unnecessary—and that her sister had no doubt heard about the infamous lovers' hideaway—Alix blushed. "I know you must be exhausted, Roberta. Let me show you to your room."

"I'll get your things out of the car," Joe offered.

"Thanks," Roberta said, handing him her car keys before he started for the door. "Michael and Kimberley's suitcases can wait till morning, I'm sure. Mine's the heavy overnight case on the back floorboard." She turned and walked up the stairs with Alix, whispering secretively. "My usual forty pounds of beauty aids, you know—"

Trying to sleep was an exercise in futility, Joe decided. He sat up, reached to switch on the bedside lamp and lit a cigarette. God, he'd never felt lonelier in his life!

The air-conditioning unit in his quarters hadn't been turned on for days, and the small house was finally starting to cool off. But his body still felt hot, just thinking about Alix. He'd only been able to give her a brief kiss, outside Roberta's bedroom, before he left them alone in the main house.

He grabbed the extra pillow from the other side of the bed and shoved it behind him. Glancing at the clock again, he saw that it was only twelve forty-five...and he wondered if he'd be able to fall asleep at all, without having Alix snuggled up alongside him, holding him, teasing him with her every touch. Funny, he told himself, how a six-night habit could turn into a lifetime addiction.

Taking a long drag on his cigarette, Joe flexed his arm muscles and groaned. He leaned back against the pillows, and the crisp white sheet slid low on his naked form.

Instead of being in a rotten mood right now, he knew he ought to be counting his lucky stars. They had made it through dinner that night without running into any of his old friends, and Mike had actually helped him out by introducing him to Alix's sister as Mr. Joe.

Roberta probably didn't know the Ferrells any better than Alix did, but he'd intentionally failed to mention his last name, just in case. All seemed to have gone well, he assured himself as he reached to crush out the half-smoked cigarette, and there was no reason for his full name to come up between now and the time she left the next day.

Hearing a faint knock on the door, he bounded out of bed. "Alix?" His hand on the knob, he heard the muffled voice coming from the other side.

"No, it's Roberta." Her voice was barely audible. "Let me in, Joe."

## Chapter Ten

"Just a minute, Roberta." Joe drew back his hand, leaving the door shut. Crossing the room quickly, he grabbed a pair of jeans and yanked them up over his bare hips.

"Be right there," he called out as he zipped and snapped his jeans, then returned to the door to let her in. "What's the matter?" He looked beyond her, toward the main house, as she breezed past him. "Is someone—?"

"Everyone's fine," she answered. "They're all asleep. I made sure of that before I came out here."

Joe closed the door, turning to face her.

"May I sit down?" she asked.

"Sure. Of course." Perplexed, he led her into the sitting room, a small alcove beside the bedroom, and gestured toward an easy chair. "Let me put on a shirt, and I'll be right with you."

"Don't bother, Joe." Her words halted him between the bedroom and the alcove. She sat down, folded her arms in front of her chest and looked him directly in the eye. "This won't take long."

Propping his shoulder against the entryway, Joe shoved the tips of his fingers into his pockets. Despite her calm manner, there could be only one reason for her to come out here in the dead of night to confront him like this. Apparently he had underestimated her knowledge of the facts.

"All right, Roberta. Go ahead."

"I'll get right to the point." Her voice was serious and unwavering. "Along with Michael's little newsflash, I saw you and Alix on the porch tonight as I drove up." She cleared her throat. "It's obvious your relationship with her has gone way beyond the handholding stage."

"Yes, it has." His eyes never left hers. "And?"

"And," she continued, "even though Alix's love life is her own business..." She stopped in the middle of her sentence, her gaze dropping to the floor for a moment before she looked back up. Her fingers moved to grip the arms of the chair. "I love my sister very much, possibly more than I love anyone else in this world, and I'll do everything in my power to see that she's never hurt again."

Joe studied the sincere look of pain in her eyes. And when he realized that this was the "honorable intentions" speech, the one normally delivered by the father instead of the protective sister, he felt a sudden wave of relief wash over him.

"Then let me put your mind at ease, Roberta." His voice was gentle but steady. "I love your sister, too. Absolutely more than I love anyone else in this world."

He walked over to her, touching her lightly on the shoulder. "You don't have anything to worry about. I assure you, I'll never hurt Alix."

"But she's been through so much. I don't think you fully understand the effect Wilton's mental abuse has had on her—"

"Oh, but I do!" Joe's back straightened. Just thinking about Wilton Smith, he had to fight to control his temper and the tone of his voice. "I knew she'd been through hell, all right. But I didn't know who or what had caused it until Saturday, when that—"

He choked back the explicit term he wanted to use, out of respect for Alix's sister, and started pacing back and forth. "Six days ago, Wilton Smith showed his face here. Within a matter of minutes, that jerk broke his own kids' hearts and called Alix everything from a rotten mother to an iceberg! He managed to put down her womanhood and her career and everything else that could possibly matter to her—"

Joe swallowed hard, but the bitter taste stayed in his mouth. "Oh, yeah," he added, his voice laced heavily with sarcasm and emotion. "I definitely understand the effect he's had on her."

"Joe! Stop pacing the floor, please, and sit down. This is difficult enough for me, without..."

He took the chair across from hers. "I'm sorry," he said evenly, clenching and unclenching his fists. "But every time I think about that man and what he's done to Alix and his own innocent little kids, I get the urge to—"

"I know," she interrupted. Her voice was almost a whisper, and a sad smile touched the corners of her mouth. "I do, too."

They sat for a moment, both of them silent, until Roberta cleared her throat again. "I know it's getting late," she finally said, her words coming out slowly and deliberately. "What I've been trying to say is that I don't think Alix can handle much more disappointment in her life."

"I don't know what else I can say to you to convince you that I love her, that I would never do anything to hurt her." He chose his words carefully, trying to reassure her. "I've done everything I can to make her happy, Roberta. Why don't you talk to her about this before you leave? If you do, I think you'll see that she *is* happy now, that she's started looking at things in a different light—especially the things Wilton's told her."

"No. I don't have to talk to her, Joe." Realizing that her blunt statement had confused him, she smiled and went on to explain herself. "I'm not blind, you know! For heaven's sake, I grew up with Alix, and this is the first time I've ever seen her looking like... a 'fulfilled woman,' to put it discreetly. I can see it in her eyes when she looks at you. I can see it in your eyes when you look at her."

He laughed, rubbing his jaw. "It's that obvious, huh?"

"It's that obvious." She leaned back, folding her hands in her lap. "No. I'm not questioning the fact that you and Alix love each other, Joe. I'm perfectly clear on that point." Her voice lowered as she watched his eyes. "What I've been leading up to is your prison record."

A lead weight seemed to drop down into the pit of his stomach. Motionless, he stared at her, not believing he'd heard her correctly.

"My sister is happy now, for the first time in her adult life, and I want that for her. I'll be honest with you, Joe. After all that I've seen and heard tonight, I think I want that for you, too." Her voice reflected her genuine concern. "Feel free to tell me if my intuitive powers are way off, but I have a strong feeling that Alix doesn't know you've been in prison."

"She doesn't," he finally answered, his tone both dismal and stunned. "But how did you know?"

"For the past forty-eight hours or so, Kimberley and Michael have talked about nothing but Joe Sinclair." A loving smile touched her face as soon as she spoke the children's names. "My niece and nephew are as crazy about you as their mother is, but I'm sure you realize that."

"Yes." His voice almost broke. "I love them, too."

"After they had mentioned your name for about the zillionth time, the connection between Sinclair and Ferrell finally dawned on me. I'm not a close friend of your ex-wife, Tammi, by any stretch of the imagination, but I do know her. I knew she'd been married to a Sam Sinclair, who'd been convicted of manslaughter sometime after their divorce. And I'd seen your picture. Only once, but—" She paused awkwardly for a few seconds. "I'm sure Alix wouldn't mind my saying this. Women tend to remember a man who looks like you do. I wasn't sure of anything, of course, until I saw you tonight."

"You're a great actress," he said, still in somewhat of a daze. "I never dreamed you knew. You treated me like an ordinary person, not like—"

"Not like what, Joe? A criminal?"

"Yes. Like an..." Ex-con seemed like such a dirty word, one that he still couldn't bring himself to say out loud.

"Well, I must admit I wouldn't have been nearly this civil yesterday when I realized who you probably were and what might be going on here. But fortunately for both of us, I've had some time to cool down and be rational.

"You know," she continued, "if I haven't learned anything else in the past few years, I think I've come to realize that things are not always as they seem. Look at Alix's situation, for instance. For ages, she had herself and all the rest of the family convinced that her marriage was happy, that . . . Well, let's just put it this way. I've decided that judging people, and especially prejudging people, can be very risky business."

"You're right," Joe said, his voice remote and sad. "Things are not always as they seem. . . ." He looked up at last, a smile of resignation on his face, and reached out to touch her hand. "Thank you, Roberta."

"Don't thank me yet," she said, smiling back at him. But then her smile disappeared completely, and she leveled him a harsh look. "Now, what are you going to do? About telling Alix, I mean."

"I don't know." All of a sudden, he sounded completely wrung out. "I've been wrestling with my conscience for weeks now, and I still don't know." He stood up, slipping his hands into his back pockets as he started pacing again. "Believe me, I've tried time and time again to bring myself to tell her. And I just can't seem to do it."

"But surely you realize that the longer you wait, the tougher it's going to be on you and on her."

"Yes, I realize that now. I only wish that I'd realized it a long time ago." He stopped short, turning toward her. "To be honest with you, I didn't let myself give it a whole lot of thought until things got too involved between us."

"Tell her now, then." Roberta watched him, her eyes shifting back and forth as he resumed his pacing. "She loves you. I'm sure she'll understand and—"

"It's not that simple anymore, Roberta!" he interrupted. "Alix needs my strength, now more than ever. She's had so damned many heartaches and problems in her life. She doesn't need mine on top of them."

"Joe, I don't think you're giving her enough credit!" She clamped her mouth shut, looking away for a moment before she continued. "I'm a fine one to talk, aren't I?" she asked facetiously. "Maybe neither one of us realizes just how strong Alix actually is. After all she's been through, all those heartaches and problems, maybe she would have never made it this far in life if she wasn't stronger than you and I put together!"

"Maybe," he replied. "I don't know. All I know is, after all the crap she's put up with from Wilton, Alix needs to prove herself. She desperately needs to prove herself to herself, not to you or to me or to anyone else."

"Yes, but have you given any thought to *what* it is she needs to prove?" Roberta took a series of deep breaths, leaning back and trying to control her voice. "Confronting this problem from your past, solving it together, might be exactly what Alix needs to help her discover the inner strength she doesn't even know she has. She's got to be told, Joe!"

"Not now, though. I've thought about it, over and over, and I simply can't justify telling her now." He ran his fingers through his dark hair. "Alix is one hell of an artist, but she's on pins and needles about this gallery showing. It's the most important thing in the world to her right now, and I'll be damned if I'm going to let anything spoil it for her!''

He turned to look at her again, his gaze intense as he went on. ''The showing's only a week away, and I can't see unloading my problems on her—not until she has that behind her.''

''Then you'll tell her after the showing?''

''Yes,'' he said with resolve. ''I'll tell her as soon as it's over.''

''Good.'' Roberta stood up. Her voice was low, but deadly serious and steady. ''Because if you don't tell her right after the showing, Joe, I will.''

Her tone held no hint of question or doubt as she went on. ''Love has been very cruel to Alix in the past, and I won't sit idly by and let her be hurt again. She's bound to find out about your prison record, sooner or later, and I sure as hell won't let her be devastated by hearing news like that from some outside party.''

''You're right. And don't worry. I'll tell her.'' He extended his hand. ''You have my word.''

''That's all I wanted to hear,'' she said as she shook his hand. ''Thank you for understanding my motives for interfering like this.''

''Of course I understand.'' He understood a lot of things now. He understood why Alix's face always held a certain gentleness when she talked about her older sister. How many women would accept the word of an ex-convict on nothing but a handshake?

''You wouldn't be out here if you didn't love her,'' he added as they walked toward the door. ''That's not difficult to understand.''

''I think I'll be able to sleep now,'' she said. ''I feel much better.''

"I feel better, too. I'm glad we talked." They stepped outside, and she looked at him questioningly. "I'm going to walk you back to the house," he explained.

"That's really not necessary, Joe." She glanced down at his bare feet. "Besides, you don't even have any shoes on."

"So what? What difference does that make?" Joe guided her along the walkway, stepping into pace beside her. "Another city girl," he said, laughing softly into the black night. "You and your sister, my dear, are cut from the same bolt of cloth!"

"I guess that's true," she agreed as they reached the main house. "Good night, Joe."

"Night, Roberta." He opened the door, walked into the kitchen after her and switched on the light over the stove. "I know you're tired. You go on to bed, and I'll lock up here when I leave."

"But I can—" She laughed when she saw his feigned look of exasperation. "I'm sorry. It's just that I'm used to taking care of things myself."

"Maybe all of that will change someday," he said quietly. He leaned back against the counter's edge, the heels of his palms bracing him, and crossed one ankle over the other. "Maybe, like your sister, you'll meet a nice country boy someday, and he'll—"

"Joe Sinclair," she scolded teasingly, her hands on her hips. "I think you're a hopeless romantic. And I also think I'm beginning to understand what you've done to my sister. Poor little Alix! I'll bet she's been totally helpless up against all that 'country boy' charm."

"Oh, yeah?" He couldn't help laughing, watching the gestures that were so much like Alix's. "Well, don't rule out what your poor little helpless sister has done to me." He smiled sheepishly. "The only reason I'm in this house right now," he confessed, "is because I figure, if I look in on her and the kids and make sure they're all right, then maybe I'll be able to sleep, too."

"Like I said, a hopeless romantic." She crossed her arms in front of her and leaned against the doorjamb, smiling softly. "Country boy, city girl," she mulled, a wistful, faraway look in her eyes. "Well, I don't think that'll ever happen for Roberta Powell, but it must be one powerful combination."

"Yeah." He nodded slowly, a reverent smile touching his lips. "It is."

Roberta stood up straight again, taking the few steps necessary to close the distance between them. "I'm so happy for both of you." She gave him a hug and then turned in the direction of her room, but not before he saw tears mist in her eyes, tears that reflected her emotional turmoil of the past few days.

"Thanks," he whispered. "Good night."

"Night."

He listened as she padded through the den, until her footsteps faded into the hushed sounds of the house, and then he opened the refrigerator and reached for a carton of milk.

"Joe?"

He turned and watched as Alix rubbed her eyes and almost stumbled down the last stair from the studio. "What, honey?" he asked, taking her into his arms and tenderly rubbing her back.

"Am I dreaming?" she asked sleepily, snuggling the length of her body against him. "Or did I see my sister kissing you?"

"You're not dreaming, sweetheart." His hands smoothed the silky, tousled fall of her hair. "She and I had a nice talk. Roberta's a special woman, you know? A lot like you." He listened as she yawned against his naked chest. "I think I could learn to love her, too."

Feeling her elbow as it gently jabbed him in the ribs, he amended his teasing statement. "In a sisterly sort of way, of course."

"That's more like it," she said, her palms going around his wide shoulders as her body started waking up, coming to life against his. "What did you talk about?"

"About you and me, mostly." He paused. "About my honorable intentions, things like that."

"Oh," she said, her breath catching in her throat for a long moment. "I thought everyone was asleep. What are you doing in here?"

"I came in to check on you and my babies." Alix felt her breath catch again as he went on. "To make sure you were all right, and to give you a good-night kiss."

She melted against him. "Why don't we go upstairs, then?" she whispered. "I'm definitely ready for my kiss."

"Give me a break, Alix," he said with a smile. "Mike's already spread it all over Dallas! One more episode and he'll be working on Bandera County, if he hasn't already."

"I guess you're right," she agreed, her lower lip pouting.

"I know I'm right." He pulled her closer, whispering against her sensitive earlobe. "But I've got a better idea."

"What?" she asked excitedly, feeling his "better idea" pressing against her flesh.

"Why don't you come out to my place?" He lifted his face, his eyes holding hers. "Where I can give you a *proper* good-night kiss?"

"Listen, Prescott, you're supposed to be a detective...a licensed private investigator." Joe's grip tightened on the telephone's receiver, and he tried to control the rage in his voice. "In this so-called case, no news is not good news. I told you last week, find my ex-wife and you'll find my brother! How tough can it be?"

"But I assure you, Dr. Sinclair, I've checked with each and every person on the list you sent me, and none of them have—"

"Then check again! Short of taking over the investigation for you, I don't know what else I can do. I've told you everything I know." His voice leveled off, his next words slow and distinct. "You've got exactly one more week on my payroll, Prescott. Seven days, and that's it."

Yanking a spatula out of the top drawer, Joe flipped the hamburger patties as he listened to the detective ramble on about "exhausting all possible leads." If he had to judge the man by his gravelly voice, he would have guessed him to be a seasoned professional. But his actual words made him sound as though he hadn't had a lick of training in his chosen field. The idiot had probably applied for his license after watching three episodes of a private eye show on TV.

"No, Mr. Prescott," Joe finally interrupted, his patience driven beyond its limit. "I don't think I'm being unreasonable. Let's simply call it an ultimatum. You might have all the time in the world, but time's running out for me." His voice started rising again. "And I'm not paying you to stand around wringing your hands while you dish out feeble excuses. Just find her!''

Slamming the receiver back into place, he turned back toward the stove and saw Alix as she entered the kitchen.

"Wow," she commented. "What was that all about?''

"Oh. Hi, honey." Trying to sound nonchalant, Joe went back to his cooking. "It was that detective who's supposed to be finding Charlie. The guy's an incompetent—" He turned down the fire under the open grill. "Never mind that. I thought you and Roberta were out by the pool watching the kids."

"We were. She still is." Alix walked over and stood beside him. "I came in to see if you'd join us for a while. Roberta's got to leave soon, and—"

She reached out to touch his arm. "Joe?" she asked, her voice hesitant. "I heard you say, 'find her.' I don't understand. If this detective is looking for Charlie, then why...?"

"Because I was talking about a woman Charlie might be with, a woman who has seemingly disappeared, too." He tossed the spatula onto the counter and turned toward Alix, running his fingers through his hair. "I know they're together, I feel it in my gut. And if he can find *her*, then I'm sure he'll find Charlie."

"Oh, darling!" She watched him, a look of raw pain reflected in her eyes. "I feel so guilty," she said, taking his hand between hers. "You've been spending all your time and energy on me and my problems when you're worried sick about your brother. Please forgive me for being so selfish. What can I do to help?"

Joe wrapped his arms around her waist, pulling her tightly against him. "There's nothing to forgive,

sweetheart, and nothing for you to feel guilty about."
He buried his face in her soft, sweet-smelling hair.
"You've been helping me all along, Alix. Just by being
with me . . . by loving me and letting me love you."

"I'll always be here for you, Joe." She turned her
head, pressing her cheek against his shoulder. "Always."

He held her as close as he could, wanting to return her
whispered commitment but knowing he couldn't—not
until he could tell her the truth about his past. The
whole truth.

And he realized, in that hushed moment of togetherness, that even if Alix could find room in her heart to
forgive him, he might never be able to forgive himself.
Without giving her one single choice in the matter, he
had made her a part of the ugliness that would forever
haunt him. She had innocently fallen in love with the
perfect, untarnished man she thought he was. And if
she chose to stand by him, the horrible, irreversible
mistake he had made would automatically become hers,
too, for the rest of her life.

"Please tell me, Joe" she whispered. "There must be
something else I can do."

Remembering his vow not to burden her yet with his
own problems, Joe lifted his face and forced a smile.
"There is," he teased. "You can get out of my kitchen
before I burn lunch. I'm not the only one around here
who's a terrible distraction, you know."

"Oh, come on, let me stay." She nuzzled his neck and
murmured, "If we ruin the hamburgers, I can always
whip up a meat loaf."

"That does it, woman," he said firmly, grasping her
by the shoulders and holding her at arm's length. "I
might be able to live through your meat loaf again—

maybe—but Roberta doesn't look that sturdy to me."
He turned her around, swatting her playfully. "Go on,
now. Get back out there and visit with your sister while
you have the chance, and I'll be there in a minute. We'll
have lunch out by the pool."

Joe watched Alix as she finally smiled and walked out
the door. Her gallery showing was exactly one week to
the day. If only that stupid Prescott would get off his ass
and find Charlie before next Saturday, he thought angrily. Alix would be a lot more likely to believe him if he
had Charlie's confession to back up his story.

He reached into his hip pocket, rifling through his
wallet for the detective's phone number. Maybe if he
called him back, told him how important it was to...
Joe closed the wallet, returning it to his pocket, and
cursed under his breath.

Alix's believing him wasn't the issue, and he knew it!
God, she trusted him completely. If that wasn't obvious before, it certainly was now by the way she had
accepted his explanation about the telephone conversation she'd overheard. Good grief, he thought, she had
even caught him the night before, half naked, kissing
her own sister! And she hadn't doubted him for a minute....

No, he told himself, she had never said or done anything to indicate that she wouldn't accept and forgive
his past. She'd never doubted or questioned him, never
pushed or pried about anything in his past—not even
about his ex-wife, for God's sake!

She had been right on target that day at the cook-off,
and he realized now that it had been nagging at him ever
since. He had to face it. He'd rationalized and made
excuses and put off telling her about his prison record
because Joe Sinclair didn't like the idea of anyone,

much less Alix Smith, seeing him as less than perfect, or even knowing that he'd been guilty of using lousy judgment. Except for that year in prison, people had looked up to him all his life, and his pride wouldn't allow him to admit his weaknesses and failures to her.

Taking the rap for Charlie had been a serious error in judgment, made more out of emotion than sensible reasoning. He had promised his mother that he would protect the boy, but it hadn't worked out the way he'd planned. Everything had gone wrong; he'd wasted a year of his life and quite possibly ruined his entire future—and Alix's too—and he didn't know if he could ever forgive his brother or himself for what had happened. He was a prisoner of his wretched past, and now, of Alix's loving faith.

Joe took the hamburgers off the grill and turned off the fire. He stood in the middle of the kitchen, staring out toward the pool deck, and watched Alix as she talked to her sister.

Seven days, he told himself. Seven more days, and then he would have to disappoint her by telling her what kind of a man she'd fallen in love with. One short week, and then Alix would know what kind of a man Joe Sinclair really was....

## Chapter Eleven

Alix stood in the open doorway of the stable. Joe, with his back to her, was busy pitching hay, and its earthy, fresh aroma was almost as tantalizing as the sight of his muscles flexing and rippling each time he swung the pitchfork.

He wasn't aware of her presence yet, but she would see to that soon enough. Her immediate plan was to stand there quietly, undetected, and enjoy the view. Ever since that first day she had seen him, she thought with a smile, her eyes had worked overtime whenever they were together. And she still couldn't get enough of him.

His shirt had been thrown over the top of one of the stalls, and a light, glistening sheen of perspiration covered his bare, sun-bronzed shoulders and back. Fascinated, Alix watched his smooth, steady, rhythmic motions, the muscles of his hard body working in perfect harmony with each toss.

Lord, how she missed that hard, strong body snuggled against her softness through the night. How she yearned for him to share her bed again. But they hadn't wanted to flaunt their relationship, considering Michael's loose mouth. And in the five long nights that had passed since the kids had gotten back home, she hadn't had one night of restful sleep. They hadn't even had many opportunities to touch and hold each other during the day, much less sleep together at night.

Joe had been aloof and worried since the day he had spoken to the detective about finding Charlie—and she'd made up her mind to try to help ease his emotional torment. She was going to do just what he'd said he wanted her to do; she would be there, and love him, and let him love her.

Yes. If nothing else, she was going to do what Joe had always done for her. He'd always been able to lift her out of her dark moods by teasing her and sharing his happiness with her, by not allowing her to take things too seriously. He had always been there for her; maybe now, she could do the same for him.

Henry and Lillie, eager matchmakers that they were, had been thrilled to oblige when she had asked them to take Kim and Mike for the afternoon. It was Wednesday, Alix reminded herself, and she had waited long enough, too long, to put her plan into action.

The wind was picking up outside, storm clouds threatening as the sky suddenly began to darken, and she heard Spirit's whinny. She would have to hurry, or they'd get soaked trying to get back to the house . . . to the studio.

Alix smoothed her white shorts and tugged at her blouse's lightweight jersey fabric, attempting to show as much cleavage as the V neck would allow. Pushing the three-quarter-length sleeves above her elbows, she realized that the soft coral top was a bit too warm for the weather. But other than the low-cut cocktail dress she'd worn to dinner the other night, which wouldn't exactly be appropriate for a horse stable, this was the sexiest thing she could find in her closet.

Kicking off her sandals, she struck a provocative pose against the open doorway and cleared her throat. "Hi there," she said, trying to keep her voice low and breathy.

Joe turned in her direction for a split second, wiping his forehead with the back of his arm, and then continued with his task. "Hi, honey. What are you doing out here?"

"I finished my last painting this morning." Jutting her hip out a little more, Alix concentrated on making her voice sound throaty and enticing. "I thought maybe you'd like to come up and see my etchings."

"I can't, Alix," he commented, barely looking at her as he worked to spread the fresh hay. "I've got to finish up here."

She ran her hand up and down the length of her upper thigh, hoping the movement would catch his eye and make him turn around. Darn it! She'd never tried to play the vamp before. If she hadn't been so anxious to get out here to him, she would have taken a few minutes to practice in front of a full-length mirror....

"Don't worry, darling," she assured him, her tone sultry. "We're alone. Henry and Lillie have the kids for the rest of the afternoon." She shifted her weight to the opposite side, gently swinging her hips, and then batted her eyelashes. "Would you like to go back to the house with me and . . . play doctor?"

"I'd like to," he answered, still not glancing her way for more than a few seconds at a time. "But I've got too much work to do today, honey."

Alix lowered her eyes, staring down at her bare feet, and realized how ridiculous she must look to him. "I'm sorry," she mumbled dejectedly. "I just thought . . . You're busy, I won't bother you. . . ."

Unable to spot her sandals through the tears welling up in her eyes, she went into the stable and started digging for them. For heaven's sake, she thought frantically, why had she worn shoes that were the color of straw? All she wanted to do was find them and get out of there, while she still had a modicum of dignity left.

God, she looks beautiful, Joe thought, propping his forearm on the top of the pitchfork as he watched her digging for something in the straw. No woman had ever affected him the way she could, with those long, shapely, bare legs, those perfectly curved hips.

He'd been so distracted for the past few days, worrying about Charlie, worrying about what it would do to Alix when he had to . . . He had almost removed himself from her, thinking that that might make it easier for her in the long run, and now he felt more like a heel than ever. Her feelings were hurt, and that was the very thing he had wanted to avoid.

Alix pulled on the one sandal she'd found and finally spotted the other one. Grabbing it, she pivoted toward the door, only to be tackled from the side. Joe yanked her back into the stable, down on top of him, and they lay sprawled on the soft bed of hay.

"I thought you were busy," she protested, her hands pushing on his hard, naked chest.

"I could never be that busy," he teased, crushing her breasts down against him. "I'm sure I have time for a break . . . in the hay."

"Is that anything like a roll in the hay?" she asked, still pretending to fight him off.

"For a city girl, you sure are quick to catch on to country ways." His lips planted light, tender kisses along the column of her throat, and she ran her fingertips through the tempting pattern of hair that covered his chest.

"I've always been a fast learner," she said breathlessly, her pulse throbbing wildly as familiar, tingling charges of current rushed through her.

"Then let's forget about playing doctor," he said, reaching up to spread his fingers through her hair and pull her face down to his. "We'll play school instead."

"I get to be the pupil?" she whispered.

"No way," he answered, his body tensing with desire. "I have the distinct impression you came out here to teach me a thing or two. So go ahead, sweetheart, teach me."

"But how can we—?" Looking sheepish all of a sudden, Alix reached beside his leg and picked up a handful of straw. "How can we make love out here? This hay smells heavenly, but it must feel . . ."

"That, my innocent Alix—" he laughed mischievously against her ear "—is why stables come complete with saddle blankets."

"Oh," she answered quickly, pulling away from him and leaping dramatically to her feet. "Then you stay right there, and I'll get one." She crossed the stable and found a soft plaid blanket close to where he'd tossed his shirt.

"Since you seem intent on pampering me," he said, smiling as she moved in front of him, "why don't you help me with these boots?"

"Gladly, sir." She dropped the saddle blanket before she turned around, her back to him, and straddled the leg he lifted toward her. Her hands on the back of the heel, she pulled the boot up toward her and slipped it off his foot, then straddled his other leg and repeated the steps.

When she turned back to face him, Joe was on his feet, standing only inches from her. He pulled her against him with a force so strong that the breath left her lungs, and she basked in the warmth of his body and the scent of clean, manly sweat as his mouth came down on hers, branding her with his hot, untamed kisses.

She moaned softly when he released her and moved back. With excruciating slowness, he undressed her, his eyes holding her perfectly still as they worshiped her naked body. And then he reached out, taking her hand, guiding it toward the button of his jeans...then the zipper. She felt him tremble as her hands skimmed the hard outline of his hips and legs, dispensing with his clothing.

The sky opened up, flashing tiny threads of lightning as Alix laid out the soft blanket and turned back to him. She listened as the rain came, drumming fiercely against the tin roof, echoing the beat of her heart.

"I've missed you so," she whispered. "I need you." She watched his eyes darken, like the storm-drenched sky, as she took him in her hand. He groaned her name and murmured his need for her.

He pulled her down on top of him, his hardness pressing against her flesh, his brilliant blue eyes drawing her into their feverish depths. The heels of his palms slid up and down the sides of her breasts in slow, exquisite torture. His thumbs circled each aroused tip, and she ached for his mouth to possess them. His lips parted then, his mouth and his tongue making them his, again, always, forever.

Suddenly his strong hands spanned her hips, lifting her, joining her to him, and she heard him gasp as she took him inside her. At this moment he was hers, and she was his, and her body and soul reveled in the wondrously uninhibited, almost agonizing pleasure he gave her. She set the pace, moving slow, then faster to the rhythm of the violent rain as they rejoiced together in the eternal act of love. She took everything he had to give, and in return, gave all of herself back, as they shuddered and cried out against each other.

His arm held them chest to chest, and they remained a part of each other as he brushed her temple with a soft kiss. Alix nuzzled her face against his throat, inhaling the hot, moist scent of him...of them. She listened as their breathing slowed gradually in unison, and she sensed the rainstorm calming at the same time. At last she felt his throat constrict, and when he spoke, his voice was low and raspy as he struggled to control his breathing.

"The first day I saw you," he said playfully, "I told myself you'd probably be hell on wheels in bed." Rather than actually hearing it, Alix felt his soft laugh as he continued. "But I had no idea...."

"I had no idea either, darling," she murmured, "until you showed me how wonderful it could be. I've never felt as happy, as peaceful inside, as I do right now." She burrowed closer to him. "I think I knew, that first day we met, that my life would never be the same again."

"I love you, Alix." His words sounded almost grave as he held her tightly, whispering into her ear, and his serious voice filled her heart with joy as he went on. "I love you more than I can ever tell you or show you. Don't ever forget that, sweetheart, no matter what."

Joe wheeled Alix's car into the crowded parking lot alongside Fischer Gallery. He pulled into the nearest space, cut the car's engine and turned to watch Alix's reaction to the nearly filled lot. Taking her hand, he held it to his thigh, and he couldn't help but smile at the excited look on her face. This was the day she had been living for, the day he had been looking forward to and yet dreading at the same time.

"Joe," she almost squealed, "look at all these cars!" She clutched his leg with one hand and the door handle with the other. "I don't think I'm ready for this."

"Don't tell me that," he said, laughing as he pried her viselike grip off his thigh. "You just spent three full hours getting ready for this. It's the first time I've ever known you to be late for anything! Now come on."

Joe helped her out of the car, admiring her unjaded spirit as she straightened her shoulders and took a series of deep, calming breaths. Before they had left her house a few minutes earlier, he'd told her how beautiful she looked, fresh and enthusiastic, every bit the soon-to-be-successful, accomplished young artist.

Her ivory raw silk dress was the simplest of styles. But on Alix, it looked like a million dollars. And she had only enhanced her sophistication by keeping it simple. The ultrafeminine dress was accented with nothing more than high heels and a clutch bag of the same creamy shade, her emerald ring and a wide wrapping of brilliant green silk around her slim waist. Her innocent, natural beauty would never cease to astound him.

Smiling proudly, Joe guided her through the double doors of the impressive gallery. And then he stepped back to allow her what she deserved—the privilege and pleasure of greeting her public alone.

Alix stood perfectly still for several moments, amazed at the crowd in attendance. She turned, her eyes searching anxiously for Joe. He was standing just inside the gallery where he had let go of her arm, and she realized in that precise moment that, even though he looked breathtakingly handsome in a three-piece suit, she would never get used to seeing him outfitted that way.

She watched him nod for her to go ahead without him, and when she understood what he was doing, and why, she smiled back her silent thank-you. Walking toward the center of the huge, open room, she was immediately surrounded by a crush of elegantly attired people, all of them "oohing" and "aahing" over her landscapes.

While acknowledging their praise, Alix kept glancing around, trying to see how Hamilton had decided to display her work. She had delivered the paintings to him the previous night, as soon as they had arrived in Dallas, but Joe and the children had been with her. All four of them had been tired from the drive, and she hadn't wanted to stay. Craning her neck, she peered beyond the throng of perfectly coiffed heads and finally spotted one of her paintings.

Just as Luci Noonan approached her, Alix drew in a sharp breath. "What's wrong, Alix?" her friend asked, gently touching her elbow.

"Nothing, Luci. I thought I saw—" She pointed toward the small, inconspicuous tag on the frame. "Has that one already sold?" she asked incredulously.

"Yes, sweetie," she said, an animated smile lighting her face. "They've all sold!"

"Every one of them?" Alix tried to keep her jaw from dropping. "All six?"

"Each and every one," the lively redhead assured her, "and don't act so surprised, Alix. You know they're all fantastic! I can't tell you how disappointed I am. I would have given anything for the fawn painting, in particular, but they were all sold by the time I arrived." Luci reached over and squeezed her arm. "I'm so proud of you, Alix."

"Thank you, Luci. I-I don't know what to say."

"Then don't say anything, except 'yes.'" Evidently seeing Alix's confusion, Luci went on to explain herself. "You've got to promise you'll let me commission your very next one. You will be staying at the ranch for the rest of the summer, won't you?"

"As a matter of fact, I will. But—"

"No 'buts,' Alix," Luci broke in. "Please?"

"All right then, I promise. I'll do something I've had in mind for quite a while now, something I think you'll like, but I'll be sure to include a fawn." Still amazed at what was happening, Alix clasped her friend's hand. "Thank you, Luci, for believing in me."

"There's no need to thank me, sweetie." She smiled genuinely and leaned closer. "I'm just happy to see you believing in yourself. It's about time, you know." Luci took one more step toward her. "It's obvious, by looking at your work, that you're thrilled with your new career. But beyond that," she whispered conspiratorially, tilting her head toward the edge of the room, "is it possible that that gorgeous hunk of a man has something to do with this newfound confidence of yours?"

Alix's gaze followed the direction Luci indicated, and she smiled as she watched Joe, his broad shoulders and back visible as he stood talking to a petite, shapely blonde. Turning back to her friend, she laughed softly. "Yes, but how did you know?"

"Because I watched the two of you as you walked in together. And because, with the exception of a few brides I've come across in my day, I don't think I've ever seen anyone looking as radiant as you do right now!"

Alix laughed, not at all embarrassed by Luci's candor, and squeezed her friend's hand again. Just then, she saw Hamilton and Roberta approaching, and Luci excused herself to make "a seventh trip to the champagne punch bowl."

"Alexandra!" Hamilton Fischer greeted her with a warm handshake. "Have you heard the good news, my dear?"

"Yes, Hamilton. But I guess it really hasn't hit me yet. I feel as if this is all a dream. Maybe someone needs to pinch me!"

"Then let me do it," Roberta said playfully, hugging her enthusiastically. "After all, that's what big sisters are for, isn't it?"

"That's what you've always led me to believe," Alix responded with a broad smile.

"Excuse me, ladies," Hamilton said. "I'm going to circulate for a few minutes and give you two a chance to talk. I'll be back, though," he assured Alix. "Several people have indicated an interest in your works, and I've promised to introduce you to them."

"I still don't believe any of this!" Alix whispered to her sister after Hamilton left them.

"I'm so happy for you, honey," Roberta confided, her voice bubbling with excitement. "And maybe this isn't the right time, but I've got more good news and I can't hold it in another minute!"

Alix's eyes brightened, but she was almost leery of asking. "Not about the house?"

"Yes, about the house. It's sold, Alix! All you have to do is sign the papers and pack up your things. They want immediate occupancy and their loan's already been approved.... And get that worried look off your face. I've talked with Wilt's lawyer, and it's all set to go through."

"Oh...." Alix gave a deep sigh of relief. "I'm glad you told me now! I'll have to change my plans and stay in Dallas for a few more days."

"Absolutely," Roberta chimed in. "We need to be at the title company early Monday morning for the signing."

Thinking of all that would have to be done, Alix's mind started reeling. "Maybe you can suggest a moving and storage firm. I'll have to arrange for the furniture to be taken care of, and then—"

"The buyers are quite impressed with the way the house is decorated," Roberta interrupted, "and they asked me if I thought you'd consider selling it complete with most of the furnishings."

Alix's eyes widened. Nothing would please her more than to get rid of any and all reminders of her life with Wilton; surely her own sister knew her well enough to realize she felt that way. "And? When they asked you, what did you say?"

"Well, I don't remember my exact words, Alix." She paused and then went on nonchalantly. "But I think it was something like, 'Does a bear sleep in the woods?'"

"Oh, Roberta," she said excitedly, wanting to shout her relief but managing to keep her voice under control. "How can I ever thank you?"

"I think the special 'family rate' will be thanks enough," she answered. "You know—double my usual commission."

Laughing, Alix caught her sister's hand and leaned closer to her. "Honestly, Roberta. All of a sudden, everything in my life is perfect," she whispered. "Absolutely perfect...."

Alix turned toward the light touch she felt on her arm. "Hi, darling," she said, smiling brightly. "Have you heard the wonderful news? All six of my paintings have sold!"

"I never doubted it for a minute," Joe told her, putting his arm around her shoulder and holding her close to his side. "Alix? Is there someplace we can talk in private?"

Roberta, quickly suggesting Hamilton's office, seemed to detect the seriousness in his voice before Alix did. "Go ahead," she added, "I'm sure he won't mind."

"Joe?" Alix asked. Noting his too-firm grip on her arm, she frowned her sudden concern for him while they headed toward the private office. "What's wrong?"

Still unable to comprehend what was going on, she let him guide her into the large, airy room and then close the door behind them. He stood with his back to her— his hand still welded to the doorknob—and stark fear mounted from deep inside her as she watched his paralyzed form.

"Joe?" she repeated, her voice echoing through the quiet office. "Please, darling. Please tell me what's wrong!"

The tension building inside her suddenly intensified when she realized his breathing was so shallow she couldn't hear it. And when he finally turned to face her, his pale, shocked expression and the agony in his eyes sent a rapid shiver of dread racing up and down her spine.

"It's Charlie," he answered at last, a line creasing his brow as he slowly continued. "He's been in the military all this time, Alix. Several days ago, they flew him to San Antonio, to the Army hospital there. He's evidently in real bad shape, honey. Otherwise, they would have treated him in North Carolina where he's stationed. He has pneumonia," he ended cryptically.

Alix moved toward him, panicked by the gravity of his voice and his words, horrified by the ghastly look of fright she had never seen in his eyes before now.

"I'm so sorry, Joe," she said quietly, her palm gently touching his rigid jaw.

"I'll have to leave right away," he said.

Putting her arms around his shoulders, she laid her cheek against him and listened to the violent, erratic beat of his heart. Her own heart ached for the torment he was suffering, and she wanted nothing more at this moment than to be able to make his pain go away.

"Would it help if I went with you, darling?" she asked softly.

"I'm sure it would, Alix," he whispered, "but this is . . . something I feel I should do by myself."

"Of course," she said softly as his arms went around her back, holding her to him so fiercely, so tightly, that she almost couldn't breathe.

"Just let me hold you one more time, sweetheart," he murmured against her hair, "before I have to go. My flight's leaving soon."

Seconds seemed to turn into minutes as they silently clung to each other in the middle of the hushed room. And when he finally pressed his lips hard against hers, she sensed not only his love, but also his desperate worry and pain.

"I'll get back to the ranch as soon as I can," he finally whispered, taking a long, deep breath and then holding her at arm's length. "I wish I could stay till tomorrow and drive you and the kids back, but—"

"No," Alix interrupted him, wanting to set his mind at ease. He didn't need to be worrying about her and Kim and Mike. "I've just found out that I need to stay in Dallas for a few more days." She also didn't want to bother him with mundane details of packing and selling the house. Not now. "The kids and I will stay here, either at my place or Roberta's. You can call and let me know your plans when you know something."

If only there were more she could do for him, she thought, watching the anxious, pained expression on his face. "You will call me, won't you, Joe? And let me know how Charlie is?"

"Of course, sweetheart. I'll call you as soon as I know something definite. In a few days, at the latest." He reached up, tenderly brushing her cheek with his knuckles. "I can see that you're just as worried about him as I am."

Joe moved away from her, running his fingers across his scalp time and again, obviously in deep thought as he paced the floor. "I'll call the Kastels from the airport," he finally said. "I know they'll be glad to keep T-Bone for a few more days, and I'll ask Henry to feed the horses until we get back. That should take care of everything, I think. Except... I want you to be sure to tell Roberta why I had to leave."

When her eyes questioned him, he smiled briefly and went on. "That night when she and I talked, she seemed a bit uneasy about my intentions toward her little sister."

"I'll be sure to tell her, then—" his concern for Roberta's peace of mind brought a tiny smile to Alix's face "—if it's that important to you."

"It's important to me," he told her.

The solemn tone of his voice prompted Alix to stop and think. Could it be that Joe was worried about Roberta's impression of him because he wanted a permanent relationship with her younger sister? Did she dare interpret this as a hint of a commitment? Her heart thudded against her chest as she let herself admit, for the first time, how desperately she wanted to believe that Joe was planning for the future. Their future...

He straightened his tie, crossing the room in quick strides, and moved her wrist to glance at her watch. "I've got to go."

"At least let me take you to the airport."

"Stay here, Alix. This is your big day, and I'd hate myself if I ruined it for you completely." When she started to protest, he stopped her by putting a finger to her lips. "Don't worry about me. I've got transportation to the airport."

"But who—?"

His finger pressed harder against her mouth, stopping her question. Puzzled, she held her breath as she watched his odd expression for what seemed like an eternity.

"My ex-wife," he answered then, his eyes never shifting from hers. "She's the one who came here today, Alix, to tell me about Charlie."

His words hit her like a blunt instrument against the wall of her heart. And it suddenly dawned on Alix that, in the turmoil of the moment, she hadn't even wondered how he had found out about Charlie's whereabouts.

"Is she—?" Alix lifted her face as she started all over again. "Is she the beautiful blond woman I saw you talking with?"

"Beauty is sometimes only skin-deep, Alix." He emphasized the word "sometimes," smiling softly as he studied her face. "To answer your question, though, yes, she is a blonde. And yes, she was talking to me."

"But I don't understand, Joe. How on earth did she know you were here? At the gallery?"

"She—" He paused for a moment, glancing away from her as he rubbed the hard muscles working in his jaw. "I guess she must have found out by way of that detective who's been looking for Charlie. I called Prescott a couple of days ago, to see if he had ever come up with anything, and I told him where I'd be this weekend."

Joe lifted her chin with his strong, steady fingers. And then he moved closer, caressing her lips with a long, slow, tender kiss that made her feel as if her heart might explode from the emotions he would forever set off inside her body and her soul.

"Just remember that I love you, Alix," he whispered at last. "Please trust me, honey. I'll explain it all to you when I get back."

"I'll be waiting for you, darling," she called after him, her voice barely audible.

But he had already turned and walked out of the room, closing the door firmly behind him.

## Chapter Twelve

I'm glad you finally agreed to get out of the house,"
Roberta commented. She turned on the walkway,
watching Alix lock her front door. "When I said 'immediate occupancy,' I had no idea you'd take me so seriously. Ease up, honey. They don't expect you to be out
of this house overnight!"

"What do you mean, 'overnight'? Estelle and I have
been working for four days now, and we're still not finished."

"You need to ease up on her, too." Roberta grinned,
opening her car door as she went on. "Mother's not
going to be thrilled if she comes back from Paris and
discovers you've worn out yourself and her housekeeper."

"Don't worry about Estelle," Alix said, smiling as
she took the passenger seat of Roberta's car. "That
woman's got more stamina than an entire team of

horses." Darn, she thought, why had she chosen those words? Horses reminded her of the ranch... and Joe.

She had tried to keep herself occupied with physical labor for the past four days, but it hadn't helped. If only Joe would call again, she thought. He had called once, the day before, but a nurse had interrupted almost as soon as they had started talking. Joe had hung up quickly to meet with one of the doctors, and Alix had to assume that Charlie's condition still hadn't changed one way or the other. She couldn't let herself dwell on it, though, she thought as she fidgeted with the hem of her skirt. It was driving her crazy with worry.

"Anyway," Alix continued, "I've instructed Estelle to take it easy for the rest of the day. Before you got here, the kids asked to take a long swim, and she offered to sit out by the pool this afternoon and keep an eye on them." She forced herself to smile as she shifted positions and looked at her sister. "That woman's a jewel. She absolutely insisted that I take you up on your invitation. By the way, where are we having lunch?"

"I thought I'd let you pick a place," Roberta said, starting the engine and steering the car along the circular drive. "Where would you like to go?"

"Why don't we eat at that little sidewalk café? The one across the street from the gallery. If you have enough time, I'd like to stop in and see if Hamilton has a check ready for me." Alix smiled sheepishly. "It's the only money I've ever earned in my life, Roberta. This may sound silly, especially when you consider the small fortune I deposited after we left the title company the day before yesterday, but I've already bought a silver frame for my first dollar bill."

"That's not silly at all." Roberta reached over, patting Alix's arm as she drove along the posh, tree-lined avenue. "You're a talented artist, Alix. You have every right to feel proud of yourself."

"Thanks." Leaning back, she settled into silence, her mind going back to the day of her gallery showing—and Joe leaving with his ex-wife. It wasn't that she didn't trust him. She did. But no matter what he had said about the woman, she was beautiful. And they had once...known each other, in the true sense of the word. Alix hated to admit it, even to herself, but that thought had crossed her mind several times in the past few days.

"Here we are," Roberta announced. "Let's hit the gallery first," she said, smiling eagerly as she reached for the door handle, "so I can treat you to a celebration over lunch. We'll do it up right, wine and everything!"

"Only if that includes something sinfully fattening," Alix told her, laughing as they entered the gallery.

"Good afternoon, ladies," an attractive woman greeted them. "Please feel free to browse, and let me know if I can be of any assistance."

"Is Hamilton in?" Alix asked.

"I'm sorry, Mr. Fischer won't be in at all today. Is there something I can help you with?"

"I don't believe so, thank you," Alix told her. "I was hoping to pick up a check, but I'll call Hamilton tomorrow."

"Then maybe I can help you," the woman replied politely, extending her hand. "I'm Gladys Thompson, Mr. Fischer's new part-time assistant. I've taken over some of his duties so that he can manage a day off now and then."

Gladys smiled as they shook hands. Turning, she stepped behind a small antique desk. "I've just finished with the bookkeeping. Are you Alexandra Powell Smith, by any chance?''

"Yes, I am."

"Congratulations on the success of your showing, Ms. Smith," Gladys said as she handed Alix the signed check. "I only wish I'd had an opportunity to see your paintings before Hamilton shipped them off Monday morning. They must have all been very special, though, for Dr. Sinclair to have been so captivated by them!"

"Excuse me," Alix said, realizing she couldn't have heard the woman correctly. "Who?"

"Dr. Sinclair, the man who purchased your landscapes."

Alix watched, dazed, as Gladys closed the checkbook and slipped it into a drawer. "Would that be Dr. Samuel Joseph Sinclair?" She still couldn't believe it, didn't want to believe it! She'd been so proud, so—

"I'm not sure." Gladys reached into the open drawer, taking out a stack of deposit slips and flipping through the ones on top. "Why, yes," she said brightly. "Do you know him?"

"Yes," she answered at last, her voice stilted. "I definitely know him." Dumbfounded, Alix clasped her sister's arm. "Please, Roberta. Let's go."

She spun around, heading for the door as the enthusiastic woman called after them. "I'll be sure to tell Mr. Fischer you stopped by, Ms. Smith. Needless to say, he's anxious for another showing!"

"Now, Alix," Roberta tried to reason, barely able to keep up with her as she made long, rapid strides toward the car. "You don't have any reason to be upset."

"Oh, no?" she almost screamed, swinging around to face her sister. "Then do you think I should be pleased, knowing that I'm such a 'talented artist,' " she said, almost choking on the meaningless words, "that my work would have never sold if Joe hadn't had pity on me and bought all of them?" She yanked on the car door, struggling to fight back the tears of anger and disillusionment that were welling in her eyes. "Please take me home, Roberta."

"But, Alix. I think we should—"

"Now!" Her voice reflected her blind fury as she got into the car and slammed the door, staring straight ahead.

Without another word of argument, Roberta came around and took the driver's seat, started the engine and turned on the air conditioner. "You are a talented artist, Alix," she stated. "And I'm not going to take you home, not until you realize you're making yourself miserable for no reason."

"Oh, Roberta," she said softly, the hot tears finally spilling down her cheeks. "How could he do this to me?" Alix buried her face in her hands, letting the tears flow freely, lacking the strength to fight them anymore. "Over and over, Joe told me to believe in myself, to have faith in my talent."

"And he was right to tell you that."

"But don't you see?" She tried to talk through her sobs. "When he bought them, he took away any value, any validity my work might ever have...."

"Please don't do this to yourself, Alix," Roberta pleaded gently, reaching over to rub her shoulder. "You're blowing this whole thing out of proportion."

"How can you say that?" Alix took her hands away from her face and stared blankly at her sister. "How can I believe in my work now that he's shown me exactly what it's worth? It's worth nothing!"

"I'm sure that's not what he meant to do. I'm sure he had his reasons for—"

"Why are you taking his side?" Alix felt rage bubbling up from deep inside her. "You're my own sister!"

"Yes, I'm your sister. And I'm not taking his side. All I'm trying to tell you is that there may be more to his motives than you know." Roberta glanced at the couple who had parked next to them. "I'm going to take you home."

They completed the drive in tense, emotion-packed silence, and as soon as Roberta parked the car in the driveway and shut off the motor, Alix eyed her suspiciously. "Why are you taking up for Joe?"

"I'm not 'taking up for him,' Alix," she answered firmly. "It's just that I'm convinced Joe cares about you, and I'm also convinced he would never do anything to intentionally hurt you."

"Why do you say that?" she asked, wanting desperately to understand, wanting desperately to hear something that would nullify what he'd done.

"You know that Joe and I had a talk the night I came to the ranch." Roberta cleared her throat, trying to steady her voice before she continued. "I wish you could have seen the look in his eyes, Alix, when he told me about the day Wilton picked up Kim and Mike. Maybe I'm not the best judge of character, but I know pain when I see it. And that's what I saw in Joe's eyes when he talked about Wilton breaking the kids' hearts and then calling you an unfit mother and an iceberg—"

"He heard that?" *Oh, dear Lord. He had even made love to her out of pity!* Or maybe his male ego had considered her some kind of a sexual challenge! Alix cringed, remembering how she'd cried in his arms after they made love for the first time, only hours after Wilton had left, and how she'd confessed to Joe that she had never—

"Please, Roberta," she moaned, "please don't say anything more. I don't want to hear this!"

"The man loves you, Alix."

"Does he?" She glared at her sister, her voice oozing with bitter sarcasm.

"Yes! And if he were here now, I'm sure he'd be able to explain why he—"

"But he's not here now!" she almost screamed. "He promised to let me know about his brother, and he hasn't done that either. Because he's off somewhere gallivanting with his ex-wife!"

"Come on, Alix," Roberta muttered disgustedly. "He doesn't give a tinker's damn about Tammi, and you know it!"

"Tammi?" she whispered, her mind suddenly reeling with the harsh reality that was beginning to surface.

Brad and Vivian Ferrell had a daughter by the name of Tammi. The blond woman's face had seemed familiar, and now she knew why. She had seen that face before in some snapshots her parents had brought back from their weekend at the Bar F.

"You can't mean Tammi Ferrell." Alix's statement had been more like a question, and she swallowed against the knot that was forming in her throat. This had to be some sort of horrible nightmare.

"No," she went on, her voice filled with conviction as she shook her head back and forth. "That just can't be. I've heard that Tammi Ferrell's ex-husband killed someone. He's in prison, for God's sake!"

"He was in prison," Roberta corrected her. "He was going to tell you, Alix, I swear. That's the reason I went out to talk to Joe that night."

"You knew all of this?" she asked incredulously. "And you never once thought you should share it with me?"

"Of course I did, Alix, but I felt you should hear it from him. Joe told me how anxious you were about your gallery showing, and he gave me his word that he'd tell you as soon as it was over. But then Tammi showed up, and—"

"And he decided it would be easier to leave with her than to stay around and risk having to tell me the truth."

In a daze, Alix stepped out of the car and slowly turned to face her sister. "Thanks for the talk, Roberta." Her voice was quiet and sad. "I must say, it was enlightening."

"Trust me, Ms. Smith," the service representative said, her telephone voice a placating drone. "We'll change the account from your name to the new owners' as of five o'clock this afternoon. You'll receive your final utility bill within the next two weeks."

Alix hung up the phone, a small, cynical laugh escaping her throat as she recalled the expression her father liked to use: Never trust anyone who starts a sentence with "Trust me." Joe had used those exact words in Hamilton's office on the day he had left. He had also asked to hold her one more time, before he had to go. And she hadn't picked up on the hidden message behind either one of the two subtle phrases.

Taking her calendar book from her purse, Alix calculated what the exact date would be in two weeks and marked it in red. Yes, she would be sure to follow up on the utility bill—

"Estelle," she said, putting the calendar away and walking across the living room to hug the woman. "I can't tell you how much I appreciate everything you've done to help me, including staying here this afternoon to wait for the storage people. As soon as they finish loading these boxes, you can lock up and go home." Forcing a smile she didn't feel, Alix tried to concentrate on the mental list she'd made. "The phones will be disconnected tomorrow from the telephone company's office, and the new owners will be moving in the next day. I think that takes care of everything, but will you be sure to call me if any problems come up?"

Estelle nodded quickly, bringing her much-used hankie to her face and then rushing out of the room and up the stairs—probably to look for the kids. Alix had assured the sweet woman over and over again that Kim and Mike would be back soon, and often, for visits with their 'Stelle. But it hadn't helped much. She and Estelle had made a fine pair the previous night...packing and crying, crying and packing.

While they had packed, the pieces of the puzzle had crept into her mind, ripping her heart to shreds as each one had fitted painfully into place. Joe hadn't had any faith in her work, or in her. If he had, he would have known that she would understand, that she would forgive him anything. In all those weeks they were together, he'd had plenty of opportunities to tell her who he really was, and that he'd been in prison.

If only she hadn't been so trusting, she thought, tormenting herself. But then, that had always been her downfall: trusting too easily, and expecting too much in

return. She had fallen for Wilton's phony charm, so
why not Joe's?

Oh, they seemed like two completely different types
of men, but they were only different on the surface.
Wilton had stuck around longer, so that he and his
slick, high-priced lawyer could manage to take her for
everything they could. But Joe didn't have to worry
about any of that; he had known from the start that she
wasn't worth a plug nickel.

And both Joe and Wilton had taken her for a fool.
Wilt had never bothered to hide his laughter or criticism, and Alix knew that her ex-husband's open, un-
disguised abuse should have been far more painful. But
every time she thought about how Joe must have
laughed inwardly, she wanted to die. With every
thought, she felt as if a knife were piercing her very
soul, jabbing and twisting and turning.

Why? she wondered. Why did it hurt so much more
now with Joe than it had with Wilt, the father of her
children, the man she had lived with for so many years?
For some reason, this was a thousand times worse!
Sinking down onto the sofa, she stared blankly at the
meaningless remnants of her past, the packed boxes that
lined the living room walls.

Alix buried her face in her hands and started crying
again, shedding hot, fresh tears that she didn't think
could still be inside her body after the way she'd been
sobbing for the past twenty-four hours. It had taken her
about twelve hours into that twenty-four to realize that
Joe had hired his investigator to find Tammi, not his
brother. In the wee hours of the morning, after tossing
and turning the previous night, alone, trying in vain to
get to sleep, it had finally dawned on her that when she
overheard their telephone conversation, Joe had been

yelling at the detective to find her. He had offered a quickly contrived explanation, and fool that she was, Alix hadn't doubted it for one minute.

Then, while her heart was still shattering over that horrible revelation, her mind drifted back to the day they had met, which must have been immediately after he'd been released from prison. And she was devastated all over again, realizing that when he had come to the ranch that fateful day, it was Brad and Vivian Ferrell he had hoped to find. With his bags all packed, he had undoubtedly come looking for their daughter Tammi, his beautiful ex-wife.

But Alix Smith had answered the door instead. Alexandra Smith, the love-starved divorcée he'd been able to read like a book from the minute he laid eyes on her. After being without a woman, any woman, for a long time, he must have taken one look at her, assumed she would be "hell on wheels in bed" and decided to stay so he could use her to occupy his summer days and his summer nights!

How many times had he talked about their wonderful summer together? And yet, she realized now, he had never actually talked about the future other than dropping hints here and there, using words like "honorable intentions" and "my babies," words he must have known she yearned to hear.

She could remember so vividly the first time he'd told her that he loved her. It was as if the words and the scene itself were carved into her spirit, to haunt her forever.... The studio, the flickering firelight, his deep, gentle voice. As they had held each other that night, he had even told her what he'd thought about her on the first day they had met: "You were so beautiful," he had whispered, "so vulnerable." And then he had made love to her, knowing that she was especially vulnerable after Wilton's verbal attack.

The telephone rang, and Alix almost tripped over the coffee table as she jumped up and raced across the room. *Please let it be Joe,* she prayed silently, trying to control her breathing as she reached for the receiver. *Please let it be him, telling me this has all been a terrible, ugly joke!*

"Alix?"

Steadying herself against the dining room doorway, she leaned back and sighed heavily, feeling as if her heart had tumbled into the pit of her stomach. "Hello, Roberta."

"Hi. I've just spotted a message on my desk that you called this morning."

"Yes," Alix said. "I wanted to tell you I'm leaving town right away. I don't know when I'll be back."

"But Alix," Roberta argued, "what if Joe tries to call? How will he know where to reach you?"

"I don't think he wants to reach me, Roberta. But if he does—" She stopped herself, realizing that she had to quit hoping for the impossible. "The kids and I are going back to the ranch."

"Do you think that's wise, honey? The way you feel right now?"

"I think it's exactly what I need," Alix said firmly. "I've got to do something, or I'll go crazy. I've got to work. I've got to start facing reality!" She paused, her voice trembling with emotion. "God help me, Roberta," she whispered mournfully. "I still love him, but I've got to start forgetting him."

"But how can you do that, Alix? At the ranch, of all places?"

"I feel like everything inside me has died and I know that's the only place I can go...to find some kind of peace." Tears started rolling down her cheeks again, and Alix wiped at them as she struggled to keep her voice audible. "I realize you don't understand, Roberta, but the ranch has always felt like home to me. It's what I've got to do."

Charlie's condition hadn't improved in five agonizingly long days, and the doctors had finally consented to let Joe into the intensive care unit for a few minutes. A strong antiseptic odor hit his nostrils as he stepped inside the door, and he remembered the day he had stood in a similar hospital room, holding his mother's hand, aching inside as he watched her pain, making a promise to her that he could never, never take back....

He'd had plenty of time to prepare himself for the way Charlie might look, and yet the harsh, visual reality of it still came as a shock. He looked pale against the white sheets, utterly lifeless.

No matter what resentments Joe had been harboring against his brother for more than a year, he knew he had to shove them to the back of his mind now—for Charlie's sake as well as his own. Slowly he walked to the bed, careful not to disturb any of the tubes and needles as he reached out to touch his brother's arm.

"Sam?"

Joe smiled as he heard the still-familiar voice, weak and muffled by the oxygen apparatus, whispering the name he'd gone by for most of his life.

"Yes, Charlie," he murmured. "I'm here."

"Why, Sam? Why did you wait so long?"

"I've been right here," Joe assured him. "For five days. But they didn't want anyone disturbing you—"

he paused, choosing words that would soothe his brother instead of frighten him "—until you had some of your strength back."

"No," he whispered as Joe leaned closer. "I don't mean now. I mean...after I left home. Why didn't you ever try to get in touch with me?"

"I would have, if I had only... Don't try to talk, Charlie. We can work this out later, when you're well."

"I've grown up a lot now," the young man persisted. "I was just a kid then, when I made those mistakes. You've made mistakes of your own. Why can't you forgive mine?"

"I can," Joe answered. "I just ... need some time to sort things out."

"My God, Sam! How much more time do you need? When I got myself into trouble, you were always there to help. Why wouldn't you let me help you?"

Charlie's dull, reddened eyes searched his, and Joe realized that a confession might just be what his brother needed in order to get better. It was possible that he needed to get it off his chest after all this time, to ask Joe's forgiveness for what he had done to him.

"Maybe there wasn't much I could have done for you while you were in prison," Charlie muttered, struggling to continue. "But I would have at least stood by you if you had only wanted me to, if you had only contacted me."

"I would have, but—"

"I know it was wrong of me...to leave home that night the way I did, without telling you where I was going or even saying goodbye.... But I had to prove to you that I could make it on my own, and I was afraid you'd try to keep me from joining the Army." He went on deliriously. "That's why I couldn't let you know where I was. Not until after I left Johnsonville that night."

Joe took Charlie's limp hand, rubbing it, not knowing what else he could do but let him talk. He listened as his brother took a gasping breath and then rambled on, his voice sounding almost desperate.

"Sam," he whispered raggedly. "No matter what you did to that man, it was an accident! I would have stood by you when you were sent to prison, if you had only given me the chance. You know that, don't you?"

Joe's grip tightened uncontrollably on his brother's hand as the cold, stark horror of the words hit him. He stood there, frozen, an icy chill of realization pushing its way up and down his spine.

He had thought all along that Charlie was guilty of hit-and-run. And all along, Charlie had assumed that *he* was the one who'd left that man to die!

"You do know that . . . don't you, Sam?"

His brother's ever-weakening voice pulled him swiftly back to the present. He loosened his hold on Charlie's frail hand, stroking it gently as he fought to contain the sudden rage he felt boiling up from deep inside him.

"Yes," Joe assured him, "I know you would have." He swallowed hard, utilizing every ounce of willpower he possessed to keep his voice calm and steady as he asked the question that had to be asked before his brother slipped back into unconsciousness.

"You've got to tell me, Charlie. If you weren't driving my car that night, then who was?"

## Chapter Thirteen

Curling up on the oversize rocker, Alix smoothed her satiny nightgown over her legs and then reached to switch off the lamp beside her, hoping darkness would keep her from seeing Joe everywhere she looked. But she knew, as the iridescent glow of moon and stars floated into the den and surrounded her, that it wouldn't help. Nothing helped.

How many times, she wondered, had Joe pulled her onto his lap while he sat rocking in the big, comfortable chair? It seemed as if she could remember hundreds of times instead of the six it must have actually been. Those six peaceful, yet gloriously exciting evenings they'd been alone together, doing things that, regardless of their routine nature, had felt heavenly to Alix: sharing a quiet dinner, teasing each other while they washed the dishes, spending time together afterward before going upstairs to bed.

But the rocker didn't feel right to her anymore, she realized as she leaned her head back and tried to relax, and neither did the bed upstairs. No, Alix decided, the furnishings felt cold now—and empty. Like her heart, like her body and her soul. She was so empty inside that there weren't even any tears left.

She had arrived here a week before. To face reality. And now, after the course of that week, Alix knew that she wasn't going to be able to forget Joe Sinclair. Not in the next week, not in the next year, not in the next eternity. That was the reality she had discovered and would somehow have to face.

Hamilton Fischer had called the day after she had arrived at the ranch, to tell her about several commissions he'd arranged, and she had been trying to work on the fawn painting for Luci Noonan. But, like everything else, the painting reminded her of Joe. She had spotted the fawn the day she'd been so jealous over the nebulous "Lillie," the day she had ridden back to the house with him, caught between the saddle horn and his obvious arousal....

"Mommy?"

Alix turned toward the moon-bathed stairway and her daughter's voice.

"Kim?" she asked, her words echoing softly through the quiet den. "What's the matter, angel? I thought you had already gone to sleep."

"I tried," the little girl answered, tiptoeing across the room and crawling up onto her mother's lap. She squirmed into position, then leaned back against Alix's chest. "How come you've been calling me 'Kim,' Mommy?"

Forcing a playful smile, Alix lifted Kim's face. "I don't know," she said, deciding to evade her daughter's question with one of her own. "How come you've been calling me 'Mommy,' Kim?"

Kim laughed a tiny, childish giggle and then settled back with a sleepy sigh. "I miss Joe, Mommy. When's he gonna be back?"

"I don't know, Kim," she whispered, holding her tightly, not wanting to make any statements that would hurt her. Alix started rocking back and forth, her heart going out to her child as she realized that Kim had never said anything like that after Wilton had left.

"The day when Joe killed that big boar," Kim said reverently, "I told him I wished he was my daddy." Each time Alix rocked back, Kim pressed her body closer to her mother's. "And you know what he told me when I said that? He told me he loves me." Kim slipped her hand around Alix's waist and snuggled even closer. "You know what else, Mommy?"

"What else, Kim?"

"I love him, too."

There were still tears inside her, she realized as she stroked her daughter's hair.

"I do too, angel," she murmured, wiping her wet cheeks. "I do too...."

Alix rocked Kim, both of them in silence, and finally walked her back up to her bedroom. She tucked her daughter into bed, handing her the stuffed dog she loved so much—the one Joe had brought her from town one day because he saw it in a store window and it looked "just like T-Bone." As Alix rubbed Kim's back and watched her fall asleep, she realized how wrong she had been to compare Joe to Wilton, to even speak their names in the same breath.

In one short month, she felt as if her life had started all over again. She felt a new confidence in herself and her abilities as a mother, as an artist, a woman, because of his influence. A man who had always been kind and gentle and caring, who had constantly set aside his own feelings to be there for her and her children, couldn't be anything like Wilton Smith.

If only Joe would call! she begged inwardly. If only he would come to her and explain. It had all started with finding out about the paintings, and the fact that he had bought them didn't even matter to her anymore. She wanted him back desperately and yet she knew she couldn't go crawling to him. Not after what had happened. If nothing else, she had her pride.

Alix stood up, brushing her daughter's cheek with a gentle kiss, and headed for the kitchen. Not bothering to go up to the studio for her robe or slippers, she took the correct key from its hook on the brass plaque, closed the back door behind her and walked quickly to Joe's quarters. She stood in front of the door, hesitating for a moment before she put the key in the lock. She was aching for him. If she couldn't have him, she could at least spend some time out here, surrounded by the things that belonged to him.

Flipping the light switch, Alix went immediately to the closet. She opened one of the folding doors and buried her face against his shirts, breathing slowly and deeply, inhaling the wonderful, intoxicating scent of Joe. Alix moaned as she brought her face up, studying each swatch of fabric, and her mind went back to where they had been together, what they had done, when he had worn each one of the shirts.

She visualized his face again, and for some odd reason she thought about the scar that had always intrigued her. It dawned on her then that she had never asked him how or where he'd gotten it. Not that she hadn't wanted to know, but every time she had reached up to skim its jagged outline, every time she had started to inquire, something he would say or do would distract her. And now, she wished that she had asked.

As she pulled on the other closet door, a colorful piece of paper caught her eye. There, balanced on the hanging rod between his shirts and his trousers, was the card she had made for him that morning, the hand drawn message she had left for him to find when he woke up and saw that she was gone. Remembering the love that had gone into that simple inscription, A.S. J.S., Alix lifted the card from its place and traced the red heart with her finger.

She threw herself across his bed . . . the bed they had shared the night he had given her a "proper" goodnight kiss, and hugged his pillow, cherishing the lingering scent she would never be able to forget, never want to forget. Over and over again, she read the card inside and out.

The thought of his sentimentality overwhelmed her as she realized how he'd had the red-and-white card displayed prominently, so that every time he went to change clothes, every time he opened the closet for anything, he would see it and be reminded of her love for him. She also realized what had been lurking in the back of her mind the whole time. Joe Sinclair, her Joe, could never be bad or evil! He could never kill anyone! Not unless there were highly unusual circumstances, or extreme provocation of some kind.

Joe was the man who had saved her daughter's life without regard for his own. And on that same day, he had shown genuine concern when he talked about his brother's safety and whereabouts.

Alix thought back to that day, remembering the sincere expression on his face when he told her that it wasn't his ex-wife who had caused his year in hell, remembering the look of torment in his eyes when he talked about not knowing where Charlie was. How could a man who was that kind and decent ever even think about—?

"Oh, dear Lord," she whispered, her hand flying up to cover her mouth as she gasped. His brother was his year in hell! He had told her that day about his promise to his mother, his promise to protect Charlie! She shuddered as his grave words suddenly crept into her mind: "My brother did something really bad...and then he took off."

Alix tossed the pillow onto the floor, jumping up from the bed and glancing at her wristwatch as she crossed the room. She turned off the light and locked the door, heading purposefully toward the main house.

It was only nine o'clock—not too late to call Henry and Lillie if she did it now, before packing her bag. And if the Kastels couldn't take care of Kim and Mike the next day, she would just have to figure out something else. Joe needed her now. And for once, she was going to be there for him.

Alix ducked her head, fighting the morning sun's harsh glare as it bounced off the hood and straight into her line of vision. She saw the exit sign directing her toward the Army post, just in time to veer to the right and off the traffic-crowded loop that circled San Antonio.

After she had quizzed Henry about the details of Joe's conviction on the phone the night before, and once again when she had taken the kids to the Davis ranch that morning, Alix knew her hunch was right. She also knew where Joe had to be; he would have called her if Charlie's condition had improved.

Henry had finally admitted that Charlie had run off with Tammi. And Alix's heart felt as if it were splintering into tiny pieces as she thought of the torment Joe must have had to endure when his brother left with his ex-wife, of all people!

As soon as Henry Kastel had hinted at the connection between Charlie and Tammi, Alix had realized that Joe had been telling the truth all along. He *had* come to the ranch looking for his brother—because it was the Ferrells' daughter who had run off with him. And he *had* wanted the detective to find Charlie, by way of the woman who would no doubt be with him.

Yes, she told herself as she steered her car into the hospital's parking lot, there was something strange about the whole ordeal. When she had pinned Henry down, he had remembered that Charlie and Tammi had left Johnsonville the same day as the hit-and-run accident. Joe's brother must have done it. Never in a million years would Joe Sinclair drive off and leave a man to die!

She tried to spot Joe's pickup truck as she looked for an empty parking space. But the huge lot was jammed with hundreds of vehicles of all sizes, shapes and colors, and she couldn't find it.

Despite the fact that it wasn't even noon yet, the suffocating, late-July heat hit her like a blistering wave from an inferno as she opened her car door and got out. She reached down, smoothing the airy fabric of her sundress, and then stretched her aching limbs after the short but tense drive from Bandera. Her legs still felt wobbly as she entered the sprawling old building and asked for directions to the intensive care unit.

"Excuse me," she asked the young nurse on duty when she found the correct station. "I wonder if you could help me? I'm looking for Charlie Sinclair. He's a patient here."

"Who?" the girl asked, adjusting her uniform's cap as she moved to an open file cabinet behind her desk.

"Charlie or Charles Sinclair. I'm sorry, I have no idea of his rank, or even his full legal name."

"He's no longer a patient here, ma'am," the nurse said, closing a manila-colored file and then going back to the chart she'd been working on. "His body went out almost a week ago."

"No," Alix whispered, steadying herself against the front of the desk. "You must be mistaken. He—"

Alix felt the blood rushing from her face, felt hot tears streaming down her cheeks as the nurse helped her to a chair.

"I'm terribly sorry, ma'am," the young woman said as she squeezed her arm. "The way you were talking, I didn't think you knew him that well. I was so busy, I didn't realize...."

"Please!" Alix grasped the girl's hand. "Don't apologize! Please just find out what the problem is. It's Charlie or Charles Sinclair." She spelled the last name slowly. "I know there must be some mistake! I would have been told if he had...if he had—" Alix stopped abruptly, realizing she couldn't bring herself to say the fatal word.

"You stay right here, ma'am," the young nurse said, prying Alix's hand away from hers and then patting it reassuringly. "I'll check on it for you. I'll be right back, okay?"

"Okay," she murmured, digging into her purse for a tissue as the girl went to the file cabinet, took out the manila folder and then moved to a station farther down the hall.

The nurse was so young, Alix thought as she dabbed at her eyes and watched the girl talking on the phone. She was probably new here. She had probably made a simple mistake.

"Ma'am," the distant-sounding voice said quietly, "I'm afraid that Charles Sinclair's body was sent to Johnsonville, Texas, six days ago at the request of his brother." She touched Alix's shoulder. "But maybe you're inquiring about a different Sinclair. I could check with—"

"No," Alix interrupted, standing up and turning toward the exit. "That...that's his hometown," she mumbled.

In a daze of horror and confusion, she left the hospital building. The sun's remorseless fire, ricocheting off the swarm of automobiles in the parking lot, threatened to blind her as she made her way to the car.

Why? she asked herself over and over, her head slumped against the steering wheel. Why hadn't Joe called her?! Why hadn't he asked her to be with him, to share his grief, to help him through this...this unspeakable tragedy?

*Because he might not want you to be with him,* an inner voice suddenly answered, the finality of the words hammering inside her brain. Alix straightened, squaring her shoulders and reaching into the glove compartment for a map before she started the car's engine. He might not want her, but if that were the case, she was strong enough to handle it. For his sake, and her own peace of mind, she had to find out.

She studied the map quickly, repeating the highway numbers aloud in their proper direction and sequence.

Not allowing herself to dwell on the hasty decision she'd made, Alix backed the car out of its space and headed out of the parking lot.

Feeling the sun as it beat relentlessly against her legs, she turned the air conditioner up to high. The drive to Johnsonville was brief, but seemingly endless, as she forced herself to concentrate only on the road signs and the traffic.

When she stopped inside the city limits for directions to Joe's ranch, the service station attendant almost sneered at the mention of the name Sinclair. But she ignored the man's look of animosity, knowing she had to ask the dreaded question. And he confirmed it for her: several days before, there had been a private funeral service for Charlie.

Alix wanted to cry again as she drove away from the station. But she wouldn't let herself. She had to be there for Joe, to be strong for him as he had always been for her.

No, she told herself as she passed under the arched Double S sign, she wouldn't cry or plead. She would say what she had come here to say, and then, if he didn't want her, she would leave.

Spotting his pickup truck parked in the far distance, alongside a huge stable, she turned off the ranch's main thoroughfare. As she sped over the single-lane road, Alix realized that a month earlier she could have never done what she was doing. In fact, she wouldn't have even gone after Joe if he hadn't helped her start believing in herself, if he hadn't forced her to recognize her own strengths and to admit and accept her weaknesses.

She saw him as she parked her car next to his truck. He didn't turn toward the sound of her car. Instead he stood motionless, his back to her as he leaned his elbows against the top of the riding pen's fence, one boot propped on the lower board.

The hot wind whipped at her dress as she closed the car door, and it reminded her of that first night on the porch when her skirt had billowed around his legs as he had held her... the night when he had touched her for the first time, and she had sensed his gentle strength....

Willing herself to have that same kind of strength, she forced her thoughts back to the present as she walked toward him, slowly, and came to a halt only a few feet behind him. "Joe?"

"What do you want, Alix?" he asked point-blank, still not turning around.

"I went to the hospital today... to ask about Charlie," she whispered, the wind carrying her voice. "I'm so sorry, Joe. I wish I could have been here to—"

"Why?" he interrupted, his back and shoulders tense, his tone harsh. "There was nothing you could do."

"No, not for Charlie. But I might have been able to help you."

"I'm all right," he answered at last.

"Are you?" Alix took another step forward. "Why didn't you tell me, Joe? About prison?"

"I knew Roberta would have told you by now," he answered dismally, lowering his head as he spoke. "She and I had an agreement. And I knew what that must have done to you, hearing about something like that from your sister instead of from me. So now you know, Alix. I'm not the perfect man you fell in love with."

He turned around then, and she almost gasped when she saw the tortured look in his eyes. "I know how much I've hurt you. You didn't deserve any of it, and I don't expect you to forgive me. So you can leave now. Now that we've said all there is to say."

"I'm not going to leave," she murmured. "Not yet. But now I realize why you couldn't tell me. I made it impossible for you, didn't I? With that...that constant gibberish about you being perfect."

"It wasn't your fault, Alix. I should have told you a long time ago, instead of lying to you."

"But you didn't lie to me...."

"I lied to you by not telling you the truth. And when I told you my ex-wife found me through that detective, I lied to you outright. She tracked me down by way of the parole authorities, Alix." He studied her eyes. "My parole officer. It doesn't sound pretty, does it?"

"It—"

"This scar you're so fascinated with—" he jerked his hand up, pointing at his eyebrow "—was given to me on my second day in the slammer by a couple of charming inmates who considered themselves to be the Welcome Wagon!" He shoved his hands into his pockets and stared at her. "Go away, Alix. You don't need my ugly past messing up your life."

"None of it matters, Joe. I can forgive you for not—"

"It does matter, Alix! I've made too many mistakes. I can't forgive myself, so how can I ask you to forgive me?"

"Forgive what, darling? Forgive you for caring? For loving your brother too much?" She took a deep breath. "For being an honorable man who did everything in his power to keep a promise he made to his mother?"

He eyed her suspiciously. "What are you getting at?"

"You went to prison for him," she said softly, "didn't you?"

"No. I didn't." He laughed a short, brittle laugh. "Until one hour before his death, Charlie thought I had killed that man and I thought he had done it!" His expression changed to a frighteningly hateful one Alix had never seen before. "One hour before my brother died, we both found out that I went to prison for my ex-wife!"

"But Joe," she muttered, shocked and confused. "I don't understand. How could she have—"

"I didn't know that Charlie was running off that night to join the Army. After Tammi dropped him off at the bus station, she was supposed to bring my car back to the house and clue me in on where he was. Well, she brought my car back, all right—after running over that man! I was asleep, and she parked it in the garage and got the hell out of there."

Alix stared at him, bewildered. "I-I'm sorry, Joe. I still don't understand."

"She kept us apart, for over a year, so that neither one of us would find out. For over a year, Tammi let me sit there rotting behind bars feeling like my insides were being ripped apart...thinking that my own brother had killed a man, thinking that she and Charlie were lovers and that they'd run off together after he had... Instead of telling me where Charlie was, she let him hate my guts for not giving a damn about him, for not getting in touch with him until it was almost too late."

"Why, Joe? Why on earth would she do something that...that horrible to you?"

"I had no idea until I confronted her. She said she was angry and irrational. It happened not too long after our divorce, and she was full of resentment toward me."

He paused for a moment, a bitterly sarcastic look touching his fiery eyes as he continued. "Yeah, she was loaded with excuses. She never dreamed Otis Brown would die. After he did, she never *dreamed* the judge would sentence me to prison. And after that happened, she knew she couldn't come forward."

Joe laughed again, that same spiteful laugh. "She was scared to death of going to jail, but it was fine and dandy to let me suffer through it. We'll just see how well she holds up!"

"What are you talking about, Joe?"

"What do you think I'm talking about?" he asked, staring at her in total disbelief. "I'm talking about making her pay for what she's done!"

"You're being irrational now! What good would it do anyone for her to—"

"How the hell can you justify what she did?"

"I'm not talking about justification. You're so caught up in bitterness over what Tammi did to you, Joe, that you've lost sight of what she did for you! Don't you realize, darling? Even though she knew you'd learn the horrible truth about what she'd done, that woman came looking for you so that you and your brother could make peace with each other before he died!"

"Is that why you came here today, Alix? To convince me that my ex-wife is a saint instead of a lousy bitch?" He glared at her now, his eyes burning with fury. "If that's what brought you here, you can just turn around and leave . . . because I'm not buying it!"

Telling herself over and over that his words were borne of vengeful rage, Alix struggled to disregard them. "That's not why I'm here," she said firmly, fighting to stay calm so that she could try to reason with him. "And I'm not saying Tammi is a saint. But don't you see, Joe? She must have some shred of decency inside her. Her secret would still be safe if she hadn't come to the gallery for you that day. Charlie could have died without seeing you—without the two of you knowing the truth about her, and especially about each other."

Her eyes pleaded with him, trying to break through the wall of hatred he'd built around himself. "Joe," she whispered, "even if it was only for an hour at least Charlie died knowing that you loved him, that you cared. At least you will always know he died in peace."

"That doesn't make what she did right."

"No, but what's done is done. Revenge won't...bring your brother back. And it certainly won't change what you've been through. Don't you think it's time you did take some of your own medicine, Dr. Sinclair?" For his sake, she willed herself not to waver. "Do your best, and don't look back."

"How can I? I'm not even welcome in my own hometown anymore! I can't even hold my head up when I walk down the street." The hollow flatness of his tone grew forceful. "Besides that, whatever I decide to do about Tammi is none of your business, Alix."

"None of my business?" she asked incredulously, almost screaming as her hands flew to her hips. "None of my business?"

"You heard me."

"Don't you dare tell me this is none of my business! What do you expect me to do? Just stand idly by and watch you make the biggest mistake of your life? If you do this, Joe, you're choosing to stay locked up in a prison of the past! You're letting your stubborn pride push you into a decision you'll regret for—"

"Stop arguing with me, Alix! Pride's got nothing to do with this."

"Oh, no? Listen. If there's one thing I know about, it's pride. For the past week, I've let *my* stubborn pride keep me from coming to you when I could have been here at a time when you needed me most. Now, if I can swallow every ounce of that pride to come here today, the least you can do is hear me out!"

"Nothing you can say is going to change the facts, Alix. I've wasted a year of my life and probably ruined my entire future for a crime my brother didn't commit." He raked his wide-spread fingers through the shock of his hair. "I don't want to talk about it anymore!"

"Shut up, Sinclair. Just shut up and listen to me! I came here today to tell you something. And whether you like it or not, I'm going to say it before I leave." Her sudden anger took over, and she raised her voice to make sure he could hear every word. "I'm not the same person I was the day we met. I've changed a lot, and I know what I want out of life. One of the things I thought I wanted was you! Just the way you are, perfect in some ways and imperfect in others." She stopped to take a breath, and then went right on talking.

"You helped me become a woman, Joe. You helped me see that if I ever hoped for a future, I would have to forgive myself for my mistakes and stop hanging on to the bitterness of the past. Well, I've done that! I've finally learned to have faith in myself. And in you. But if you can't stop wallowing in bitterness and self-pity, as I did for so long, then I don't want you in my life!" She stood there, feeling awkward all of a sudden, not knowing what to do next.

"That's ... that's all I have to say," she sputtered, turning on her heel and heading straight for the car.

"Alix?"

His voice stopped her in her tracks. She turned to face him, her chin held high as he called to her.

"Before you go, I've got something for you."

Alix felt her breath catch in her throat, and she walked slowly toward him, meeting him halfway. She watched as he reached into his breast pocket, pulling out a worn-edged, tattered envelope from behind his cigarette pack ... next to his heart ... and then handed it to her.

Her eyes scanned the simple handwritten message on the front. *For Alix, on her day.* She looked up, her gaze locking into his as she silently questioned him.

"I was going to give this to you after your showing." A gentleness touched his eyes as he studied her. "I have your paintings, Alix."

She stared at him, her face solemn as she remembered the pain of finding out. "I know," she whispered.

Her fingers trembled as she opened the envelope and took out a folded card. At the same time, a gold chain fell from its place inside and into her hand. Hanging from the delicate chain was a gold pendant—a small artist's palette. Six tiny gems, each one a different stone from the next, formed a brilliant circle on the palette.

She held the gold charm in her palm, moving it back and forth, watching its colors glisten in the bright sunlight. There was a ruby, an aquamarine, a diamond, a sapphire, an emerald and an amethyst; each the same size, each making its own unique statement of beauty and perfection.

Alix unfolded the card, and tears welled behind her eyes as she read the inscription inside.

Six jewels, for six priceless treasures of art—the collection, and recollection, of our first season of love.

  The paintings were no longer yours, Alix, and they weren't mine. In that one perfect summer month, they became OURS, forever, and I couldn't let them go—

I'll always love you.

Joe

"Alix?" he asked softly. "Now that you've pounded some sense into me—" he paused for what seemed like an eternity "—do you think you might want to be . . . a country girl? On a permanent basis, I mean?"

"No, Joe. I don't want to be a country girl." A small tear rolled down her cheek as she looked up into his serious, dark blue eyes. "I want to be *your* country girl. And yes," she added, a smile of total joy touching her face. "Permanently. Forever. . . ."

"Oh, Alix," he whispered, pulling her into his arms and crushing her against him. "I wouldn't let myself hope—"

"Sinclair?" she breathed, lifting her face so that her eyes met his. "Just shut up . . . and kiss me. . . ."

# Silhouette Special Edition
## COMING NEXT MONTH

**CHEROKEE FIRE—Gena Dalton**
It was Sabrina Dante's silver spoon that Cherokee cowboy Jarod
Redfeather couldn't trust. The two lovers came from opposite
worlds, but the Indian heritage taught them to overcome
their differences.

**A FEW SHINING HOURS—Jeanne Stephens**
Fifteen years ago, Quinn left for Vietnam, not knowing about the
daughter he had given Kathleen. Now he was back, hoping that
love could make time stand still.

**PREVIEW OF PARADISE—Tracy Sinclair**
Travis couldn't resist rescuing Bettina from being sold at an
auction by nomad chieftains. But a valuable amulet had been
stolen, and his damsel in distress was the number one suspect!

**A PASSIONATE ILLUSION—Tory Cates**
Tempers flared when Matthew accused Lissa of not being able to
act. He wanted her to bring illusion alive with passion—passion
as real as the hunger he could no longer deny...

**ALL MY LOVE, FOREVER—Pamela Wallace**
They were adults now—not lovestruck teenagers. But even after
the hurt of raising their child alone, Carolyn still loved Rafe. She
only knew she wanted him...more than ever before.

**FORWARD PASS—Brooke Hastings**
Federal drug agent Liz Reynolds never intended to win a trip to
Hawaii with star quarterback Zack Delaney. But now Zack was in
for the most challenging game of his career.

## AVAILABLE THIS MONTH:

**RIGHT BEHIND THE RAIN**
Elaine Camp

**SPECIAL DELIVERY**
Monica Barrie

**PRISONER OF LOVE**
Maranda Catlin

**GEORGIA NIGHTS**
Kathleen Eagle

**FOCUS ON LOVE**
Maggi Charles

**ONE SUMMER**
Nora Roberts

# Take 4 Silhouette Romance novels

# FREE

Then preview 6 brand-new Silhouette Romance® novels—delivered to your door as soon as they are published—for 15 days without obligation. When you decide to keep them, pay just $1.95 each, *with no shipping, handling or other charges of any kind!*

Each month, you'll meet lively young heroines and share in their thrilling escapades, trials and triumphs...virile men you'll find as attractive and irresistible as the heroines do...and colorful supporting characters you'll feel you've always known.

Start with 4 Silhouette Romance novels absolutely FREE. They're yours to keep without obligation, and you can cancel at any time.

As an added bonus, you'll also get the Silhouette Books Newsletter FREE with every shipment. Every issue is filled with news on upcoming books, interviews with your favorite authors, even their favorite recipes.

Simply fill out and return the coupon today!
*This offer is not available in Canada.*

**Silhouette Books, 120 Brighton Rd., P.O. Box 5084, Clifton, NJ 07015-5084**

---

### Clip and mail to: Silhouette Books,
**120 Brighton Road, P.O. Box 5084, Clifton, NJ 07015-5084**

**YES.** Please send me 4 Silhouette Romance novels FREE. Unless you hear from me after I receive them, send me six new Silhouette Romance novels to preview each month as soon as they are published. I understand you will bill me just $1.95 each (a total of $11.70) with no shipping, handling, or other charges of any kind. There is no minimum number of books that I must buy, and I can cancel at any time. The first 4 books are mine to keep.          **BR18L6**

| | |
|---|---|
| Name | (please print) |

| | |
|---|---|
| Address | Apt. # |

| | | |
|---|---|---|
| City | State | Zip |

Terms and prices subject to change. Not available in Canada.
SILHOUETTE ROMANCE is a service mark and registered trademark.          SR-SUB-1

# AMERICAN TRIBUTE

## Where a man's dreams count for more than his parentage...

*Look for these upcoming titles under the Special Edition American Tribute banner.*

---

### CHEROKEE FIRE
**Gena Dalton #307–May 1986**
It was Sabrina Dante's silver spoon that Cherokee cowboy Jarod Redfeather couldn't trust. The two lovers came from opposite worlds, but Jarod's Indian heritage taught them to overcome their differences.

---

### NOBODY'S FOOL
**Renee Roszel #313–June 1986**
Everyone bet that Martin Dante and Cara Torrence would get together. But Martin wasn't putting any money down, and Cara was out to prove that she was nobody's fool.

---

### MISTY MORNINGS, MAGIC NIGHTS
**Ada Steward #319–July 1986**
The last thing Carole Stockton wanted was to fall in love with another politician, especially Donnelly Wakefield. But under a blanket of secrecy, far from the campaign spotlights, their love became a powerful force.

## AMERICAN TRIBUTE

*American Tribute titles
now available:*

---

**RIGHT BEHIND THE RAIN**
**Elaine Camp #301—April 1986**
The difficulty of coping with her brother's
death brought reporter Raleigh Torrence
to the office of Evan Younger, a police
psychologist. He helped her to deal with
her feelings and emotions, including love.

---

**THIS LONG WINTER PAST**
**Jeanne Stephens #295—March 1986**
Detective Cody Wakefield checked out
Assistant District Attorney Liann McDowell,
but only in his leisure time. For it was the
danger of Cody's job that caused Liann to
shy away.

---

**LOVE'S HAUNTING REFRAIN**
**Ada Steward #289—February 1986**
For thirty years a deep dark secret kept them
apart—King Stockton made his millions while
his wife, Amelia, held everything together.
Now could they tell their secret, could they
admit their love?

# Take 4 Silhouette Special Edition novels
# FREE

## and preview future books in your home for 15 days!

When you take advantage of this offer, you get 4 Silhouette Special Edition® novels FREE and without obligation. Then you'll also have the opportunity to preview 6 brand-new books —delivered right to your door for a FREE 15-day examination period—as soon as they are published.

When you decide to keep them, you pay just $1.95 each ($2.50 each in Canada) *with no shipping, handling, or other charges of any kind!*

Romance *is* alive, well and flourishing in the moving love stories of Silhouette Special Edition novels. They'll awaken your desires, enliven your senses, and leave you tingling all over with excitement...and the first 4 novels are yours to keep. You can cancel at any time.

As an added bonus, you'll also receive a FREE subscription to the Silhouette Books Newsletter as long as you remain a member. Each issue is filled with news on upcoming books, interviews with your favorite authors, even their favorite recipes.

To get your 4 FREE books, fill out and mail the coupon today!

## *Silhouette Special Edition®*

**Silhouette Books, 120 Brighton Rd., P.O. Box 5084, Clifton, NJ 07015-5084**